~~I Do!~~ Do I?

Ruchita is a triple gold medallist from the Indian Institute of Foreign Trade, New Delhi. Her best-selling novel, *The (In)eligible Bachelors,* was awarded the Awadh Samman in 2012. She works in London, where she lives with her husband. Ruchita blogs at www.smilethesmile.blogspot.com.

~~I Do!~~ Do I?

RUCHITA MISRA

HarperCollins *Publishers* India

First published in India in 2014 by
HarperCollins *Publishers* India

P-ISBN: 978-93-5136-332-3
E-ISBN: 978-93-5136-333-0

2 4 6 8 10 9 7 5 3 1

HarperCollins *Publishers*
A-75, Sector 57, Noida, Uttar Pradesh 201301, India
77-85 Fulham Palace Road, London W6 8JB, United Kingdom
Hazelton Lanes, 55 Avenue Road, Suite 2900, Toronto, Ontario M5R 3L2
and 1995 Markham Road, Scarborough, Ontario M1B 5M8, Canada
25 Ryde Road, Pymble, Sydney, NSW 2073, Australia
10 East 53rd Street, New York NY 10022, USA

Typeset in 11.5/14.5 Dante MT by
R. Ajith Kumar

Printed and bound at
Thomson Press (India) Ltd

Ma, Chacha, Sid, Diva and Neharika,
For you are the wind beneath my wings.

1

4 January 2013, 7.00 p.m.

It's official.

We are on red alert. There is no mistaking it.

Mum is a rather spectacular shade of red from all the stress. Nothing can be less than perfect now, else Mum will murder someone.

I am not kidding.

No, seriously, I am not.

Like really, I am not.

'Kasturi,' Mum said to me yesterday, staring thoughtfully at the curtains that she and Ramu had just spent hours hanging. 'Have you ever noticed the curtains in Purva's house?'

'Hmmm,' I said noncommittally, busy texting Pitajee. Pitajee, officially known as Amay – only no one calls him that now – is one of my best friends, who has just been offered a fantastic, front-end job with a hi-fi investment banking firm in Mumbai. I am, of course, trying my level best to dissuade him from taking it.

'Are theirs better?' Mum asked in her fake-disinterested voice.

'Maybe…' I said, still busy texting. The word was out of my mouth before I could stop myself.

'Maybe? *Maybe*?' shrieked Mum, and I readied myself for immediate flight. No one – I repeat most emphatically – *no one* should be around Mum when she gets all shrieky.

New curtains have been bought, stitched and hung. All in less than twenty-four hours. Don't ask me how. Ramu does not know either, but he is borderline hypertensive and is running a high risk for a heart attack.

Ramu, you say? I know what you're thinking – in this day and age, who has help called Ramu? How seventies is that? Well, to be fair, it's only Mum and Dad who call him Ramu; I prefer the infinitely more fashionable 'dude'.

'Kasturi bitiya, doodh bol rahe hain hum,' he says when I call our landline and he happens to answer the phone. And then he laughs, each time, without fail.

I digress. If there were ever a championship at digressing, I would win the gold – no questions asked. I think it would be fun to participate in a digressing championship. Anyway, I digress again … coming back to today, the house is resplendent and gleaming, ready to welcome the guests. Mum is in a frenzy, trying her best to do everything at once, Dad is a little annoyed for he is unable to really comprehend the magnitude of the situation and Ramu is wondering if he has put salt instead of sugar in the gulab jamuns (he has done that before, mind you). The point I am trying to make – or rather was before I digressed again – is that everyone is so busy that no one is really bothered about how I am feeling. No aunt putting the aanchal of my sari over my head and telling me how pretty I look. No mum getting teary-eyed, no kurta-pyjama-clad dad looking at me with Alok-Nath-ish pride in his eyes.

After all, the ladke waalas are coming home.

And that brings me to Purva. At twenty-eight, Purva, a doctor at the prestigious AIIMS hospital in Delhi, is two years older than me. In the two years that we have been together, I have realized that he and I are as different as two people can possibly be. My unending madness starkly juxtaposes with his calm serenity. My hollers that reach neighbouring countries contrast well with his shy smile. And my complete lack of commitment to work can hardly be compared to his dedication for the ailing.

deep sigh

'Why are you not ready yet?' Mum asked, walking past and not waiting for me to even answer. 'Ramu! The flowerpots! The Dixits will be here before we know it and they will see the flowerpots looking all shoddy! Who will want to marry a girl whose flowerpots are all shoddy?'

Somehow, in my head, something about this sentence seemed very, very wrong. However, I had little time to react with the indignation that such a sentence merited because the doorbell had just started ringing.

'Oh my god!' Mum shouted to no one in particular. 'They are here! The Dixits are here!'

No one said anything except for Sultan, our family dog who, excited by Mum's shrieks, began chasing his tail and barking uncontrollably. I love Sultan but, sadly, I have no delusions about his IQ.

I sighed and closed the door of my bedroom to shut away the madness. I desperately needed a moment to myself. I stood in front of the mirror and a sari-clad girl stared right back at me. The sari was Mum's choice. Whatever said and done, there is no denying that she has extremely good taste in clothes. Even if I say so myself, the light pink of the sari set off my complexion beautifully. I took my time doing my hair, twirling strands of it around my finger before pulling it all in a low, elegant bun. Mum had planned my look for the evening and had sent me the link to a YouTube video titled, 'How to make low bun like princess' many weeks in advance.

A lot was going on in my head. It was odd having Purva and his folks visit mine like this. It made things seem all official and grown-up. Was I ready to grow up? Probably not. But then would I ever be ready to grow up?

I decided to not answer that question. Instead, I picked up the rather huge rose that Dad had plucked from our garden earlier in the day and stuck it into the bun, exactly as Mum had shown me.

I breathed deeply. I looked elegant, demure and err ... unrecognizable. A small smile played on my lips as I wondered what Pitajee would say, were he to set eyes on me right now.

I had been told that I was to stay inside my room and not emerge till I was called. So I sat down and thought. Thought of Purva. Quiet, calm, sensible, wise Purva.

Soon, sounds of excited chattering from the living room reached my diamond-adorned ears. Mum was laughing that maniacal laugh of hers. I sighed. The maniacal laugh was a clear indication that she was stressed out. Poor Mum.

I sat twiddling my thumbs for some time and then decided to check Facebook and Gmail. Another friend was getting married and no new emails had popped into my inbox since I'd last checked it about two seconds ago.

I turned around at the sound of the purposeful clicking of heels.

'Bettaaaahh,' said Mum in a weird accent. Really, where does she get this accent from? It pops up every now and then, particularly when she has company she wants to impress.

'Mum,' I said, getting up, my heart beating fast.

'Oh Kasturi,' she gushed, and I almost smiled, 'your hair is disgusting!'

My face fell. Mum, of course, did not notice. She tried to do something with my hair, but gave up in about a second. 'It is beyond salvation,' she said dramatically, 'Let it be. We don't have time.' She paused and seemed to think. 'Do you want to cover your head with the pallu of your sari?'

'*Mum*!' I said, indignantly.

'Okay. Okay,' she said pacifyingly. 'It's fine, let's go. You will look?' she asked, looking expectantly at me as the two of us walked towards the living room. We had been through this drill many times in the last week.

'Demure,' I replied, mechanically.

'You will not?'

'Scowl.'

'Or?'

'Stick my tongue out at anyone,' I said, scowling and sticking my tongue out.

'You will?' she asked.

'Smile.'

'And?'

'Touch feet of Dadi and Nani?'

'And?'

'Not talk much.'

'And?'

Was there another 'and'? I thought. I had hardly paid any attention to Mum as she had trained me for the 'Session with the Dixits', as she liked to call it.

'And?' Mum said, stopping now, the living room just a few steps ahead of us.

'I will be nice to Purva,' I said, scowling even more.

Mum seemed satisfied. 'Let's go in,' she said.

And in we went.

2

7.15 p.m.

'Bahu,' someone said in a feeble voice as soon as I walked into the living room, flanked by Mum on both sides. I am not kidding, Mum *can* be on both sides of me at the same time. No, really, I'm serious. It's just another of her superpowers.

I looked around, smiling awkwardly at everyone, too dazed to really notice the faces, desperately clutching at the sari that suddenly seemed too loose around my waist.

'Focus, Kasturi, focus!' I said to myself. 'You are a woman of the twenty-first century; you can handle this. You can handle anything.' I was vaguely aware that the tall, broad form of Purva was standing somewhere close by. So dazed was I that I did not even acknowledge the man I had decided to marry. Also, in all fairness, it had just struck me that I needed to pee very urgently.

Next to Purva was his mum, the only person other than Purva and my own family that I recognized. She smiled sweetly at me and kissed my forehead.

'Yo! Bhabhi Jaan!' said a voice that was, rather disturbingly, as familiar as it was unfamiliar. I turned around and came face to face with a man who looked like Purva. Only he was not Purva. I looked at him puzzled and spotted Purva smiling widely in the background. This was one introduction he had been dying to make.

'Kasturi, this is Vikram, my brother. Vikki, Kasturi...' said Purva, in his characteristically quiet voice. My eyes darted from one face to the other. How could two different people be so similar, I thought, struck again by the two faces that looked at me with almost identical smiles plastered across almost identical faces. I had seen pictures of Vikki, of course, but seeing him in person was another surprise altogether.

My parents have been lovely and whatever I might say about my mum, I have had the most perfect life with them. Except for one thing that I have always missed. It is a void that friends, toys and cousins have not been able to fill: a sibling.

'Hello!' said Vikki, taking my face tenderly in his hands. 'How did a monkey like Bhaiyya find someone as beautiful as you?'

I giggled.

'My bhabhi gorgeous-est,' said Vikram, his face shining with such love that I felt my throat tighten. I knew it right then, in that one moment, that Vikki and I would be friends for life.

'Bahu,' said the same voice that had called out to me earlier, feebler this time, but tinged with unmistakable annoyance. I would have barely noticed it, had not everyone begun to stare at me. Mum nudged me and began to nod her head so vigorously in the direction the voice came from that for a second I was worried that her head would drop off. I brushed away the gruesome image.

'What? Bahu? Me?' I said indignantly to myself and turned around to face an elderly lady who had found herself the largest, most comfortable sofa our drawing room had to offer.

Naniji? Or Dadiji? Seeing that both the grey-haired lady and Purva's mum had the same hawk-like nose, I concluded that it was the former.

Would it not be absolutely fabulous if I scooped towards her feet, saying, 'Charan sparsh, Naniji'? I would then be the would-be bahu – note the 'would-be' please – who not only does charan sparsh at the drop of a hat but also knows all the relatives by face. Do they even make those anymore? Oh yes they do! Meet Kasturi Shukla. Tada!

With *Kyunki Saas Bhi Kabhi Bahu Thi* playing in the back of my head, wondering if I should have, after all, covered my head with the pallu of my sari for added effect and almost revelling in the fact that all eyes were on me, I walked demurely towards Naniji. Bending low, I said loudly – so that everyone could clearly hear me – 'Charan sparsh, Naniji,' and, after a pause, added, 'Pranam, Naniji,' just for extra effect. Go full throttle, I say. No half-baked nonsense from the woman of substance that I am.

There was deathly silence for a second. Puzzled, I turned to look at Mum and knew that something had gone horribly wrong when I saw that her face was getting redder by the second. The elderly lady cleared her throat, opened her mouth to say something and then closed it again. Further examination made it abundantly clear to me that something about our little exchange had disturbed her deeply; she seemed to be having trouble breathing.

What had happened?

Dad hurried up to me. 'Beta,' he said, looking stricken, 'Naniji is here.' He pointed to the dark corner where a frail lady with snow-white hair was sitting, a slow smile on her beautiful face. I turned around in slow motion to face the lady whose feet I had just touched. Now I was having trouble breathing. 'Mausiji,' said Dad, cringing visibly.

'Aaah,' I said, trying control the damage. 'Badi Mausiji?' Aunty had an elder sister, I knew, who was older than her by almost a decade. That would make sense, right? And make me look less terrible. I mentally patted my back. Quick thinking. Decisions on the go. Strategizing on the fly. That's me. Give me a bad situation and I will emerge shining.

'Purva's mum's youngest sister,' said Dad wearily.

That was when I caught sight of Purva. The dark clouds of a guffaw, ready to break free, were evident on his face. He coughed a fake cough, trying his best to cover up.

'Kasturi,' said Purva in my ear, in what he meant to be a disapproving tone. His eyes, however, danced with mirth.

'What am I supposed to do?' I muttered angrily under my breath to Purva. 'After all ... inki twacha se inki umra ka pata hi nahi chalta!'

This time Purva and Vikki, who were both standing close enough to overhear, made no attempt to fake it. Their identical guffaws rang loudly in my drawing room. The actual naniji was the first to join the boys and, before I knew it, everyone was laughing at the would-be 'bahu rani' who did not know where to look.

Mausaji slapped Dad's back and Mausiji managed a weak smile. The younger cousins joined in the laughter. Seeing everyone in splits, my mum began to laugh rather hysterically, so much so that I got really worried after about a few seconds.

However, I have just one question to ask.

Why me? Every bloody time.

3

8.00 p.m.

I was in the process of being kissed on the cheeks by another unknown elderly lady when I heard Vikki yell. 'Here they are!' he cried, pointing towards the door.

I looked up to see Pitajee and Anu bound in, hand in hand, like two cheeky monkeys. Right. It's time for the all-important introductions. The goofy Pitajee, officially known as Amay, is my best buddy. Purva says Pitajee and I do each other no good and that he does not know who is a worse influence on the other. I will have to grudgingly agree.

Pitajee is mad. I am mad. Our combined madness, however, is greater than the sum total of our individual madnesses. That, my friend, is the sign of the truest kind of friendship. Nothing is as much fun or as crazy without Pitajee around. He does not shy away from yanking my hair or pinning my hands behind my back and twisting my arm till I agree with him. Of course, I keep my dignity intact and do not resort to such uncouth behaviour. Instead, I have, in the glorious past, locked him inside the bathroom for four hours, thrown his mobile phone out of the car in *a Zindagi-Na-Milegi-*

Dobara-esque moment of purpose and even crank-called his boss with a heart-wrenching tale of how Pitajee had ditched me for a prettier girl.

And yet, we mean the world to each other. I will never forget the night when I had just discovered the truth about Rajeev, and Pitajee cradled me in his arms as I howled like a baby. I will not forget how, when I was roaming the streets of Delhi looking for a job, he used all his connections in the corporate world to get me interviews. And I will never undervalue how he always leaves for me the better, bigger slice of my favourite pizza.

And then there's Anu. Anu – short for Ananya – is my other best friend. Anu and I were part of the same management training program and even though we work in different places now, we continue to share an apartment in Delhi. Anu and Pitajee, who, incidentally, met through me, are also madly in love with each other.

Seeing them standing there, hand in hand, grinning idiotically, I could not help but dramatically bring my hands to my mouth in genuine surprise. These guys were not supposed to be here. I looked at Purva, who was walking towards them, a surprised look on his face.

'You guys!' he said, slapping Pitajee's back.

'Yes,' said Pitajee, winking at me from across the room. 'Us guys. And who is that mataji in the corner there?' he asked, pointing in my direction.

8.10 p.m.

Family members surrounded us with great fanfare. Purva's

family seemed to be getting very excited about something that they clearly had up their sleeve. One of Purva's aunts made us stand in the centre, flanked on either side by parents and guests.

While Mum looked decidedly uncomfortable, Dad did not notice anything odd. The frequency with which the ladke waalas were exchanging conspiratorial looks with one another was steadily – and worryingly – increasing. Vikki pulled out something from his bag that looked a lot like the bazookas I had seen on TV. Only it was not. It was one of those fancy cameras. He smiled at me and walked a little distance from us to take his position as the photographer of the evening.

'What the hell are the Dixits doing?' murmured Mum, looking around surreptitiously, as though she were a spy in a hostile country.

'Relax, Ma. Chill,' I said, shrugging my shoulders, getting very worried myself. I needed to pee.

'So,' began Arvind Mausaji in a very important voice. 'Can I have your attention, please?'

'*May* I have your attention please,' muttered Purva under his breath. The grammar puritan, I thought benevolently, stealing a glance at the kurta-pyjama-clad doctor standing beside me. Purva is, if I were to be honest, not the most handsome man on this planet. Don't get me wrong; he is not bad-looking. His large, intelligent, black eyes fanned with long lashes give him a sharpness and an innocence that I find very appealing. Thick, wavy hair frames a wise, calm face. Good-looking, yes, but let's just say you won't confuse him with Tom Cruise or Hrithik Roshan. Clad in a maroon-and-beige kurta, which was, I have to say, uncharacteristically fancy for the jeans-and-white-tee Purva, he did look quite handsome. My cousin Mili would not stop staring at him and I debated the pros and cons of taking off my expensive heels and hitting her on the head with them.

Mausaji cleared his throat and launched into his speech. 'Times have changed. They have! They have! My father used to buy bread that cost seventy-five paise and now I buy bread for seventy-five rupees.'

'Seventy-five rupees!' exclaimed Mausiji, her mood obviously still foul. 'Is your bread made of gold?'

Mausaji glared at his wife and then continued. 'So, times have changed. Gone are the days when the girl's family was any different from the boy's family.' Mausaji paused. It did not sound grand enough. 'In fact, I will have to say that gone are the days when *anyone* was any different from *anyone* else,' he said with a flourish. He fidgeted a little bit, pulled up his pants and patted his belly. Though everyone nodded their heads in agreement, I doubt if anyone – including Mausaji himself – was able to make sense of this valiant declaration.

Not the one to be impeded by logic or sense, Mausaji continued. 'So it's easy to see…' he paused and looked around dramatically, 'that we are all the same. We are one!' he said with a theatrical sweep.

It was now my turn to disguise a laugh into a cough. The mental image of everyone in the room rolling into each other and becoming one just would not leave my head. Purva, his lips twitching, patted my back.

'Now that we are all one,' continued Mausaji, 'it is time to

... do something about those who stand in front of us.' He had, quite evidently, lost the plot.

'Prabhaji,' said Mausaji, bowing gracefully towards Mum, who beamed in return. 'Allow me to do this.'

'Sure,' said Mum in an instant.

I glared at her. Do you even know what Mausaji has up his sleeve, I asked silently, getting quite worried. Anything could happen now.

Mausaji smiled. Dad looked extremely bewildered. I still needed to pee.

'Allow me, Mrs Shukla,' said Mausaji, 'to present to you the engagement ring.'

'What?' I said.

'What!' exclaimed Dad.

'What?' cried Mausiji.

Mausaji blatantly ignored us and continued to smile at Mum. Dad look decidedly uncomfortable when Mausaji began to walk towards Mum with the little jewellery box in his hands and a silly smile on his face. Mental images of Mausaji going down on one knee in front of Mum while a horrified Mausiji looked on made me feel very weak.

Mausaji, blissfully unaware of the panic he was causing, cleared his throat, preparing himself to speak. 'We know that every parent dreams of their daughter's engagement. However, today is Purva's father's birthday. It would mean so much to us if, in his memory, Kasturi and Purva got engaged today. That way we would have included in the ceremonies that wonderful man whose time on the planet was cut short so suddenly.'

Someone sniffed. Finally Mausaji was getting the kind

of response he had been hoping for. Better late than never. Encouraged, he continued. 'That man was the greatest doctor that ever lived. The greatest *man* that ever lived. The greatest *soul* that ever lived. So kind, so gentle. And if you agree with this, Prabhaji, it will be a very generous gift from your family to ours, for which we shall remain indebted to you for life. We know it is a surprise, but it would mean so much to us … so much, so much!'

'Bhai Sa'ab,' said Mum, wiping her eyes, though I am sure I did not see any tears. 'Please, please go ahead. We have but the greatest respect for the memory of Dr Dixit and would love to include him in every way possible.' Then she paused, looked at Dad and, as an afterthought, asked, 'It is okay, isn't it?'

Dad, too dazed to say anything else, nodded his head.

'Smile!' shouted Vikki as he began to furiously take pictures.

'Hurray!' shouted a bespectacled little boy from Purva's family, clearly delighted that the boring monologue was now over.

'What?' said Purva, sparing a hand over his forehead. He had come for a meal but it seemed he was also getting engaged.

'What?' I said, looking around in bewilderment.

'H … how?' asked Purva, wide-eyed with surprise.

'I know!' I exclaimed. We were now babbling indignantly to one another, as the relatives busied themselves in hugging each other.

No one, of course, bothered with us and before I knew it, in the midst of claps and cheers and flower petals that appeared from nowhere, Purva had put a ring on my finger and I had put a ring on his. And just like that, working on autopilot, we were engaged.

'What just happened?' I asked, looking at the ring on my finger.

'I have no clue,' said Purva, shaking his head. 'I think we just got engaged.'

The mothers clasped us to their chests. Dad got all teary-eyed. We went around the room touching relatives' feet and were fed so much kaju katli in the process that I was sure I would be sick. It was about ten minutes later that I found myself in a quiet corner with Purva. Alone at last, just the two of us...

Mum walked by, smiling knowingly and then paused, turned around and winked.

At Purva.

I could do little more than roll my eyes.

'We are engaged!' said Purva once Mum had gone, his face expressing mild surprise.

'You know, Purva,' I said, putting my hand in his.

'Yes, darling?' he said tenderly, leaning in so that his face was but a few inches from mine.

'I really, really need to pee.'

4

9.00 p.m.

I grimaced as I straightened my back. Anju Aunty – Purva's mum – had just given me *another* tour of her side of the family. The following had happened in the last twenty minutes:

Number of times I was kissed: twelve.

Number of times I was told that I was very pretty: fourteen (Yay! Whoop! Whoop! Don't I love it?).

Number of times I was told that Purva is a very lucky man to have found me: seven (Smug smile of agreement).

Number of times I bent down to touch someone's feet: twenty-nine.

Being the would-be daughter-in-law was already proving to be back-breaking work (no pun intended).

The bespectacled six-year-old boy from Anju Aunty's family who had followed me closely as I met every person in the room now went up to his mother, tugged at the pallu of her sari, pointed a thick finger at me and asked, 'Mummy, who is that girl?'

His mother smiled a warm smile and looked benignly at her cherubic little son. 'That's your new chachi,' she said.

'Thaathee?' the boy repeated with a drawl.

'Chaa-chee,' said the mother.

'Tha-thee,' said the boy, sucking his thumb and jutting out his chin.

'Say cha,' persisted the mother.

'Cha,' repeated the boy obediently.

'Chee,' said the mother.

'Chee,' the boy agreed.

'Cha-chee,' said the mother.

'Tha-thee,' said the boy obstinately.

The mother took a deep breath and I knew that she was reaching out to the ocean of patience that God creates in would-be mothers during the nine months of pregnancy. Out of the blue, the boy started screaming and crying loudly. He began to wipe his eyes with the back of his hands, though I could clearly see that there were no tears. The drama, I thought indignantly, feeling for the mother with all my heart.

'Why are you crying now?' said the mother, looking at me exasperatedly. I nodded sympathetically and a glimpse of the future – a dozen kids clinging to me, screaming 'maa-meee' – flashed in front of my horrified eyes. My head reeled. My heart beat faster. The image was gone in a second, but it left me feeling weak. A wave of panic swept through me. I had just got engaged. What happens next? Marriage? Then kids? Then more kids? Then *their* kids! Where does it all end? Had I thought this through? Oh dear!

My line of thought was disrupted as the sounds of the boy, sobbing most pitifully, reached my ears.

'What happened, darling?' asked the mother.

'She did not,' Darling said, looking accusingly at me and

jabbing a pudgy little finger in my direction. What, in the name of the heavens above, had *I* done? Or not done?

'She did not what?' pressed his mother.

'Thathee did not touch *my* pheeet,' he screamed and then proceeded to bawl his lungs out.

Darling stamped his feet and before his mother could look beseechingly at me, logic dictated that I scutter away – and scutter away I promptly did.

9.02 p.m.

Dazed, I walked into the kitchen where another little scene awaited me.

Mum, for reasons best known to her, was standing in the middle of the kitchen, holding a pakora in each hand, her face wet with tears. Ramu and Dad were both standing at attention on either side of Mum, ready to spring into action should she have the meltdown she seemed so dangerously close to.

The person with his arms around Mum, however, was Pitajee. No surprises there, really. Defying logic and sense, Pitajee and Mum have grown, of late, rather thick. Though they have little in common, they seem to get each other. That, as Pitajee once told me with a profound look on his face, is all that matters.

Much like Darling, Mum also pointed a finger in my direction and, clutching the pakora to her chest, burst into tears. Really, what was wrong with everyone? It seemed that all I needed to do was to merely appear for people to burst into tears.

Pitajee nodded his head sympathetically. What had I done now?

'Eight-point-five,' said Mum in a tearful voice.

Pitajee nodded his head.

'Twenty-six,' said Mum.

Pitajee nodded his head again 'Twenty-eight, Aunty, if you count…'

'Oh yes, see … twenty-eight! And now…' Mum gesticulated with her hands. Someone had gone away? She was shooing me away?

Pitajee seemed to understand and he nodded his head. He was about to say something soothing when Mum burst into a fresh set of tears and, petrified, I scuttled away. From the corner of my eye, I saw Pitajee give Mum a big hug.

What was wrong with the world?

9.03 p.m.

Everything.

9.15 p.m.

This night seems to conspire against me and refuses to end.

After the obligatory round of dancing, Purva's cousins, colluding with mine, decided they wanted the newly engaged couple to play *some* games. After a few minutes of negotiations, Purva and I agreed to play *one* game.

The game was going to be fairly straightforward. They would ask me five questions about Purva and ask Purva five questions about me. Simple. Whoever got the maximum number of correct answers won. Everyone sat around in the living room, gently nibbling on the food that there was no dearth of and stared expectantly at us.

'Bhabhi,' began Purva's cousin Pinki.

I continued to eat and no one responded to Pinki. How rude people can be, I thought lazily to myself as I chased a pakora on the plate.

'Bhabhi,' she repeated.

Purva nudged me and it dawned on me that it was yours truly who was the 'bhabhi' in question.

Anu and Pitajee giggled with sheer delight at my obvious shock. I hate it when they do that. With friends like these, who needs enemies?

'Umm … err … yes, yes,' I said hastily.

'Bhaiyya's turn first. We will ask him five questions about you. First, you wait for him to answer and then you tell us if he was right or not.'

'Okay,' I said.

'So here we go! Purva Bhaiyya, Kasturi Bhabhi's favourite restaurant is?' Pinki said, putting on her fake game-show-host voice that drew a couple of laughs from the audience.

'Saravana Bhavan, Connaught Place,' came Purva's calm voice the next instant. Everyone turned their eyes on me. I nodded demurely, trying desperately to look shy. Images of soft, round idlis danced in front of my eyes.

'Bhabhi's favourite book?'

'*Villette*,' said Purva without hesitation. I nodded my head again.

'Question number three. Bhabhi's favourite movie?'

'*Dilwale Dulhaniya Le Jayenge*,' said Purva, smiling.

'That even I knew!' exclaimed Pitajee indignantly.

I nodded my head. I have seen *DDLJ* 126 times, the last eleven times with Pitajee.

'Excellent, Bhaiyya! Question number four. Kasturi Bhabhi's favourite colour?'

Purva took his time to deliberate, which surprised me. We had gone shopping last week when he had all but shot himself in the head as we hunted for a salwaar in the right shade of pink. 'Mauve,' he said, after a pause.

'Wrong!' said Pitajee the next instant with a superior smile on his face. A glorious glare from Anu, and Pitajee visibly shrank.

'Wrong,' I agreed, smiling.

Purva's family let out a collective groan as if the son of the soil had let his country down.

'And for the final question,' said Pinki, quite the game-show host. 'Which is Kasturi Bhabhi's favourite Bollywood song?'

Pitajee and I giggled in chorus. Even Purva smiled. *'Hum kalein hain toh kya hua dil wale hain,'* he said, smiling and shaking his head.

Everyone in the room – including Anju Aunty who had spent the better part of last year sending me parcels of Fem's reputed bleaching cream that loudly promised to make you five shades fairer in the blink of an eye – laughed.

I nodded my head.

Once Pinki had finished laughing, she cleared her throat. 'Four out of five. Great score but not unbeatable!'

'Now Kasturi's turn,' said Anju Aunty, settling into her chair, as if the real circus show was finally about to start.

I gulped. What if I got nothing right?

'I will help,' mumbled Pitajee discreetly in my ear.

I gulped further. Even Pitajee knew I was going to need help. Purva winked at me. I took a deep breath. Of course I could do this.

'Kasturi Bhabhi,' said Pinki, 'Bhaiyya's favourite Bollywood actress is?'

Hmm ... I thought hard for the next few seconds. The mind, invariably, went back to last week. Purva, Pitajee and I had had a very animated discussion about Sridevi (mostly about the plastic surgery though). Purva seemed to have a lot to say. 'Sridevi,' I announced, loudly and confidently.

Everyone looked at Purva who looked a little surprised. An instant later, however, he nodded his head.

'Yay!' yelped Pitajee.

'See, my daughter-in-law,' said Anju Aunty, proudly pointing a finger at me. I could have won a gold in the Olympics and Anju Aunty would not have been this proud of me.

'Purva Bhaiyya's favourite food?'

'Chinese?' I said, doubtfully.

'That's *your* favourite food, you idiot!' hissed Pitajee in my ear.

Before I could retort suitably to Pitajee who had stooped to a new level of low by calling me names on my engagement day, a round of applause resounded in the room. Purva had nodded his head and I had two correct answers.

It was then that I realised that the game was not as difficult as I had thought it to be. And boy, was I good! Before I knew it, I had announced, with unwavering confidence, that Vegas was

Purva's dream holiday destination, cricket was his favourite sport and meditation relaxed him.

I had also, surprisingly, given five correct answers.

With great joy, and amidst tremendous cheering, Anju Aunty clasped me tight to her chest. A girl who knew her son so well had to be given her due, after all. I think she got a little carried away and, in the flow of the moment, removed a gold bangle from her wrist and clasped it around mine.

'Your prize, my darling Koochie,' Anju Aunty said proudly and proceeded to smack another kiss on my forehead.

'Koochie!' I heard Pitajee repeat to Anu, sounding delighted beyond measure. 'Kasturi's mom-in-law calls her Koochie.'

My heart sank. I knew, just from the sheer delight in Pitajee's voice, that I would rarely be called Kas again.

Terrace, Shukla Residence, 11.00 p.m.

Most of the guests had gone. The house looked like it always did after a big party. Dishevelled.

Anju Aunty, Mum and Dad were downstairs, talking in hushed tones, discussing the surprise engagement and the upcoming wedding preparations. Purva and I sat on the terrace on a rotting wooden box that had survived more monsoons than we had thought possible, under the stars that blinked happily. We sat in comfortable silence, my head resting on Purva's shoulder, letting it all sink in. The white crescent of the moon bathed us in its pristine white. Anu and Pitajee sat on the floor of the terrace, holding hands.

'We're engaged,' Purva said, smiling down at me.

'I know,' I said, twiddling the expensive solitaire that glittered joyfully on my finger. 'Is this Anju Aunty's choice?'

'No, mine,' said Purva, moving his head closer to mine. 'Only I didn't know that I was going to put it on your finger today.'

I stared at the iridescent rock, transfixed by how much the mute stone signified.

'Let me show you something, Kas,' said Purva, gently tugging the ring out of my hand. I marvelled, yet again, at how gentle his touch always was. He pointed to the inside of the thick band and handed it back to me.

'Your smile fills my heart with joy,' the cursive hand of the inscription read.

'My smile fills your heart with joy?' I asked, tilting my face to one side and smiling my widest.

'Yes,' he said, lightly tapping one cheek. 'Especially when you smile *this* smile.'

Pitajee and Anu, who were sitting further away, now turned to look at us.

'Guys, shouldn't we get going?' said Anu.

'Yes,' said Purva, nodding his head.

There was one more thing that I needed to speak to Purva about and I put a hand on his arm to draw his attention.

'Yes?' said Purva.

'Who is your favourite actress?' I asked, pouting.

Purva laughed for a good minute before he placed a finger under my chin and pulled up my face. 'I love you so much Kasturi!' he said, his eyes dripping with unadulterated adoration.

'Your favourite actress, Purva?' I insisted, my voice low and glum.

'Madhuri Dixit. We Dixits kind of rock, you know,' he said, grinning from ear to ear.

'Food?'

'Mexican.'

'Dream holiday destination?'

'Paris, with you.'

'Favourite sport?'

'Tennis,' he said, but hurriedly added, 'though I do like cricket,' when he saw my face fall further.

'What relaxes you?'

'Looking at you goofing around,' he said, smiling.

I grimaced. I had zero correct answers and, as always, Purva had made sure that I bore no public embarrassment.

'Do you want this gold bangle? This was the prize for the winner, you know.' I asked, pouting and pointing at the gold bangle that Anju Aunty had given me.

Purva guffawed. 'You absolutely crazy girl,' he said, smiling as he planted a tender kiss on my forehead. 'I love you.'

'I love you too,' I mumbled and leaned in for a kiss. Purva always kisses slowly, as if he has all the time in the world. For him, I know the earth stops spinning. Sometimes, just sometimes, I feel a little bit like I know he feels. But mostly…

'Koooochhiiiieee, Beta Koocchhiiieee,' a voice came from downstairs, breaking the spell.

To my sheer horror, I realized that it was not Anju Aunty's voice. Mum. Mum, who had spent twenty-five years calling me Kasturi, was now calling me Koochie.

'Koochiieeee Beta...' said Mum again, as I looked on,

appalled. 'Come down, Beta ... Anju Aunty is leaving.'

Pitajee clasped his hand to his mouth and laughed uncontrollably for an eternity before he regained his composure. Looking down the staircase, he shouted at the top of his voice, 'Kooochiiee is here, Aunty ... she is coming down now! Koochiiee,' he said, keeping his face straight with obvious difficulty, 'let's go down.'

I stuffed the pallu of my sari into the waist band, turned around sharply and, without any warning, lunged for Pitajee's jugular. Purva and Anu tried, in vain, to stop me.

'Bhabhiji!' shouted Pitajee, shaking with laughter, right before my hands clasped around his neck. 'You are the very epitome of poise!'

Before long, we had all tumbled into a mass of limbs, one on top of the other.

5

Vijaywada & Sons Headquarters, Delhi, 11 January 2013.

'That just cannot be true, Mum!' I said into my cell phone, aghast at what I had just heard. I twiddled the ring on my finger, still not quite used to it. I could not believe my ears. My cubicle partner – P.P. Padma – busy tapping away at her laptop, glared angrily at me.

'It is, Koochie Beta!' Mum hollered in return.

'What are you saying?' I said, too shell-shocked to even reprimand Mum for calling me Koochie. In the last week, after I left home to come back to Delhi, I had had eleven fights with Mum. Seven of them were because of 'Koochie'. I digress.

'The truth,' said Mum.

'Say it again,' I said, disbelievingly.

'Arjun is in love with you.'

'Dear Lord!'

'Don't "Dear Lord" me, Beta. It's rude. If you were younger, I would have spanked you for this.'

'Okay, sorry,' I said, meekly. 'How do you know that Arjun

loves me, given that even I don't know that?'

'He told me ... I mean he told you.'

'What? Mum, what are you blabbering about?'

P.P. Padma cast me a glance that would have made even a dead man turn cold. I ignored her and continued to chat with Mum, my legs resting on the table next to the desktops.

'Okay, let me explain. He sent a package addressed to you.'

'Okay...'

'So I opened it.'

'Mum! How can you open my mail?'

Mum ignored me and continued. 'And out came a CD. I put it into my laptop and it was a voice-recording. Frankly speaking, Beta, there was a lot of gibberish in it. I think he was reciting some poetry, which made no sense to me. There was some nonsense about stars looking like your eyes or maybe your eyes looking like stars ... which, of course, is a ridiculous thing to say; stars are like dots, they don't resemble eyes either in shape or form. Anyway, after a lot of dilly-dallying, he finally came to the point and said that he has loved you since he first saw you. But it doesn't make sense either.'

'Why doesn't it make sense?'

'Now I know we first met his family when you kids were a year old. So if I were to believe him, he has been in love with you since you both were one, which is ridiculous,' said Mum, doing some quick maths.

Arjun is my next-door neighbour, occupant of the famous A/138 apartment. To be honest, he is quite cute but I have never fancied him. He and I were at school together, then went to the same mathematics coaching centre and then the same engineering college. Thankfully, we parted ways after that and ended up in different business schools. I distinctly remember a time, in class six, when I hit him on the head with a ruler, after which he was taken to the infirmary and given twenty stitches. He still bears the scars. If that were not enough, in engineering college, I was cheating from his answer script and *he* got caught. I know I am very mean; still I can't help but giggle uncontrollably when I think of that.

Why he would ever fall in love with a girl who displays a distinct streak of violence at the tender age of twelve and grows up to become a cheat was beyond me. Anyway, people do strange things.

'This is weird,' I said, staring at the little black bindi that adorned P.P. Padma's forehead.

'Yes!' said Mum.

'Then?'

'Then I got angry. How can you send a courier like that to the girl's mother, of all people? These boys have no sense of decorum and protocol. It's fine if you are in love with a girl, but go tell the girl! Why send a CD recording to the girl's mother?'

'But Mum, he didn't send it to you,' I said feebly, my head reeling.

'Whatever. Now don't go around defending him,' said Mum, chiding me. 'I called up Leela Aunty and told her that your wedding is fixed. I told her to convey this to her rowdy son…'

The world swam in front of my eyes. Poor Leela Aunty.

'Kasturi!' I heard my boss, Mr Vijaywada, holler in the background.

'Mum! I need to go now,' I said impatiently.

'Why?'

'Mum! I am in office, that's why.'

'So?' she asked innocently. 'Pankudi Aunty and I chat for hours when *she* is in office'

'Mum!'

'Oh okay,' said Mum half-heartedly and hung up.

'Kasturi!' Mr Vijaywada hollered from his cabin once again. I sighed.

P.P. Padma tucked a strand of religiously oiled and very long hair behind her ear and looked disapprovingly in my direction. The daggers in her eyes, I thought philosophically to myself, will kill me one day.

I smiled apologetically, feeling, as I always do when I am on the receiving end of that stare from P.P. Padma, quite small. One day, I vowed to myself, I will tell her I am not as bad as she thinks I am.

P.P. Padma is the EA to the MD. Tall, thin and dark, with long hair that she generally keeps oiled and tied in a ponytail, P.P. Padma is undoubtedly a force to reckon with. Irrespective of what she wears, a tiny black bindi adorns her forehead without fail.

When I was new to the organization, I had asked her a question that turned out to be the final nail in the coffin within which our potential friendship lay, already dead. 'Why don't you take the bindi off your forehead?' I had asked her, meaningfully eyeing her jeans and ridiculously pink, frilly top.

She stared at me, stunned, unable to speak for the next few minutes. Is she having a heart attack, I wondered as I saw her face turn purple.

'Take off my bindi?' she asked incredulously, in a low growl.

I cowered under her glare. 'No ... no … I mean … why not take this one off and put on a pink one instead of the black one … err … to match your pink top...' I fumbled. P.P. Padma said nothing and simply turned away, disgust written on her angry face.

With that innocent suggestion, I knew I had squashed any chance we had of becoming friends. However, there are other reasons for this friendship to not have bloomed. P.P. Padma is more dedicated to work than I would have thought humanly possible. The aim of her life is to serve the MD. The aim of my life is to make the MD suffer. Our interests, ideals and work ethic clash, rendering this friendship effectively impossible.

'Kasturi!' Mr Vijaywada hollered from his cabin, interrupting my line of thought. I yawned again, not bothering to cover my mouth and turned my attention towards the Facebook page open on my screen.

'Kasturi!' Mr Vijaywada hollered for the fourth time.

I rolled my eyes. Not a moment of peace in this god-forsaken office, I thought to myself. The day was indeed not turning out well.

'No harm in working once in a while,' Padma muttered under her breath, loud enough for me to hear. I turned around sharply to look at her.

'I'm sorry?' I said, belligerent, yet dangerously polite. 'Did you say anything to me?'

'No, not to you, just to myself. General observation,' she said in her thick south Indian accent. She continued to stare at her laptop, allowing herself a rare, small smile.

'KASTURI SHUKLA!' screamed my boss, giving me a start.

I will deal with P.P. Padma later, I told myself and, giving her one final stare, stormed off in the general direction of Mr Vijaywada's office.

Mr Swaminathan Vijaywada – the MD of Vijaywada & Sons – is, if nothing else, a fair man. He pays me half of what he should pay someone with my qualifications and I do half the work that someone in my position should do. It is a simple arrangement. Our goals are contradictory. I try to get him to increase my salary and he successfully resists. He tries to get me to increase my working hours and I successfully resist. However, in spite of the situation, the two of us get along fairly well, much to the disdain of P.P. Padma.

The door to his office was open and I stormed in, still piqued at the comments of his faithful EA.

'Morning, Mr Vijaywada,' I said angrily.

'Morning,' he said, looking meaningfully at the small antique alarm clock on his table. Our meeting was scheduled for 11.00 a.m. and it was already 11.15.

I smiled apologetically, feeling no remorse. 'I was busy making the presentation, Vijaywada Sir,' I said meekly. Both of us knew that was untrue.

'I called out your name twice,' he said accusingly.

'Five times,' I said to myself. 'Sorry sir, I did not hear it even once,' I said, making a sad face.

His face softened. 'Ear problem?' he said, shaking his head sadly.

'Yes, sir,' I nodded my head. I sighed a deep, sad sigh, befitting the occasion. Mr Vijaywada looked at me with pity in his eyes, shaking his head sorrowfully. Poor girl, fairly incompetent and partially deaf. Whatever will happen to her, he seemed to think to himself.

So, yes, Mr Vijaywada thinks I am partially deaf. I'll delve into the long story of how that came about later. Suffice it to say that I do little to correct it.

'Okay, so moving on. How are we coming along with the PowerPoint?' he asked, referring to the presentation that I was making to suggest ways of increasing brand awareness.

I was walking back to my cubicle after the meeting, out of which nothing useful had emerged, when my cell beeped.

'Emergency meeting. Premarital issue. Same place. Right after Purva's shift at the hospital,' the unusually dry text from Pitajee read.

'What has happened now?' I wondered to myself. I got a distinct feeling that all was not well in the world of Pitajee and Anu.

I sighed as I sat at my desk and flicked Facebook open again.

Sweet 'n' Chilly Café, AIIMS, Delhi, 8.00 p.m.

I nervously twiddled with the ring on my finger. The four of us were sitting in dismal silence around the table, the red bottle of ketchup staring dolefully back at us. Purva was bleary-eyed; it had been yet another thirty-six-hour shift at the hospital. The mood of the group was sombre for obvious reasons. Anu and Pitajee had just dropped a bomb.

'So what exactly did Ahya say?' asked Pitajee. Ahya Goswami is Anu's rather corpulent and stern mother. She also happens to be an IAS officer, fully capable of instilling the fear of God in the heart and soul of any man on this planet. That she is not very popular in our group is evident from the fact that none of us call her anything but Ahya.

'That I should not even think of marrying you. If I do, she will chase you to the ends of the world and kill you,' said Anu, her face glum and voice matter-of-fact.

The five-hundred-kilo Ahya Goswami cut a threatening figure even while standing still and I could understand why that little shudder ran through Pitajee's body when Anu repeated the threat. No one would want to be chased to the end of the world by Ahya.

'So what do we do?' asked Purva.

'Kill Ahya?' Pitajee asked innocently. I nodded my head in vehement agreement.

'Shut up or I will kill you,' threatened Anu, but her eyes were not angry.

'What about Govind?' asked Pitajee, referring to Anu's father, who was a widely-respected IAS officer as well. Let's just say that he is not known to be soft-hearted.

Anu shook her head. 'He is dead opposed to the match.'

'But why?' I asked. Pitajee, of course, has no brains but he is good and kind and from a very reputed B-school and also an investment banker. (It is a universal truth that you do not need to have brains to get into a good B-school or land a job as an investment banker, but let's not get all controversial here). Surely he would be considered a 'good match'?

'Mom and Dad think I should only marry an IAS officer.'

'MBA graduates are no good?' I asked indignantly, mentally brandishing my MBA degree in front of Anu's eyes.

'Marry an IAS officer so that you can spend half your life in a village without ever being able to remember its name?' contested Pitajee, equally indignantly.

'Do you want to spend evening after evening sitting on the stage as the wife of the chief guest?' I continued.

Pitajee shot me a 'thanks-buddy' look. 'Or spend them getting ready for cocktail parties?' he added.

'Or get together with the other wives and throw kitty parties?' I piped up.

'Or cut ribbons when the local school opens a new lavatory?' Pitajee chipped in.

'Or flirt with your IAS husband's IAS boss, whose wife is too busy flirting with *his* IAS boss to bother?'

'Or...'

'Shut up, you two,' glowered Anu, interrupting Pitajee. I gave him a 'tell-me-later-okay?' look.

Anu settled the dupatta of her salwar-kameez. Ever since her parents have refused to allow her to marry Pitajee, Anu has taken to wearing chikan salwar-kameezes. Her growing love for theatrics is becoming quite evident to us. 'They even have a boy in mind,' she added in a small voice.

'What?' I almost shouted. This was news.

I noted that Pitajee had stilled, all the goofiness disappearing in an instant. 'Boy in mind for what?' he asked.

'A boy for me to marry,' said Anu.

'When did this happen?' asked Purva.

'This morning.'

There was silence as the four of us exchanged looks, the gravity of the situation not lost on us. The silence was broken a few seconds later by Anu. 'There is more…' she said in an even smaller voice.

Three pairs of eyes turned towards her.

'They are meeting the boy's parents this Sunday. If the parents like each other, they want me to meet him by the end of this month.'

The Goswamis meant business and we knew enough of Anu's parents to know that it would be a very bad idea to cross their paths. Ahya's wrath was enough, but Ahya and Govind combined were a force that even Anu shrank from.

May the force be with us.

6

Anju Aunty's Apartment, Sarojini Nagar, Delhi, 20 January 2013, 5.00 p.m.

Most doctors have a horrible sense of humour. Anju Aunty, a gynaecologist, is no exception. My cheeks and spirit hurt as I smiled, yet again, at her attempts at humour.

Of late, I have made it a point to visit Anju Aunty at least once a month and try to call her up once in two weeks. I have reminders in my phone and little crosses on the calendar at work to remind me of these visits and calls. Protocol, Pitajee calls it. One would think that being professional women, Anju Aunty and I would have a lot of professional things to talk about ... hopes, dreams, aspirations...

Sorry to disappoint you, but we don't.

For example, the last time we spoke, Anju Aunty spent a lot of time explaining to me the various types of dal one should always ensure one's kitchen is well-stocked with. Another time she told me how best I can manage the maid. Before that, it was a monologue about boiling milk or something equally important.

I digress again. This evening, I came to Anju Aunty's apartment to spend some time with her and then have dinner with Purva and Vikki, who were to join us later. The conversation so far had been fairly uneventful.

She spoke, I listened.

She spoke and I smiled.

She continued to speak and I continued to smile.

This seemed to be going fairly well, until now.

'So, Beta,' said Anju Aunty chattily. 'What colour would you like your wedding lehenga to be?'

'Umm…' I thought, frantically. Funnily enough, it had never struck me that I would need a lehenga for the wedding. 'Umm … red, I think.'

'Very good. I will buy it for you.'

'Thanks, Aunty,' I said, smiling again. My cheeks were already hurting from all the smiling I had been doing since I had entered the house.

'Just like the one we bought for Betu's wedding,' she said, as if Betu were my bosom buddy.

'Ji Auntyji,' I said, nodding my head. 'But Aunty, who is Betu?'

'Arre!' said Anju Aunty, surprised that I did not know this important personality. 'Betu! Gilli Masi's eldest daughter!'

'Err ... Gilli Masi?' I asked, hesitating. Why would anyone in their right minds name their child 'Gilli', I wondered to myself, as I waited for Anju Aunty to reply.

'Gilli Masi, Lata Taiji's youngest daughter-in-law!'

I gulped and did not voice the burning question that gnawed at my insides. Who, for god's sake, was Lata Taiji?

'Ohhh…' I said, slapping my forehead gently. 'Lata Taiji … of course! I must have confused her with someone else, I think,' I said, seemingly disappointed with my memory.

'Don't worry, Beta,' said Anju Aunty kindly. 'I know, you must have confused her with Mala Taiji's youngest daughter-in-law's eldest daughter.'

My head reeled for an instant. God, please help me. 'Really? Why do you think that happened?' The words were out of my mouth before I could stop them.

'Mala Taiji's youngest daughter-in-law's eldest daughter is called Beti! That's why!'

'Her name is Beti?' I asked, disbelievingly. Really, there was something wrong with the way this family named its daughters! Thoughts of having a daughter named Bitiya Dixit, or something equally insane, struck me.

'Of course! That's why you must have confused the names! Beti and Betu are so similar.'

I tried to collect my thoughts as Anju Aunty looked at me, confused at my confusion. Really, I could not be the ideal daughter-in-law if I did not know who Beti and Betu were.

'Of course! That is exactly why I got confused,' I agreed, smiling jubilantly.

'Good! Very good!' said Anju Aunty, her face beaming with joy, now that I looked a little less zapped. 'I am glad you know who Mala Taiji is, at least,' she said, smiling kindly. 'Lata Taiji's daughter-in-law's daughter-in-law did not even know who Mala Taiji was!' she added, conspiratorially. 'Even after she got married!'

'Really?' I said, aghast at how cheeky daughters-in-law were getting these days. I made a mental note to ask Purva who Lata Taiji was. And Mala Taiji. And Betu. And Beti.

'So how are your cooking classes coming along?' asked Anju Aunty, just as I brought the cup of tea to my mouth.

'Cooking class? Which cooking class?' I asked nonchalantly, eyeing the samosas that were on the table. I had already had five and Anju Aunty was now watching me with raised eyebrows as I stretched my hand out for the sixth one.

'Which classes?' she asked, seeming zapped. 'You told me you've been going for cooking classes every day for the last four weeks?'

I almost sputtered out the tea I was about to swallow. I vaguely recalled lying to her about it and, having uttered the lie, I had completely forgotten about it. 'Ji … ji…' I stuttered. 'Of course … they are good fun and I am learning so many new things…'

'Really?' said Anju Aunty, beaming with the sort of pride that only a mother-in-law in the making can beam with. 'What did you learn in your last class, Beta?'

'Umm…' I fumbled, trying to think on my feet but blanking out instead. 'Pizza!' I cried.

'What?'

'Pizza!' I said jubilantly, smacking the arm of the sofa in my excitement.

Anju Aunty eyed the cloud of dust that arose from the sofa disapprovingly. 'But did not you say that it was an Indian cooking class?'

Why do I have to go overboard when I lie?

'Oh yes!' I recalled now how I had told her how much Indian cooking excites me and how I would love to be able to cook delicious Indian food for family and friends after the wedding. It was all coming back to me.

Slowly.

'Beta,' she said, making a visible effort to reign in her patience. 'Are they teaching you how to cook Italian food? If that is the case, you should ask them to return your money. If they don't, let me speak to them. This is not done. In fact, call them up right now. Right now. I will shout at them and get your money back,' she concluded, her cheeks red with indignation.

'No ... no...' I said, panicking. I began to rack my brains. 'Actually, that's the other cooking class I go to.'

Deathly silence for a few minutes.

'You are attending two cooking classes?' Anju Aunty said slowly, unable to hide either her surprise or delight.

'Ji,' I said, looking down shyly at my hands that were now neatly folded my lap. 'Two classes – one for Indian cooking and the other for Italian,' I purred in a soft, demure voice.

'Arre ... my darling,' she crooned as she came to me and affectionately patted my head. I had just won about a trillion brownie points and mentally high-fived myself. I wondered if I had moved Anju Aunty enough for her to take off the other gold bangle and press it into my hands. 'So, what did you learn in your last Indian cooking class?' she asked, as she made her way back to her sofa. The lone gold bangle rolled around her wrist as she sat down and sipped from her cup of tea.

I looked around helplessly. The madness would not end.

'Mughlai parantha,' I said, amazed at how that came out of me. For god's sake, I have never even seen, leave alone eaten, mughlai parantha.

'Ohh … that is very nice! How do you make it, Beta? The recipe?' she said, sipping her tea and looking expectantly at me. This was exactly the kind of chai-time conversation that Anju Aunty had dreamt of having with the bahu – swapping recipes, discussing dal and talking about boiling milk. I gulped. The world swam around me. Why does this always happen to me?

'What is the need for that, Auntyji? I will cook it. Someday,' I said glibly.

Anju Aunty laughed delicately, pleased with her future daughter-in-law's promise to cook mughlai paranthas. 'Why some day, Beta?' she said chirpily.

My heart stopped beating as I raised my eyebrows, wondering where all of this was heading.

'Why don't you make it today?' she said, throwing up her hands gleefully.

I could literally feel my eyes pop out. I shook my head.

'Today?' I asked, to clarify.

'Right now!' she said, in a happy sing-song voice and then paused 'Why? Any problem, Beta? Aren't you here to spend the evening till Purva and Vikki return?'

There was no way out.

'Oh … yes … yes ... no … Auntyji …I mean no problem … I will make tandoori parantha today.'

'Mughlai,' she said gently.

'Eh?' I asked, lost.

'Mughlai parantha, Beta, mughlai,' she corrected me, smiling.

I felt faint. What does Mughlai parantha even look like, I wondered, allowing Anju Aunty to lead me to the kitchen so that I could cook Mughlai paranthas for her, Vikki and Purva.

7

The Kitchen, Anju Aunty's Apartment, Delhi, 6.30 p.m.

I took a deep breath and looked around.

'So, Beta, what should I get for you?'

'Mughlai parantha,' I said ruefully.

Anju Aunty laughed heartily. 'Good sense of humour, Beta,' she said and I tried hard not to grimace. 'So?' she continued.

'So, what?'

'What are the ingredients?

'Ahh.'

'Hmm?'

'Ahh,' I said. After a couple of minutes, during which a debate raged in my head, I said 'flour' with a finality in my voice.

The bell rang before Anju Aunty could say anything. She hurried out.

6.32 p.m.

Internet. I immediately fished out my phone but the stupid browser would not work.

I felt my pulse race, my heart beat faster, my breathing become difficult.

6.33 p.m.

Mum. Without further ado, I dialled her number.

'Betu,' said Mum chirpily.

'Mum, don't call me that,' I said curtly. The recent conversation with Anju Aunty about the Betus and the Betis was still fresh in my mind.

'I call you "Koochie", you have a problem. I call you "Betu", you have a problem with that also. What should I call you?'

'Use the same name you have used for the last quarter of a century,' I said in a firm voice.

Silence.

'What have I called you for the last quarter of the century?' said Mum, perplexed.

I groaned out loud. 'Kasturi,' I reminded her.

'Oh, that,' she said, a little disappointed.

'You chose the name, Mum!' I said.

'But Beta…'

'Mum, I need help,' I cut in. There was no time to lose. 'Mughlai parantha,' I said, urgently and cryptically.

'Okay. What do I do with them?' Mum said, her voice mimicking mine.

I snarled in frustration. 'Mum! How do you make them?'

'I don't.'

'What!'

'I don't make mughlai paranthas!'

'Why not?'

'I believe in feeding my family healthy, nutritious...'

'Mum!' I cut in again. 'I really need...'

'Kasturi,' said Mum, now cutting me short. 'How many times do I have to tell you that it's rude to speak when someone is trying to say something? These CAT coaching centres, they actually teach young people how to not let others complete their sentences. That is why all you MBA people...'

'Mum ... I just need the recipe,' I wailed, now close to tears.

'Kasturi, Beta, you are losing it ... I am getting worried. Do you want me to book an appointment with the doctor? Pankudi Aunty's friend was ... you know ... behaving a little like you and they took him to this doctor for the mentally challenged and...'

I cancelled the call. I could hear Anju Aunty speak with someone at the door. There was no time.

6.36 p.m.

'Pitajee,' I barked into the phone.

'Darling.'

'Shut up.'

'I'm hurt.'

'I don't care...'

'How rude!'

'Shut up!'

'Okay.'

'Mughlai paranthas!'

'What about them?'

'How do I make them?'

'How, and more importantly, why would I know?'

'Idiot, I know you don't. Google it for me'

'Why?'

'I don't have time to tell you why.'

'I won't Google anything unless you tell me why.'

'How uncool!'

'Waiting for the whole story. I have all the time. Remember, you don't.'

That maniac! I quickly told Pitajee the whole story.

'Serves you right,' he said politely.

'Shut up.'

'For lying to someone who is like a mother to you!'

'Shut up!'

'Don't ever lie again.'

'Shut up!'

'Be a little more ladylike.'

'Shut up!'

'Okay. Here is the recipe,' said Pitajee finally and began to rattle off the recipe that I tried hard to memorize.

'You want to thank me?' said Pitajee pointedly after he had finished.

'No, but I want to say something else...' I said in a soft voice.

'Go ahead, darling.'

'You are a maniac,' I said politely.

'So are you, my love,' retorted Pitajee.

'And that is why we rock,' I said, now smiling. I could hear Pitajee smile too as he wished me luck and hung up.

9.30 p.m.

I was sitting at the dinner table, when my cell phone beeped.

'How did the paranthas turn out?' Pitajee's text read.

'Horrible,' I replied.

'Poor you.'

'It gets worse.'

'?'

'My parantha was so bad that…'

'That?' came Pitajee's message, the next second.

'Anju Aunty has asked me to stop going to the cooking classes she thinks I go to. They are obviously no good.'

'HAHA. Not bad!'

'There is more.'

'?'

'She has called up a friend of hers who runs cooking classes for brides-to-be and specializes exclusively in making Indian bread.'

'Dear lord.'

'Yes, dear lord. Anju Aunty has paid for thirty classes. I will have to go twice a week.'

Although Pitajee was about forty kilometres away from me, I could almost hear his crazy laugh.

8

Our Apartment, Delhi, 27 January 2013, 1.00 a.m.

What was that, a squeak? The door opening? Maybe it was a burglar breaking in? Where was that fake plastic pistol I bought from the Diwali mela? Oh no, I'd left it in the office.

Note to self – bring fake Diwali-mela pistol from office and keep it by the bedside.

1.01 a.m.

Not a burglar … a cat maybe?

1.02 a.m.

Two cats? Cats talking to each other? One cat and one burglar? One burglar and his cat?

Still groggy, my head spun.

Was my brain playing tricks on me? Side effect of the cough medicine Purva got for me? Would I begin to hallucinate and die from hallucinations?

This seemed to make sense.

Maybe.

1.03 a.m.

Was that Anu crying?

3.00 a.m.

Anu and I met when I started working in India Telecom Private Limited, where both of us were part of the same management trainee programme. We shared a room during the induction and had been flatmates since then. Through break-ups and patch-ups, leaking taps and overheated boilers, absent maids and milkmen who would not leave, Anu and I had emerged stronger than ever.

In all these years, I had never found Anu awake in the middle of the night, in tears.

'Anu!' I said aghast, rushing to her side. 'What's wrong?'

'I love Amay,' she said, referring to Pitajee.

'Oh yes, of course,' I said, sitting down beside her on the bed. The warm glow of the lamp cast a melancholy shadow on the hunched-up body, racked with sobs. 'What's happened, Anu?'

'Mom and Dad are adamant, Kas. They won't listen to me.'

'Everyone errs, Anu, even our parents. You know my mum, don't you, how she sometimes does the wonkiest of things but whatever she does, she does with the best intentions. All we need to do is convince Ahya and Govind that Pitajee is the best for you. They really do want you to be happy,' I said, grabbing hold of Anu's hands.

Anu shook her head. 'Mom called me today…'

'And what did Ahya say?'

'That Dad has a weak heart. He has gone for various tests over the last couple of months…'

'Oh, come on,' I groaned. 'So you should just marry whichever guy they want you to? Else dad will have a heart attack?' I asked, my voice dripping with sarcasm.

Anu did not reply.

'Anu, this is nonsense. Govind is one of the sturdiest men I know. He eats like a healthy stallion,' I said, recalling, with a shudder, the seven paranthas our cook had made for him the last time he had come to visit his daughter. Suffice it to say, thanks to my recent interactions with Anju Aunty and the subsequent cooking classes, anything vaguely related to paranthas was prone to make me shudder.

Anu gave me a stern look. 'His heart, Kas…'

'Oh, come on, Anu! This is just a cheap trick Ahya is playing on you.'

'Whatever you say, Kas. I know I won't be able to fight this…'

'Which is why Ahya has come up with this master plan. To silence you!' I said, feeling anger surge inside me.

'You know, Kasturi, I never understood what love was…' said Anu, a faraway look on her face. 'I probably still don't. But I feel physical pain if I think of a situation where Amay is not with me. I see murder if I imagine Amay with someone else. I … I just … love him,' she said, looking helplessly at me.

'Why do you love him, Anu?' I asked her, more out of curiosity than anything else.

'I just do, Kas. I don't have one reason, I don't have many reasons, I don't have *any* reasons ... I only know that I love him and I love him with all my soul,' she said, shrugging at me.

Stupidly, I shrugged in return. I got her.

There was silence for the next few minutes as the two of us sat on Anu's bed, lost in our own thoughts.

'My dad cried when I left for engineering college,' she said quietly.

I patted her hand and tried hard to get rid of the deeply disturbing image of the stallion-like Govind Goswami crying.

'He used to teach me history, a subject I truly hated, for hours before my exams.'

That, to me, sounded a lot like torture, but well, Anu seemed to think differently, so I let it be and nodded my head sympathetically.

'He would take me to ballet class ... Bharatanatyam class .... oh my,' she said, getting teary-eyed now.

He would *drag* you to dance class, I said to myself but patted her back nevertheless.

'Why should I have to choose one over the other?' she asked me.

'I know it won't come to that, Anu,' I said firmly, a familiar surge of anger rising in my chest.

'I know it *will* come to that, Kasturi,' Anu said, equally firmly.

Pitajee and Anu are the world's goofiest, cutest couple. They have to, have to, *have to* be together.

I will stop believing in love if their relationship does not work out.

5.00 a.m.

Talking to Anu has stirred something inside me … something that I had hoped I had buried deep. Memories from more than two years ago have been plaguing me for the last hour, as I lie in my bed, staring at the whale on the ceiling.

About six months ago, in a fit of love for me, Pitajee had attempted to surprise me by sticking a glow-in-the-dark whale on the ceiling of my room. We still have lengthy discussions about what prompted Pitajee to think that I would like to have a grinning, glow-in-the-dark whale on my ceiling to stare at me every night. It was this glow-in-the-dark whale that I now stared at as I thought about Rajeev, surprised at the deep, seething, painful yearning that seared through me.

Have you ever read about those loose women who have affairs with their bosses? And wondered who those girls are?

Well, I was one of them … I know, I know … grossly unprofessional and all that but … well … that is what happened. In my defence, Rajeev was the most handsome man I had ever set my eyes on and I fell madly in love with that gorgeous face the moment I walked into his cabin. Just like that, in one moment, as if someone had flicked on the switch, I fell in love. That he seemed as interested in me certainly helped matters. To put it really mildly, he swept me off my feet. He was the knight in an embroidered waistcoat, carrying a sword in a scabbard and I was the pretty damsel in an off-shoulder white gown. Yes, it was as pathetic as that … really.

All turned very sour then when I caught him red-handed with his girlfriend. The *other* girlfriend. The *real* girlfriend.

How does it feel to be cheated on? I saw the question written on the faces that looked sympathetically at me during that time. Now, however, I will answer it. It's quite simple really. First, you take the sharpest sword known to mankind. Heat it over a crackling fire so that the metal is molten red. Impale it in your chest and then slowly turn it around.

That is how it felt.

Oddly enough, tonight, the pain, the shame, the humiliation of being cheated on, did not come to me in the rushed bursts it still did sometimes. Tonight, I thought about how it felt to be that madly in love with someone. I don't know if you will understand what I say now … but … let me give it a try. I love Purva with all my *mind*. He makes sense and, most importantly, he loves me more than I love him.

Rajeev, I loved differently. I threw caution to the winds and loved him with my heart. I could think about something he had said for days on end. I could, probably, kill for that one look from him. He would stand at the other end of the room and when our eyes met, smile that beautiful smile of his and then wink at me – a quick, secret wink meant only for me. It was like we had a secret language that no one else could understand. Not that anyone else mattered. There was electricity between us … there was mad attraction … there was fire…

As these thoughts danced violently in my head, a shudder, a fear ran through me and I hurriedly, frantically, dialled a number.

'Kasturi, honey, is everything okay?' came Purva's calm voice the next instant.

'I am fine, Purva … I just wanted to hear your voice,' I

said, holding the phone to one ear and hugging a pillow to my chest. No, I am not fine … something is wrong … why … why am I thinking of the past?

There was silence on the other end for a few moments.

'Are you scared, Kasturi?' he asked, in his calmest voice, which, to my tired and worried ears, sounded like a well-loved lullaby.

'Yes,' I said. I am so, so, so scared, Purva. Scared of myself.

'Are you freaking out about the surprise engagement?'

I said nothing.

'Everything all right, Kas?' he prodded further.

'What if something does not work out, Purva? What if something goes wrong?'

I could hear Purva smile. If he were with me, I know he would have pulled me into a hug and I would have felt better immediately.

'See, I am not going anywhere … and you are not either … or…' he said, now laughing, 'if you change your mind and think of wandering away, I will just pull you closer towards me.'

'You will pull me closer?' I asked.

'I won't let you go, Kasturi.'

Please don't let me go, Purva. Please don't.

'Do you want me to read something to you?' he asked.

I nodded my head and then remembered that he could not see me. 'Yes, please.' I said meekly.

I heard Purva smile again. For reasons best known to the cosmos, Purva's voice, generally a low, quiet baritone, calms and soothes me like nothing else can. Listening to him speak is my meditation.

'You little devil! I can just find a book on cardio surgery. Will that do?'

'Are you in the hospital?' I asked.

'Yes, I am … but don't worry, I am between shifts. This book will do?'

'Does not matter,' I said, desperate to hear his voice.

'Fine, then close your eyes and try to sleep,' he said. I obediently followed instructions.

In five minutes, with the phone stuck to my ear, I was fast asleep, sleeping a dreamless sleep.

9

2 February 2013, 1.00 a.m.

I don't mean to sound like a teenager who owns a pink phone and a purple bunny ear-cover, but my birthday is not far away!

Yay!

7 February 2013, 2.00 p.m.

'Purva, darling,' I crooned into the phone as P.P. Padma glared at me.

'I know your birthday is round the corner,' said Purva, laughing loudly.

'Bye, then,' I said. My job was done.

2.30 p.m.

That P.P. Padma hates me is beyond any doubt. How *much* she hates me, however, is worthy of being discussed in a panel chaired by the respected Arnab Goswami.

The nation needs an answer!

2.31 p.m.

I was lazily nibbling a piece of chocolate when Mr Vijaywada popped over for a chat. Before he sat down, I quickly alt-tabbed the Facebook page that I had been mulling over for the last two hours.

'Kasturi,' he said loudly, obviously conscious of my deafness.

'Mr Vijaywada,' I said politely, hurriedly gulping down the piece of chocolate.

'Ear okay today?' he asked gently.

I waited to see if a spasm of guilt would rack my soul. When nothing happened, I smiled even more widely. 'No, sir,' I said, shaking my head. 'Today is quite bad. Please be a little loud.'

'Oh,' said Mr Vijaywada, his face falling. 'I MEAN OKAY,' he said, loud enough for people in Chennai to hear. I giggled mentally, wondering when this would ever stop being funny. I looked up at him with the most angelic smile that I could muster. P.P. Padma glared at me.

'I have a proposition for you, Kasturi,' continued Mr Vijaywada, in a loud voice.

'Yes Sir?'

'How about heading strategy for Vijaywada & Sons?' he said, smiling widely.

Ha. Ha.

'At my current salary? No Sir,' I said, returning his smile. I wondered if I should add some nonsense about needing money for ear surgery, but decided to let it go.

'Then we will increase it!' said Vijaywada, smiling benignly.

I looked at P.P. Padma who was typing furiously, her ears red. Could this get any better?

The ears. Now is a good time to tell you the story of how I came to be deaf.

It all started in the first week I joined Vijaywada & Sons. I had only recently broken up with Rajeev and that fateful day, when Vijaywada repeatedly called out to me, I was sitting at this very desk, bawling my eyes out, unable to get over what Rajeev had done to me. Pitiful and pathetic, I was in no position to go speak to Vijaywada. Or anyone else on the planet. When Vijaywada marched to my work station, angry, he stopped short when he saw a red-eyed, red-nosed girl dabbing at her eyes.

'Oh my gawd,' he said, rolling the 'god'. 'What is wrong, bachche?'

It was nice of him to bother, but I wasn't going to confess my miserable story to yet another sympathetic face. 'Nothing, Sir,' I said, trying hard to stop the tears. The image of Rajeev would not leave my mind.

'Why are you crying?'

'No Sir, I am not,' I said, as tears streamed down my face.

'Arre,' said Mr Vijaywada indignantly, 'I called you again and again and when you did not respond, I had to come here, and look what I find … Kasturi in tears! Did anyone say something to you? Padma? Yes, Padma? Is it Padma?'

Oh dear!

'No Sir, not Padma … it is … er …' I looked around, frantically, scratching my ears.

'Your ear?' said Mr Vijaywada thinking that I was pointing towards my ears.

'Umm … yes … I guess,' I added, shrugging. This was as bad as anything else I would have come up with.

'What! Your ear?'

What? My ear? Why the hell did I just say that?

'Umm … yes, Sir.'

'What happened to your ear?'

My brain worked fast. 'I go deaf every once in a while,' I said jubilantly, smacking the table in front of me. 'That would explain why I did not hear you call out to me.'

'What?' said Mr Vijaywada, shocked.

'Yes Sir, I have met hundreds of doctors … spent hours in hospitals … taken all sorts of medicines … but nothing has changed. These tears, Sir,' I said, melodramatically, 'that you see staining my cheeks at the moment, are but a testimony of my anguish, my frustration at not being able to lead a normal life ... with ears … that … that…' I left the sentence incomplete for two reasons:

It sounded tragic and melodramatic.

I did not quite know how to end the sentence.

'Of course,' said Mr Vijaywada, looking stricken beyond measure. 'Of course … oh my! I did not know this. I am sorry, Kasturi…'

'That's okay, Sir. This is not your fault,' I said, sniffing piteously. 'Life is not fair.'

Mr Vijaywada nodded his head; my words had hit a raw nerve. 'It is not, Kasturi, it certainly is not,' he said, shaking his head.

I tilted my head as if staring into space, hopefully appearing to pontificate on life and its unfairness. 'What has life done to you, Sir, if you do not mind my asking?'

Mr Vijaywada sighed. 'All I want,' he said, shaking his head again, 'is one son. What I have,' he said, and paused, 'are four daughters.'

I tried not to giggle.

'Not that I don't love my girls, I do. But … just that … I want a son to play football with … to go fishing with.'

'You play soccer, Sir, and you fish?' I asked brightly.

'Errr … no … not really … but … you know…' he stammered, 'I could...'

I tried hard to not laugh as it struck me that the CEO of Vijaywada & Sons did not have a son. I remember that day well; it was the first time since the break-up with Rajeev that I had felt like my old self again.

That was more than a year ago. P.P. Padma, of course, figured out my little lie very early on, but Vijaywada has remained blissfully – and thankfully – unaware. Ever since that day, Mr Vijaywada had sported a soft spot for me, favouring me blatantly over others in our small office, excusing the stupidest mistakes with a smile. The advantages of the little lie, therefore, have consistently outweighed the moral implications.

4.30 p.m.

Vijaywada has passed by my desk thrice since our little discussion and has each time spared a gentle hand over my head.

5.00 p.m.

I was about to leave for home when Vijaywada came to my desk. Overcome with emotion at the great deed he was about to do, he put a hand on my head again and said, 'Kasturi Beta, you are like a daughter to me. My fifth daughter.'

I almost choked on nothing.

10.30 p.m.

I was waiting outside Purva's hospital in the evening when Pitajee called. Purva had been in surgery the whole day and asked me to come over to the hospital so that we could grab a quick meal before he headed back into the ward.

'Dost,' I said, in a happy voice. Purva was late and waiting made me feel very bored.

'Kasturi,' he said.

I could not remember the last time Pitajee had called me Kasturi.

'I am going to Mumbai tonight.'

'Oh my god,' I said. That Pitajee's voice was laden with worry and stress was not lost on me.

'To meet that stupid Ahya.'

'Oh my god.'

'They like Saumen, the IAS guy, and think he's God's gift to women and Anu would be the luckiest girl if she can marry him and his car with the red beacon light.'

'Oh my god.'

'They now, urgently, want Anu to meet the guy.'

'Oh my god.'

'So, I am going to meet Ahya and Govind,' he said. I heard the slight shudder in his voice.

'Oh my god.'

'To see if Anu and I can make them see how much we love each other and that Anu does not really need a car with a red light.'

'Oh my god.'

'I am so scared, Kas … I will have to face the collective wrath of Govind and Ahya…'

'Oh my god.'

'Kasturi?'

'Yes?'

'Please stop saying "Oh my god"?'

'Oh my god … I mean … sure...' I said, numbly.

10

Our Apartment, 12 February 2013, 2.00 a.m.

I woke up with a start.

Disoriented, I looked around, taking in the familiar surroundings of my room. The glow-in-the-dark whale grinned idiotically at me. I shook my head. That will have to go sometime soon, I promised myself again.

I had had a dream, a dream about a man … a dream that had made me so restless that I sat in my bed, wide awake. Was it something to do with Purva? Dad? Pitajee?

7.00 a.m.

Who *was* it? The restlessness that I felt in the dream was so intense that I can feel it even now…

3.00 p.m.

I was sitting in the office staring at P.P. Padma's bindi when, pretty much like it happens in Bollywood movies, flashes from the dream began to come to me.

It was about a wedding ... *his* wedding...

7.00 p.m.

'Mooli ke paranthe today!' said Veena Aunty, the instructor of the cooking course, and I groaned out loud, making no attempt to camouflage my disinterest. Twice a week, I now suffered unadulterated torture in the form of these classes. As Veena Aunty and Anju Aunty are bosom buddies who caught up on a regular basis, I did not dare miss a single class.

Veena Aunty cast a disapproving look in my direction; I was far from the ideal pupil. 'Pushpanjali,' said Veena Aunty, looking pointedly at me and talking to her favourite student, 'how excited are you to learn the tricks of making the perfect mooli ke paranthe?'

Now Pushpanjali, I suspect, has been born to marry. Her big day was drawing close and, having spent a lot of time abroad, she was keen to transform into a Hindi-speaking, parantha-cooking bahu that her in-laws could be proud of.

'Bahoooot, bahoooot!' she said obediently in a thick accent.

Veena Aunty clicked her tongue. Correct answer, Pushpanjali, I thought ruefully as I poured two full glasses of water into a bowl that contained a handful of flour.

'Not glasses! Table spoon! T-B-S-P. Not G-L-A-S-S,' said Veena Aunty, looking dismally at the milk-like fluid that was in front of me.

She shook her head and walked away. She was close to giving up on me. That was when, as I ran my hands through the watery mix, it hit me.

The dream. The man in the dream. Not Purva, not Dad and not Pitajee.

Rajeev.

7.30 p.m.

I can see patches of the dream now. It comes to me in bursts. In my dream, Rajeev is standing on the stage, about to get married, surrounded by people. Through the crowd, as his to-be-wife speaks to him, he spots me and stills. Transfixed, his eyes follow me as I leave the room. Sometime, somewhere later, Rajeev and I are standing face to face and he tells me he can't marry anyone else and neither should I.

That was when I woke up.

9.00 p.m.

There is something deeply disturbing about my dream. I was so distracted during the cookery class that I made perfectly round and absolutely delicious paranthas. I suspect that the 150kg, ghee-loving Veena Aunty was closer than ever to a heart attack when I presented the sumptuous paranthas to her. I should not do this too often; after all, I do not hate her enough to have her blood on my hands.

They say dreams bare your soul, spill out to you your most intimate fears and reveal your innermost desires. Was there something that the dream was trying to tell me? It is true that I have been thinking more and more about Rajeev of late. It has been two years since I last saw him and I am still dreaming about him. It does not make sense. Rajeev hurt me and I still smart from the stings of his adultery. And yet…

I am very confused and very tired and wish Purva were not as busy as he is.

10.00 p.m.

I don't.

10.01 p.m.

I don't.

10.02 p.m.

I don't. I don't. I don't.

10.05 p.m.

It is ridiculous to even suggest that. Of course I don't.

10.15 p.m.

I don't. I am not one of those women.

10.30 p.m.

I don't. I don't.

I don't. I don't. I don't. I don't. I don't. I don't. I don't. I don't.

In case you don't get it, I don't.

11.10 p.m.

Okay. I do.

I still miss Rajeev. Sometimes so badly that it hurts.

11

13 February 2013, 11.00 a.m.

'Kasturi.'

'Mum.'

'I have a blog now.'

I sputtered out the coffee I had just taken a mouthful of. 'You have a what?'

'A blog.'

'A *what*?'

'A blog. You get this web address and it's almost like having an online diary. It's quite cool. I can…'

'I know what a blog is, Mum!' I said, interrupting her.

Web address. Online diary. Quite cool. Was that really my mum I was speaking with? What had happened to her?

'Then, darling, let me send you the link to mine. It is time you have it,' she said nonchalantly before cancelling the call, leaving me pretty much gasping for air.

When will Mum cease to surprise me?

11.05 a.m.

To put it rather simply, I stared. Stared without blinking at the computer screen in front of me. Stared with my mouth gaping open.

Not only does my mother have a blog, she has had one for about three months. She has only recently decided to come out in the open with it. Anyone visiting Mum's blog would have no doubt about what he will get from the page; the blog is, after all, titled rather unabashedly, 'Pearls of Wisdom'.

I checked the number of followers and did a double take. Eighty-four!

In a matter of three months? Is Mum headed for cyber glory?

2.00 p.m.

I feature extensively on the blog. To protect my identity, I am not called Kasturi on the blog. For reasons past understanding, I am mostly referred to as Pimple. Dad is called PkP – Pimple ke Papa, as she explains in brackets. To make matters worse, I come across as a spoilt, irresponsible teenager. Is that how Mum perceives me?

Our Apartment, Delhi, 15 February 2013, 6.00 p.m.

Pitajee was sitting on the deewan in our living room, his head in his hands, occasionally looking up to stare dismally at Anu who was sitting a little farther away on the sofa. I sat next to him, one hand loosely slung around his shoulders in a silent show of solidarity. Purva had just come from the hospital, and, seeing Anu in tears, had rushed to her side. He now had his arm around her shoulders and was wiping tears off her face.

'Are you okay, Anu?' he asked in his low, gentle voice.

Anu nodded her head, looked up at Purva, then promptly buried her face in his chest and burst into tears. Taken aback at the outburst, Purva cradled Anu, all the while gently murmuring something in her ear. Pitajee and I exchanged a look. This was not good.

'So what exactly happened?' asked Purva.

'I met them, that's what happened,' said Pitajee, as if that explained it all.

Purva looked quizzically at Pitajee and then at me.

'Well … Ahya threw a fit,' said Pitajee, looking up. 'Which is quite bad in itself. Then Govind joined in and he threw another massive tantrum.'

For no reason the image of two elephants stamping their feet and demanding ice lollies came to my mind. Being the true friend that I am, I stifled my giggles.

'And?' asked Purva, his face serious.

'They asked me to get out of Anu's life.'

'What do you mean? Why are they saying no?'

Pitajee grimaced.

'Govind actually called out to some servant and asked him to show me out.'

'Polite way of telling someone to get lost,' I added helpfully.

'Thanks, Kas, just in case anyone here had not figured *that* out,' said Pitajee, managing a grin. I pulled him closer and playfully tousled his hair.

'Are you kidding me?' exclaimed Purva.

'No Sir, I am not,' said Pitajee, nodding his head. 'They asked me a few questions, decided that I would not be able to provide Anu the lifestyle she is used to … I am not an IAS officer, you see. I could have somewhat redeemed myself had I managed to get an IIM A,B or C tag or an engineering degree from IIT, but since I have not, they concluded that I should be simply thrown out of the house.'

'And the caste bit,' I added, most helpfully.

'Thanks, love,' said Pitajee, throwing a sarcastic grin in my direction. 'Yes, that Anu and I are not of the same caste does not help matters.'

'Do you want to consider giving the IAS exam?' I said, brightening up. It could be the perfect solution to the problem. 'You could wear a kurta-pyjama, oil your hair generously, take an apartment in JNU and not come out of it for days. We could line your room with books, which you could spend days and days studying. You could also buy a guitar and play songs on it in during the few minutes you are not studying.'

'I … I … could … I guess…' said Pitajee doubtfully.

Anu managed a weak smile. 'No, sweetheart. You won't. I can't have you change your career just to please my parents.'

I have to admit that Pitajee looked fairly relieved. 'I have a friend who has been giving the exam ever since he was two and has still not cracked it,' he muttered to me.

'Guys, parents eventually understand. They'll take their time, but they will come around,' said Purva optimistically.

There was silence in the room for a few seconds.

'I don't see that happening,' said Anu, voicing the thought that everyone was thinking.

Things were bleak. So bleak that they were almost black.

10.30 p.m.

'You are very quiet today,' said Purva, looking up from his book and staring intently at me.

'No, no, no,' I said vehemently.

A small smile began to dance around Purva's lips as it often does when he tries to prise something out of me. He put aside the thick book he had engrossed himself in after dinner and took my hands.

'What's wrong, Kas?' he asked as he fiddled with the ring on my finger.

How does he know, each time?

'I am worried about Pitajee and Anu,' I lied. Agreed, I was worried but at the moment it was not thoughts about them that tormented me. The worst kind of fear is when you are scared of yourself. And I was. I was very scared of what I could do. I felt like flotsam bobbing on the sea at the mercy of the waves, desperately looking for something solid to cling to and make my way ashore. My only hope was Purva.

'Why do you look so scared, Kas? They will be fine … it will work out. It always does.'

'And if it doesn't?'

'Then, as they say, it is not the end,' said Purva.

By this time, I was standing very close to Purva and he had an arm around my waist, his chin touching my head. He had been performing surgeries all day and reeked of the typical hospital smell that I had grown to absolutely love.

'And there you go!' he said, grinning.

'Eh?'

'You are sniffing for the hospital smell,' he said.

Time to roll my eyes and crinkle my nose.

'Don't like it?' he said, tapping my head.

'No.' I said, promptly.

'Liar!'

Giggling, I threw my arms around his neck and he wrapped his around my waist. We stood like that for a few moments in companionable silence. Purva buried his face in my hair and breathed deep. I could almost feel the stress, tension and anxiety leaving his body.

Poor guy, I thought to myself, he works hard to save lives most people have given up hope on. If he can't spend enough time with me, that doesn't mean that I start hyperventilating about a man I was in love with a lifetime ago. It's no excuse, I said to myself, hugging Purva tighter.

Purva immediately withdrew a few inches away from me, surprising me yet again by how sensitive he was to each change in my mood, movement and thought.

'You okay, Kas? ' he asked again, looking intently at me and placing a light hand on my head.

'I am not *okay*, Purva,' I said in a fake hoity-toity voice. 'I am cool, sexy and very, *very* glamorous.' I finished it with a sophisticated arch of the eyebrows and a coy look at the nails.

Purva burst out laughing. 'I get worried when you are not monkeying around, Kas,' he said and lightly kissed my lips.

'Wait!' I said and he stopped, surprised.

'What?'

'You know…'

'…that it's your birthday in two days?' he said, groaning.

'Yes,' I said, laughing.

'You monkey!' he said, laughing and pulling me closer.

12

Our Apartment, Delhi, 7 March 2013, 2.00 a.m.

It's 2.00 a.m. and I am sitting upright in my bed; sleep is as far away from me as is possible. Is this going to become some kind of a nocturnal ritual now?

Go away Rajeev, go away!

Shoo!

Boo!

3.00 a.m.

Do you think Rajeev has married his binge-drinking girlfriend, Teena?

3.01 a.m.

No.

3.02 a.m.

Yes. He is married, I am sure. Married with three kids. Three fat, screaming kids who throw tantrums at the drop of a hat.

The image of Rajeev's (other) girlfriend, all fat and stodgy after not being able to get rid of the post-baby fat, came to my mind and I heaved a sigh of deep satisfaction. I closed my eyes, folded my hands and prayed fervently that Teena had put on at least 500kg. It would be poetic justice and we all like poetic justice.

4.00 a.m.

I can't sleep, so I am in the kitchen making mooli ke paranthe. Rajeev is probably awake too, sharing the marital bed with his grumpy, obese wife and screaming kids.

As I smeared one perfectly round parantha after the other with generous dollops of ghee, I knew that somewhere in the cosmos, Veena Aunty was dying of an unexplained heart attack.

The unfairness of life.

9.30 a.m.

There is something horribly and hopelessly wrong with P.P. Padma.

The forehead is missing the bindi. Is this the end of the world? A year late, but here nevertheless?

10.00 a.m.

I am the one who has been up all night because of a man who cheated on me two years ago and is probably married to his (other) girlfriend and P.P. Padma is the one who is grumpy.

Really?

11.00 a.m.

P.P. Padma has snapped eleven times this morning. I counted.

Seven times at me (have I ever had the chance to mention how much she loves me?), twice at the peon and twice at Mr Vijaywada, who is now scurrying around the office on tip-toes, trying his best to keep out of P.P. Padma's way.

The woman is transformed into a crazed, vile witch. Not that she was not one before.

Noon.

Do you think Rajeev ever thinks of me after all these years?

12.01 p.m.

No.

12.05 p.m.

Definitely not.

12.06 p.m.

What if…

2.00 p.m.

God fearing, I-go-to-the-temple-everyday, I-will-die-the-day-I-miss-puja P.P. Padma just used the F-word.

What is wrong with her?

3.00 p.m.

I walked into the ladies' room, humming my own, rather charming version of 'Happy Birthday ... toodle doo ... to me' and stopped dead in my tracks. Sitting on the floor in front of the wall-length mirrors was P.P. Padma.

Although that in itself was shocking, (not the fact that she was sitting, but that she was doing so, cross-legged, in the ladies') the real thing was yet to come. Sensing me walk in, P.P. Padma turned around. She was, I deduced immediately from her red eyes and tears, crying bitterly.

Oh dear! My first reaction was to flee from the scene of danger. P.P. Padma had been in a vile mood today and given that she looked borderline hysterical, I was quite sure that she was capable of physical assault. Something, however, stopped me from doing that. And before I knew it, to my utter shock, I found myself sitting cross-legged, right next to P.P. Padma on the bathroom floor, gingerly extending a shaking hand towards her rather broad and dangerously muscular shoulders. Idly, I wondered how bad it would hurt were P.P. Padma to turn around and thwack me on the head.

'I don't bite, you know,' said P.P. Padma caustically, turning angrily to face me.

'Yes, yes,' I said weakly and found myself patting her shoulders. The surprises life throws at one.

P.P. Padma glared at me, tears streaming down her face. I looked on, mesmerized. It had never crossed my mind that one could glare and cry at the same time. I made a mental note to try it sometime.

'I mean ... no, no, of course you don't.'

'Don't what?' she said impatiently.

'Bite.'

'What? Who bites?'

'You bite.'

'What! Are you suggesting that I *bite*?' she said in a low growl, sounding remarkably like something that *could* bite.

'I mean…' I said, nervously, 'you don't bite … I mean…'

I decided to shut up. Speaking was not helping.

P.P. Padma and I sat in silence. A weird kind of comfortable silence.

A little later and very meaningfully, I cleared my throat. 'Are you okay?' I asked.

'You can leave,' was her curt reply.

'No, it's okay. Don't answer my question if you don't want to,' I said meekly and crossed my legs so that I was sitting more comfortably. I spent the next couple of minutes tossing the tear-stained tissues in the air, stopping when Padma glared at me … yet again.

I then fiddled with my phone, sent a couple of text messages to Pitajee, who did not respond, forwarded a few rather lame jokes to Dad, who also did not respond, and sent a virtual kiss to Purva, who did not respond either.

'I have a boyfriend,' said P.P. Padma, suddenly.

I rolled my eyes at her and laughed. She could be funny too! This was turning out to be a day of revelations.

Silence reigned supreme as P.P. Padma glowered at me.

Oh dear! She actually has a boyfriend? I immediately straightened my face and tried desperately to disguise my guffaw into a groan.

'And … and…' faltered the mighty Padma.

'And?'

'He won't take me to meet his mom!'

'Big deal! Don't meet the mom. Trust me, no good comes out of meeting the boy's mother,' I said, forcefully smacking the bathroom floor with my hands, my mind wandering to the parantha-making classes.

'Tiger,' she said, then shook her head when I looked blankly at her. 'My boyfriend, Tiger, loves me but … I think … I think he does not think his mother will approve of me.'

I bit my lip and tried not to comment on the name of her boyfriend. It was not the time to say anything about it. I vaguely recalled a friend in engineering college whose dog was called Tiger and I had found even that deeply amusing. Who calls a dog Tiger? Would that mutt not grow up with a deep rooted identity crisis?

'Why?' I asked instead.

P.P. Padma pointed a finger at her face and cast such a sad glance in my direction that my heart melted for the gawky girl.

'P.P. Padma,' I said, 'looks don't matter!'

'It's easy for you to say that … you're pretty; men fall for you left, right and centre. And even if it were not your face, there's your personality. You…' Padma seemed to be lost for words for a minute and I looked at her encouragingly, '…you … bring sunshine into the room … guys just can't help … hell, if I were a guy, I would have a crush on you…'

My eyes and ego grew to the size of Jupiter in a matter of nano seconds. P.P. Padma is not that bad, I thought, chewing my lower lip thoughtfully. Maybe I had misjudged her all this while. And no, it had nothing to do with the compliments she had just thrown my way. I am not, I repeat, I am *not* that shallow.

'So … err … that sunshine bit that you were talking about … is it, like, my dress, or you think it's because of my….'

Another glare from Padma and I shut up.

'So what's the big deal about him not taking you to see his mom?' I asked after a few moments.

'How do you think we will ever get married if I don't even meet his mom?' she asked the rather pertinent question.

'True,' I agreed.

'Tiger loves me for the person I am, but I overheard him talking to his friend. He is sure Aunty will not like me because … because … I am not pretty enough!'

'P.P. Padma!' I interjected, trying to exclaim indignantly at the regressive line of thought. However, it is tough to say 'P.P. Padma' and sound indignant. Try it, if you don't believe me.

'I don't know why I am telling you all this...' said P.P. Padma, tearing up. 'You will just make fun of me…'

'P.P. Padma,' I repeated, more sternly.

'Please,' she said, equally sternly. 'No one calls me P.P. Padma. Call me Padma.'

I smiled. 'Padma,' I began again, with authority this time, 'you have a pretty face.'

'What utter rubbish!'

'Shut up and listen,' I said, shocked and pleased with the firmness of my voice.

'Okay.'

'You have a pretty face. You just don't know how to present yourself.'

'What do you mean by that?' asked Padma, intrigued.

'Will you trust me?' I asked, with a smile on my face.

'I guess so,' she said, shrugging.

'When are you meeting Tiger next?'

'At eight, tonight.'

'Okay, let's go,' I said.

'Go where?' asked Padma.

'Dolby's beauty parlour and the shopping mall,' I said, winking at her.

Ten minutes later, the peon, who was well aware of our frosty relationship, stared open-mouthed as Padma and I walked out of the office building together, smiling widely.

8.02 p.m.

'THANK YOU, KAS!' Padma's text read.

I smiled, benignly. A good haircut, proper make-up and nice clothes can solve each and every problem in this world.

'I LOVE YOU! <3,' was the next message, a few minutes later.

I smiled further. While there are certain things I cannot do, there are many that I can. One of these is knowing when I have made a new friend. I switched on the television and tried to concentrate on the news piece about a fire that had broken out in a slum in the city.

I looked at the clock and smiled. Just four more hours.

Wohoooo.

13

2 April 2013, 00.01 a.m.

It is THE day. It is the birthday.

Wooohoooo!

00.03 a.m.

'Happy birthday!' Pitajee and Anu shouted in unison, as they burst through the door of my room. Pitajee was carrying a huge bunch of balloons and a box of cake.

'Happy birthday, Kas!' said Anu, planting a wet kiss on my cheek.

'Happy birthday, Kas!' mimicked Pitajee, planting a wetter kiss on the other cheek.

'Ewwwkkks,' I yelped, but the two of them had pulled me into a tight hug. Before long the cake had been brought out of the box.

'Pineapple!' said Pitajee, with a flourish.

I rolled my eyes and Anu smacked Pitajee on his shoulder. 'I told you she doesn't like pineapple-flavoured cake!' Anu said, mortified.

'What do we do with cake that the birthday girl does not want to eat?' said Pitajee, narrowing his eyes wickedly at me.

'Lord, no! NO!' I shrieked, the moment I understood what Pitajee was going to do with the cake. I made a wild dash for the door but Pitajee's powerful arms had grasped me by the waist and, in spite of my yelps and screams, a few seconds later, I had foul pineapple cake smeared all over my face and hair.

'What about cutting the cake? We didn't even do that!' said Anu, laughing.

'Worry not!' said Pitajee, pulling up his collar and winking at us. I immediately felt very worried.

Pitajee used his hands to pull out a chunk from the debris that was once a cake.

'Yuck!' I said, disgusted.

'You are a pig, Amay,' said Anu, laughing nevertheless.

Pitajee, immune to our reactions, planted a big candle in the chunk of cake he had pulled out and lit it.

'Cut it. Now,' he commanded.

'With? Where is the knife?'

Pitajee and Anu looked blankly at each other.

'You lazy people!' I shrieked, laughing. They had forgotten to get a knife!

'Use your finger,' Pitajee suggested. Anu looked like she was about to puke as I did exactly as I was told. Pitajee played happy birthday on his phone and began to sing with a lag, completely out of tune. Anu began the song a few seconds after Pitajee and sang it to some tune from *Dabangg*. It was in that mish-mash of hugs and laughter and shrieks and out-of-tune singing that I cut a chunk of pineapple-flavoured birthday cake with my finger.

As the song ended, high on giggles, we collapsed on my bed into a pile of cake-smeared arms and faces.

Pitajee got out of the bed and switched off the light.

'What? Why?' I objected. Pitajee crawled back into the bed and the three of us lay on our backs. I stared, open-mouthed, at the ceiling.

'Buddaayy gift,' shouted Pitajee, gleefully.

The glow-in-the-dark whale now had a friend! A glow-in-the-dark elf!

In all this madness, I had not even realized that Purva had not called to wish me a happy birthday.

8.00 a.m.

'Bachche,' said Anju Aunty.

Your son has not even called. Ninety-eight out of 140 batchmates from B-school, including someone called Pranav, whom I have no recollection of ever having studied with, have called.

'Namaste, Aunty,' I said, trying hard to keep my voice polite.

'Happy birthday, Bahu Rani,' she said.

Ugh.

10.00 a.m.

No call. Two hundred of his cousins have, however, called to wish 'Bhabhi'!

Hmph.

1.00 p.m.

'Dad.'

'Yes, Beta.'

'Purva has not even called.'

'Why? Why was he supposed to call?' asked Dad.

'Dad! You just wished me a happy birthday. Don't you think Purva should have done the same by now?'

'Oh,' said Dad, trying hard to keep the surprise out of his voice. 'He has not?'

I have never been more peeved.

2.00 p.m.

Padma ordered a cake for me. I cut it listlessly, my head wrapped in thoughts. Vijaywada, whom I have been avoiding, gave me a hug and a notebook with my name on it.

'For you to make grand strategy plans for Vijaywada & Sons,' he said, beaming.

I was so low that I did not even pretend to not have heard him. I did not crack a single joke about Vijaywada's gift.

Not even one in my head.

4.00 p.m.

'Maybe he has a really big surprise planned for you in the evening,' Padma suggested.

I brightened up, immediately. Yes, I am sure that is the case. He will call me up any time soon, laughing and teasing.

7.00 p.m.

I closed my eyes and sat at my desk in front of the laptop. One hundred and seventy-four friends had posted birthday messages on my Facebook wall. Purva had still not called.

I had received seven texts from Anu and Pitajee, asking me to come out for a special birthday dinner. I had ignored all of them. Both of them had tried in vain to reach Purva. He was busy in the OT, the nurse had said each time. In the darkness that now surrounded me, I travelled back two years. I could still remember how Rajeev had made me feel on my birthday. Special. Very special.

I sighed. Could I stop thinking about Rajeev. I smacked the table in frustration.

10.00 p.m.

Why am I comparing this to the last birthday I celebrated with Rajeev? What is the point? Rajeev cheated on me and probably does not even remember my name now.

10.03 p.m.

How does it matter if one person did not call me on my birthday? Why don't I look at the hundreds of others who did?

10.04 p.m.

I don't want to cry.

10.05 p.m.

I won't cry.

10.06 p.m.

Okay, just a little bit. After all, this has been a fairly disastrous birthday.

10.07 p.m.

The idea was to shed a few dignified tears, not bawl my head off like this.

10.11 p.m.

Almost mechanically, my fingers flew over the keyboard and before I knew it, Rediffmail was open. Without thinking, and blinking away tears, I typed in the username and password I had not used in two years.

'There will probably be nothing from Rajeev...' I mentally prepared myself.

After my break-up, I had abruptly cut off all ties with him. Anu used to work with Rajeev and he had tried to communicate with me through her when all else failed. I had deleted all the email accounts I had used then, changed my phone number, found a new job ... I had done everything that I could to take myself away from Rajeev. Except for this one thing. Why I had not deleted this account, I cannot quite tell. What I can tell you is that I have not opened the account since the day I had caught Rajeev red-handed with Teena.

Until this moment.

I was hurting. This was my last birthday as an unmarried girl and all I wanted was to feel a little special. I wanted Purva to ... to ... make me feel special ... and he had not even called. I had contemplated calling him many times during the day but my ego had got in the way each time. 'Why are you doing this?' I muttered to myself. 'What do you want to see?'

The email account was now open. It took a minute for it to all register as I hurriedly wiped away tears with the back of my hand, stunned. A couple of quick clicks and my heart skipped a few beats. Soon I was sitting ram-rod straight in my seat, too shocked for words. My inbox contained 827 unread emails from Rajeev – at least one each day since I had seen him with Teena.

The subject line of the one on top of the pile simply read, 'Happy birthday, my special girl, a very very happy birthday'.

The email had been sent at 12.01 a.m. today.

14

I opened a random email from Rajeev. The subject line read, 'A new start'. Curious, I read on.

Dear Kas,

Today was my first day at LBS. As I walked into class I could not believe that this was really happening to me. I had done it!

The GMAT exam, the applications, the interviews and finally the admission. Even though I don't think you read my emails, I cannot thank you enough. You are my inspiration, Kas.

Thank you.

Rajeev.

I opened another email.

Dear Kas,

I am working hard at LBS. At the end of the tunnel I see that MBA degree that so many covet, and I know you would be proud of me. This is hardest I have ever worked and I can see some results already. Maybe I am not empty in the head after all.

Words can inspire. They can become wings that can be used to soar high. You had so much faith in my abilities, Kas. Whenever I doubt myself, I go back to our time together and in front of me flashes your innocent, trusting face, telling me that I can do whatever I set my mind to. I did not believe you then, but I have faith in your words now.

Your words, Kas, spoken with such innocence, have stayed with me, visit me often and always give me strength and hope.

Thank you.

Rajeev.

'He got through LBS,' I said to myself, amazed and impressed. Out of the blue, a quiet evening spent near India Gate, almost two years ago, flashed before my eyes.

'You don't like to work in the corporate world, do you?' Rajeev had asked, his dimple presenting itself to me in all its glory.

I shook my head.

'Then what would you like to do?'

'Study further, do another MBA perhaps,' I said.

'But you already have a fabulous degree,' he had said, inching closer. His deodorant, heady and intoxicating, wafted towards me in bursts as the wind changed directions.

'I want another degree ... from...'

'From?' he said, smiling.

'London Business School,' I said, shyly.

Rajeev looked at me, his mind elsewhere.

'You should try too…' I said.

'Would that make you proud of me?'

'I am already very proud of you, Rajeev … but yes, I would

be super-proud of you if you got through LBS!'

Rajeev had smiled a slow smile and the gorgeous beauty of his face distracted me yet again.

My phone rang, bringing me back into the present. It was Purva. I looked at my watch; it was 11.35 p.m.

I ignored the phone and turned to another email from Rajeev, dated December last year.

This one had an attachment.

Dear Kasturi,

I am in Vienna for a two-day break and guess what? It is snowing! Here is a picture of the hotel's front lawn.

I miss you.

Rajeev

I opened the attachment and drew in a sharp breath. There was a picture of Rajeev, standing in the middle of what can only be described as a pool of snow. Packed in clothes and looking, if possible, even more handsome, he held in his hands a stick. He was looking up at the camera, grinning as he wrote with that stick the 'I' of 'KASTURI' in the snow.

I closed my eyes, unable to take it all in. What about Teena?

A quick search threw up some emails that had the word 'Teena' in them. I opened one, my heart pounding.

Dear Kasturi,

Today, I booked a date for the GMAT exam and am already feeling nervous. If you were still part of my life, Kas, I would just sit by your feet and put my head in your lap. I don't think I have ever written an exam like this – armed with hours of prep, notes, practice tests and all.

I smiled.

I can almost see you smiling when you read this. I am sure this appeals to the geek in you

Teena got married yesterday, to some fellow her folks found for her in a matter of days. Kas, I know you probably feel that I never loved you ... and that it was Teena all the way for me...

It was and then it was not.

I wish I could explain it all without sounding like the scum of the planet ... but I can't. I thought I was in love with Teena, but I was not. I thought I was never going to fall for you but ... guess what? I did. I fell in love with you so spectacularly that I don't think I will ever be able to forget you or forgive myself...

I miss you. I miss your smile. I miss your bright, twinkling eyes. I miss you. I miss you so very much.

Rajeev.

I sat still for a few minutes, my head in my hands. What had just hit me?

3 April 2013, 4.00 a.m.

I sat with my head in my hands, eyes swollen from the frenzied reading of the last three hours. Each email had been read and, some that had resonated more deeply than others, reread. Memories came rushing back to me in waves, each bigger than the last, each bringing with it a searing pain that I did not know what to do with.

And now I understood all that they say about your first love.

There was a desolate longing in Rajeev's emails that I knew was real. He was trying very hard to be the man I'd thought I'd been in love with … how could I not be affected? As I had moved on, found love and created a new life for myself, Rajeev had clung to my aspirations for him and was now dedicating his life to fulfilling them.

For too long, Rajeev had been the bad guy, the man I was best without. Rajeev's remorse shook something inside me. And the one question that had been niggling around me for the last few days finally dared to raise its ugly, monstrous head.

Was I still in love with Rajeev?

15

3 April 2013, 7.30 a.m.

'Koochie Beta,' chirped Mum. I had managed to fall asleep by five in the morning and the last thing I needed was Mum calling me 'Koochie' at seven.

'No,' I groaned.

'No what?'

'No, I don't want to talk to you when you call me Koochie,' I said, snuggling comfortably under the blanket. I knew this call would last a while.

'You know the first word you learnt to say?'

I groaned. Not this story again.

'"No". That was the first word you said. There I was, sitting next to you near the potty and you...'

'Mum!' I said, cutting her short. I could not hear *that* story again. In fact, I did not want to ever hear anything that began with me near the potty.

'Okay, tell me, what is wrong with "Koochie"?' said Mum.

'Mum!' I said, exasperated. 'What is right with "Koochie"?'

'It's so cute.'

'Mum! It is *not*!'

'In other news,' said Mum, sounding a little hurt and changing the topic, 'Anjuji called yesterday.'

'To say what?'

'She wants you to wear a yellow sari for the actual wedding ceremony.'

'And?'

'I said, behenji, the lehenga will be so expensive, she should at least wear it for the jaimala and the wedding.'

'But Mum, in our family don't brides always wear a yellow sari for the wedding ceremony?'

'Of course,' she said. I could hear her smile.

'Mum!' I said, exasperated, 'Why are you uselessly picking fights?'

'Anyway,' she said, laughing. 'What did you and Purva do for your birthday yesterday?'

I made a face and then realized that Mum could not see me.

'Nothing.'

'What do you mean?'

'He did not even call me.'

Wrong. He had called me fifteen times from eleven-thirty at night to two in the morning, after which he had left me a couple of messages.

'What?'

'Yes.'

'This is scandalous! Why?'

'I don't know.'

'Hmmm … you must ask. I am sure he has a reason.' said Mum.

I grunted.

'I have some more news,' she said gleefully.

'What?'

'The wedding date has been fixed.'

'Whose wedding date?' I drawled, lazily stretching myself. There was silence. I sat upright. 'My wedding?' I asked slowly.

'Yes, your wedding. Remember, you are getting married?'

I didn't say anything.

'To Purva,' Mum added helpfully.

'Oh,' I said, the hundreds of emails from Rajeev still dancing in my head.

'6 August,' said Mum.

'Eh?'

'Your wedding date, Beta. 6 August.'

'Oh,' was all that I could come up with.

8.00 a.m.

The bell rang impatiently. I had already called in sick at work, citing issues with my ear, and disliked the injustice of being forced out of bed at this unearthly hour. Anu had left at five in the morning today to be with her mum in Pune. Ahya had rung up the previous afternoon, bidding her eldest child to drop everything and come home. She refused to give her a reason, leaving Anu to imagine the worst. Anu, of course, dutifully decided that there was something wrong with Govind's heart.

'There can't be anything wrong with Govind's heart,' I had said.

'Why?' she had asked, looking hopefully at me.

'Because he doesn't have one,' I had said, before collapsing into giggles.

The doorbell rang again, bringing me back to the present. I

shook my head, an old habit, hoping that in doing so, I would be able to rid myself of the noise that was making my head ache. I trooped to the main lobby, hitching up my pyjamas, and opened the door.

Purva.

Feeling anger surge inside me, I turned around abruptly and walked right back in, shutting the door on Purva's face. I almost ran the last few meters to my room and threw myself down on the bed, breathing in deep bursts.

Purva walked in slowly behind me and put a hand on my shoulders. I shook it away.

'Kasturi,' he said gently. 'Look here.'

I sat still on my bed with my back towards Purva and my hands crossed across my chest.

'Please?' he pleaded.

I sat unmoving.

'Please,' he repeated, gently turning me around. I narrowed my eyes in surprise as I looked at him. Purva's hair was tousled and his eyes looked weary. It seemed like he had not slept in ages.

'I am sorry, Kas,' he said in a soft voice.

'All I wanted was to spend time with you on my birthday,' I said in a small voice, looking at my hands.

'Kas, I'm very sorry…' his voice trailed off.

I noted, then, that his eyes seemed heavy with sleep…

'You did not call me the whole day! Who does that?'

'An idiot,' he said, grinning. Not a fresh-faced happy grin, but a sad grin that failed to reach his eyes. The anger I had been harbouring inside me now seemed to ebb away just a little bit.

'Have you eaten?' I asked, in spite of myself.

'Not in the last thirty-six hours,' he said, shrugging his shoulders.

Without another word I got up, went into the kitchen and returned with sandwiches and milk.

'Eat,' I ordered curtly, and handed the tray to him. Purva's amused eyes followed my every movement. He smiled, took the tray from my hands and placed the food on the bed. He then took my hands in his.

'Dheerbahi slum caught fire ... you might have seen it in the news...' he said, staring at my hands 'They brought all the casualties to AIIMS. I was the doctor in charge. A school … seventeen kids…' he shook his head, reliving the memories. 'I saw forty-seven people die … bit much even for me,' he finished with a weak smile.

'Oh,' I said. So this was why no one could reach him. The anger that had already begun to ebb was now quickly being replaced by immense guilt and shame.

'I am sorry, Kasturi. I know this birthday was important to you. It was important to me too, but I … I could not get away,' he said in his characteristic low, grave voice, his intense gaze searching my face, reading each thought as it passed through my head.

'You have not slept either, have you?' I asked, smiling.

'I need to go back in an hour,' he said, shaking his head.

'Eat this,' I said, pointing to the food, 'and sleep on my bed. I will wake you up in an hour.'

Purva stared at me without blinking for a few minutes. He then got up, stretched himself to his full height of six feet and, pulling out a nicely wrapped box from his backpack, handed it to me.

'Happy birthday, sweetheart,' he said in a voice so low that it was almost a whisper. 'I love you.'

Simple words, earnestly spoken by the tired man I loved, found their way straight to a place somewhere deep in my heart. I hoped fervently that Purva's gift would be a box of expensive chocolates or a piece of jewellery. Anything more and I knew I would be in tears.

I unwrapped the gift and found myself staring at something that was very familiar.

For my seventh birthday, Mum and Dad had gifted me a musical box. Open it and a pretty delicate ballerina twirled to Mum and Dad singing happy birthday to me. I had spent an entire year doing nothing else but opening and closing the box. Predictably, it broke from overuse. Even then I could never let go of the turquoise box with the twirling ballerina inside it. It stayed with me when I left home for engineering college, came back home with me when I finished, went with me to B-school, came back home again and now was – or so I thought – with me in my apartment.

A spruced-up, sparkling-new version of the same box was now in front of me.

'Open it,' said Purva, staring intently at me.

The ballerina from my childhood appeared and, to my utter delight, began to slowly twirl around.

I shrieked with joy. However, before I could even look up at Purva, the sound of Mum and Dad singing happy birthday reached my stunned ears. Dad had taken this box to so many repair shops but it could not be fixed.

'Is this a new box?' I asked, bewildered. Mine broke almost

twenty years ago and repeated attempts to put it right had failed.

'No,' said Purva. 'The same one.'

'But that one ... it ... it didn't work...'

'This has been my project for the last two months,' he said, smiling proudly, his face suddenly looking a little less tired.

'Oh my god,' I whispered to myself as I rubbed the turquoise box in wonder. It was almost like being reacquainted with a lost, yet integral, part of my childhood. The mystical, magical, wonderful music box.

The thought behind the gift tugged at the strings of my heart and I felt my throat tighten. There is something so sacred about childhood, so pure and innocent that in touching a bit of mine, Purva had given me the best gift possible. Clutching the box to my heart, I looked up at Purva, only to find him staring at me.

'I...' I tried, but stopped. 'The ... the...' I tried again, now deeply embarrassed at the tears that were beginning to stream down my face.

'Shh,' said Purva, looking mortified and bending low to wipe my tears with his hands. 'Silly girl...'

The tears refused to stop.

'This ... this ... is...' I blubbered.

Purva pulled me closer and I drew towards the comforting wafts of chloroform like it was a magnet.

'Shhh ... hey ... come on ... don't cry ... please...' he pleaded softly. Purva took my face in his hands and kissed my moist eyes. Each kiss, each word so tender and so full of gentle, innocent love that I could do little to stop the fresh wave of tears. Wrapped tightly in Purva's arms, feeling the safest I could possibly feel, images of me huddled over my laptop, reading email after email from Rajeev, flashed before my eyes and brought a fresh wave of guilt-ridden tears.

What the hell am I doing?

Purva, you are too nice, too good and too honest to be with someone like me.

16

5 April 2013, 5.00 a.m.

No, of course I will not open Rediffmail to see if there is an email from Rajeev today.

9.00 a.m.

'Any calls from Anu?' I asked, turning to look at Pitajee. In return for aloo paranthas cooked by me, Pitajee had agreed to drop me off at office twice that week. As he drove his fancy car, I munched on an apple, reflecting on the advantages of knowing how to cook. My paranthas, when I cook them now, turn out perfectly round and very soft. I am officially the type of parantha-making daughter-in-law that any mother-in-law would be proud of.

'Yes.'

'What? What did she say?' I said, surprised.

'I don't think there is anything wrong with Govind.'

'There will never be anything wrong with Govind,' I said ruefully.

'So…'

'So we don't know why Ahya called Anu home.'

Pitajee put his foot on the break and car came to a sudden halt. Turning off the ignition, Pitajee turned around to face me.

'What are you doing?' I asked, taken aback.

'Kas,' said Pitajee, his jaws set firm. 'Why am I not good enough?'

I put a hand on Pitajee's.

'Is it just because I decided to sit for the MBA entrance and not the IAS exam? An exam will decide whom I get to marry? Or is it something else? Why am I not good enough?' he fumed, frustration darkening his usually good-humoured face.

'You may not be good enough for Ahya and Govind, but for Anu you will always be the best … and that is what really matters, does it not?' I said, smiling.

Pitajee stared at me for a moment, opened his mouth and then shut it again.

'You will always be good enough for Anu, Pitajee,' I repeated.

For a moment, the darkness lingered in his eyes and I wondered what he would say next. But the dark clouds lifted from Pitajee's face and the sun shone clearer. The old, lovable Pitajee was back.

I smiled a very maternal smile.

'Sometimes, I begin to doubt us … but your words … they … you rock, Koochie,' he said, grinning from ear to ear.

I thwacked his head with my purse.

'Bhabhiji!' he squealed and pinned my hands behind my back.

11.00 a.m.

I won't open the email account.

1.00 p.m.

I won't.

2.00 p.m.

I should not.

3.00 p.m.

I should not and I will not.

4.00 p.m.

Is there any harm in just reading the subject line?

5.00 p.m.

No.

7.00 p.m.

Subject line – 'My deepest regret and a picture'.

Dear Kasturi,

I have many regrets, but the biggest is the way I treated

you. I will never forgive myself and I spend a lot of my time and energy, trying to become the person you thought I was.

The one person very happy about this is my mother, who speaks very fondly and very often about you.

I am also sending you a picture from yesterday. This is with Jon, who heads the mergers desk, at BNP Paribas, here in Europe. I worked very closely with him in the last few weeks and, right before this picture was taken, he asked me what kept me so motivated all the time. I smiled and said nothing and he asked me if it was a girl. I said yes, her name is Kasturi.

He smiled knowingly. Only he did not know the entire story. If he did, he would be shocked.

I miss you terribly ... more so with each passing day.

Rajeev.

I opened the attachment and stared at the suited-up Rajeev. His diamond ear-studs were gone and he had started wearing spectacles which gave him a very intellectual look. A lot of things about him were very obviously different. The only thing that remained the same was that he continued to look utterly handsome.

9.00 p.m.

'Dad! Sorry, I missed your call,' I said, as I washed dirty utensils with the phone stuck between my right ear and shoulder.

'What are you doing? What's that noise?'

'Washing dishes.'

'Sounds more like you're throwing them around.'

'Same thing.'

'Agreed.'

'So, how are things?' he asked.

That is one loaded question, Dad. Rajeev is sending me an email a day and has been since the day I caught him with Teena. Teena is married to another man and Rajeev is now getting an MBA degree from the best business school in the world. He is also grovelling in misery and desperate for me to reply. I, on the other hand, am thinking more about Rajeev than about the man I am engaged to.

'All good,' I said.

'Are you sure?' he asked.

'Yeah…'

'Wanna get married in the Taj?' asked Dad. I laughed out loud. Dad is very entertaining when he tries to use slang.

'What?' I said, laughing.

'I am going to book the Taj reception hall for the wedding.'

I said nothing.

'Kasturi? Are you there?' Dad asked.

'When, Dad?' I asked.

'Tomorrow.'

'Dad,' I said, after a pause, 'is it always supposed to be magical … meeting the boy, getting to know him, getting married…'

Dad laughed. 'No … more often than not, it is far from magical but…' he paused, '… it has to feel right even when it is not magical.'

What if it suddenly stops feeling right? And something else that was all wrong begins to feel right?

10.00 p.m.

Exchange of text messages with Anu –

'Kas, are you there?'

'Yes, how is Govind's heart? *sarcastic look*'

'I am getting engaged. Day after tomorrow.'

Midnight.

Delhi flew past me as I stared steadily in front of me, eyes on the road, my mind elsewhere. I felt sullen and shocked in equal measure. Shifting to fourth gear, with Mum's warning about road rage resounding in my ears, I let a Honda City overtake me. Although I liked this stretch of road from the airport to my home, images of Pitajee's shocked face kept coming back to me.

I had just dropped Pitajee off at the airport. He had left in a desperate attempt to stop Anu's engagement. I looked at my watch; the flight to Pune would have taken off by now.

I really, really hope it works. Both for their sake and mine.

10 April 2013, 10.00 a.m.

Subject – 'Deer and their eyes'.

Dear Kasturi,

All my friends here know about you, the girl I love. The girl who is so angry with me – rightfully so – that she will not even read my emails.

Yesterday I went to Richmond Park for an early-morning

run. During the two hours that I ran, all I thought of was how much you would have liked it. Sometimes I do this, you know, wonder about what your favourite places in London would have been had you been here with me. Anyway, so coming back to the park ... I know without any doubt that you would have loved it! There are deer everywhere, sitting in groups ... and oddly enough they remind me so much of you.

I know what you are thinking ... What? Deer remind him of me!

Well, their gorgeous, kohl rimmed eyes did for sure. Your eyes are beautiful, Kas, very beautiful. Alive and always dancing with mischief. Sometimes I wonder when it was that I really and truly fell in love with you ... neither a particular time nor a particular incident comes to mind ... just your eyes ... dancing with mirth, dark with anger, alive with mischief ... always so full of expression. I have been thinking about them since yesterday.

I always miss you, Kasturi, but today ... even more so...

Rajeev.

1.00 p.m.

I need to talk to someone.

Pitajee is not answering his phone and I have just left him my sixth voicemail telling him that I need to:

a) know what is happening with him and Anu.

b) tell him something important.

I don't have a good feeling about any of this.

2.00 p.m.

What am I thinking?

Indira Gandhi Airport, Car Park, Midnight.

Pitajee sat stone-still, his usually smiling face devoid of any expression. I had just picked him up at the airport and we were now sitting slumped in the car. I had not even bothered to turn on the ignition.

'Say that again,' I repeated, aghast.

'Anu is getting engaged to Saumen Dutta tomorrow. I tried to talk her out of it, but she is too worried about Govind's heart to … to…'

I put a reassuring hand on Pitajee's shoulders. 'I don't understand it Kasturi … why … why can't she just say no?

'Pitajee,' I said, helplessly.

'You know what, Kas, I'm done with Anu … it's all over.'

I turned my head sideways to stare open-mouthed at Pitajee. There was an air of resolute determination about him that scared the wits out of me.

'Have you lost it, Pitajee?' I said, not willing to believe him. Anu and Pitajee are meant to be together … theirs was one story that had to have a happy ending. Had to.

'It's over, Kasturi. It's all over … I don't understand Anu's behaviour but it's over,' he said, shaking his head as if he could not quite believe it himself.

There was silence in the car for a few moments.

'I need to tell you something too,' I said meekly, already afraid of how he was going to react. I had spent many hours thinking this through and finally knew what I wanted to do.

'Go on?' he said, raising his eyebrows.

I gulped.

'I cannot marry Purva,' I said, jutting out my chin, obstinately. It was Pitajee's turn to now stare at me aghast.

'Are you kidding me?' he said, shocked.

I shook my head.

'Why?'

'I don't know,' I lied, unwilling to share the real reason with him.

'Have you lost it, Kas?'

Yes, I probably have.

17

Café Coffee Day, Green Park, Delhi, 3 May 2013.

Purva stared at me, his eyes wide behind the spectacles I had gifted him for his last birthday. His face registered confusion.

'I'm sorry, Kas, what do you mean by that?' he asked me, the smile vanishing now. The two of us were sitting in the café near AIIMS, one of our usual hang-outs. I had spent the last two days tossing and turning, a gazillion thoughts in my head. Finally, I had come to a decision; a decision that was about to wreak havoc in everybody's life.

'Purva,' I said, staring at my fingers, 'I cannot do this.'

'Do what?'

'Get married…'

Purva continued to look confused. My comment had blind-sighted him, I knew. It broke my heart to do this, but I knew I could not live this lie any more.

'You don't want to marry me?' he asked, slowly, fiddling with the sides of his spectacles, which he always did when he felt nervous.

'I don't want to marry anyone,' I said, emphasizing 'anyone'. As if that helped.

Purva remained silent for a few seconds, as thoughts and consequences of this conversation filled me with a weird concoction of dread and nervousness.

When he looked up, which he did a little later, his eyes were red. Red and oh-so-terribly sad. So sad that I felt I could not breathe. I hated myself with all my heart for doing this to Purva.

'Why, Kasturi?' he asked softly, without the aggression that I had prepared myself for.

'I … I don't know…' I said, tears gathering in my eyes, as I stared unblinkingly at Purva. I wanted to lunge forward, hug him and tell him I was joking and this would all be over. But I could not … I couldn't live like this … this fake life where I pretended that my heart beat only for Purva.

Desperation closed in from all sides and a fat tear rolled down my cheeks and splattered on the paper napkin on the table. 'I don't know…' I repeated.

'Is it something I said? Something I did?' he prodded gently.

I shook my head.

'Then?' he asked.

'Purva … I don't feel ready … at all…' I said.

'Kas,' he said, grabbing my hands, 'these are just nerves! Don't worry, you don't have to do anything … nothing will change. You … you stop those stupid parantha classes … everything remains the way it was, the way you like it.'

Purva spoke breathlessly and I sobbed throughout, looking down, not daring to meet his eyes.

'It's not easy for me, Purva … but … I … I can't … just can't…'

'Why? What has changed? I … I…' he trailed off.

I closed my eyes. I hated seeing Purva like this. I hated being the person who was doing this to him. With trembling fingers, I removed my engagement ring and placed it on the table between us.

'Do you need more time?' he said, subconsciously pushing the ring towards me.

I closed my eyes and shook my head. 'Purva … if I don't feel I will be able to give you or our relationship a hundred per cent … I will not, and should not, marry you.'

Purva stared at me, his face now gradually clearing.

'I did not see this coming…' he said after a pause.

'Neither did I!' I said, swallowing hard.

Our eyes met; his shocked and mine desperate.

'You don't love me anymore,' he said, calmly, more to himself than to anyone else. 'Probably never did.'

A knife went through my heart as Purva quietly took the ring and put it in his pocket.

18

6 May 2013, 9.00 a.m.

'You've lost it, Kas,' said Pitajee's text.

'I know,' I replied.

6.00 p.m.

'Pitajee,' I said, into the phone.

'I hate you, Kas,' he said.

I stayed silent for a minute. 'You do, don't you?' I asked him.

'I don't want to lie to you about this, Kas, but I hate what you have done … I fail to see the logic,' he said, in a dry voice.

'Did you speak to him?'

'Speak to whom?'

'Purva!' I said, exasperated.

'Oh, you mean the man you ruthlessly ditched?'

I cancelled the call, anger surging inside me.

6.01 p.m.

'Kas,' said Pitajee, calling me up the next instant.

'Don't talk to me,' I said angrily.

'This is not us,' he said, his voice sad. 'We never fight like this.'

'I know,' I said. 'We never do. Everything has changed, Pitajee…'

'I met Purva,' he said, interrupting me.

'And?' I said, crossing my fingers. 'Is he all right?'

'Yeah. He told me what you had said to him. He seems to have doubled shifts and is working enough for forty bulls…'

'Is that all? Did he say that I was horrible?'

'He will never say that.'

'Why?'

'Because he loves you too much for that.'

I could say nothing to that because I knew he was right.

'Anu?' I asked.

Silence for a few minutes.

'Ask her. I don't care now,' he said abruptly.

I slumped back into my chair. What had happened to the four of us?

Life, said a little voice in my head.

7 May 2013.

'In case I haven't told you this before, you've lost it completely, Kas,' read Pitajee's text.

'Shut up,' I wrote back.

9 May 2013.

In a bid to distract myself, I have been spending a lot of time toying with the pearls of wisdom (read: Mum's blog).

Extract from a post titled, 'Comparisons that should not be made':

> *It is grossly incorrect to compare your life with that of those around you. Doing that will only make you feel smaller because there will always be someone with better health, a bigger career, a prettier wife. Remember, each of us has his own share of ups and downs. Experience the ups with quiet dignity and go through the downs with quiet dignity. The key to happiness is a stable mind. A stable mind, not given to troughs and peaks, while difficult to attain, is a beautiful mind.'*

Extract from another post titled, 'What you owe to yourself':

> *We go about life doing whatever it is we consider to be our duty towards our friends, family and society. What we forget often, I am afraid, is the duty we have towards ourselves.*
>
> *Do you know what the biggest duty you have towards yourself is?*
>
> *I will put it simply.*
>
> *Your biggest duty is to help yourself become the best you can possibly be.*

I sat and read the last line a couple of times. It was powerful stuff, I had to say. My mind went back to what I had done to Purva and wondered if that had signified the worst in me.

Moving to other matters now, the number of followers of

the blog is now an unbelievable 612. She has become some kind of cyber Shri Prabha Shankar.

My Parents' Home, 10 May 2013, 3.00 p.m.

'Give me one good reason,' Mum thundered, as she furiously paced the living room.

I closed my eyes, trying hard to block out both the anger and the questions.

'One good reason,' she repeated, jabbing a finger in my direction.

Dad, Mum and I were sitting in the living room. Two days ago, I had announced to them that I no longer wished to marry Purva. Before the day had ended, the e-ticket to a flight home had arrived politely in my email.

After many rounds of arguments, where Mum mostly seemed to ask me to give her one good reason, we still had not made much headway.

'Prabha,' said Dad, 'leave us alone.'

'What? Why? Why should I leave my daughter alone? I was the one who gave birth to her, not you.' Then she changed tack. Do you know how horrible it was for me to call up Mrs Dixit and request her to postpone the wedding for the time being? Do you have any idea how stupid Kasturi is?'

'Prabha,' Dad said, his voice dangerously calm, 'Please leave us alone.'

Mum cast one look at me and stamped away, leaving Dad sitting at the dining table, alone with me.

'Beta,' said Dad, 'have you spoken to Purva since you came here?'

I shook my head.

'I see you are not wearing the ring.'

'I gave it back to him,' I said.

Dad seemed lost in his thoughts for a few seconds. 'It stopped being magical and it stopped feeling right?' he asked in a low voice. I had to hear those words to start crying again. I felt relief wash over me; finally someone understood.

I nodded my head.

'Why did it stop feeling right?' he asked me, his voice gentle. When I did not answer for a long time, he continued. 'Kasturi, it's okay for things to not make sense sometimes. I am on your side. We are in this together. Tell me what's going on in your head and we can sort this out together.'

I began to cry bitterly, anger, frustration and helplessness taking over. Why did I have to feel this way? Why?

Dad patted my head.

'It's Rajeev, isn't it?' he asked in a whisper.

I looked up at him, stunned. How did he know? I debated whether it would be a good idea to deny this, but decided against lying.

'Yes,' I said in a low voice.

Dad looked on intently at me.

'I still think of him all the time,' I said in a low voice.

9.00 p.m.

'You have lost it, Kas,' Pitajee's text read.

'Get lost,' I replied, immediately. 'Anu?' I texted again.

'Get lost,' he replied, within seconds.

11.00 p.m.

Subject line – 'I miss you'.

Dear Kasturi,

I miss you so much more today, there seem to be strings, strong though invisible, that connect me to you. I can never get too far away from thoughts about you.

I miss you.

Rajeev.

11 May 2013, 10.00 p.m.

Dad and I sat in his bedroom watching another rerun of *Big Boss* when he looked up at me and, completely out of blue, asked me about Rajeev.

'What's he doing these days, do you know?' he asked.

I nodded my head. 'LBS ... MBA.'

'Have you spoken to him?'

'Not since ... since...' I trailed off. Not since Teena.

'Is he married?' Dad asked.

I shook my head and told him about the emails and all the information I had gathered about him from the daily email updates.

'One email each day?' asked Dad, surprised.

'Sometimes more than one,' I said, shrugging.

Dad said nothing and turned around to face the TV. Mum came in, in a big hustle.

'Pankudi,' she said, 'keeps asking me about the Dixits! What am I supposed to say to that?'

Dad shrugged and I tried to look ashamed of what I had done.

'Kasturi,' said Dad, now looking at me thoughtfully. 'Meet him.'

I almost sputtered out the water I had just taken a gulpful of. The things parents say!

'What?' I said, in an appropriately screechy voice.

'Yes.'

'Yes to what?' said Mum, looking first at Dad and then at me, suspicion written large on her face.

'Are you kidding me?' My heart had started racing excitedly. Meet Rajeev? After all these years?

'No,' said Dad gravely. 'In fact, I insist that you meet him as soon as possible.'

'Meet whom?' asked Mum.

'Rajeev,' said Dad, turning around to face Mum.

'Have you lost it?' asked Mum, staring at Dad.

11.00 p.m.

'Dad must have a reason,' I said to Pitajee. It was late in the night and I had just told Pitajee all about Rajeev's emails and Dad's comment.

'Kasturi, I don't trust Rajeev. At all,' Pitajee sounded grave. I could picture him shaking his head, his face serious.

'He is a changed man, Pitajee … and I … I can't help the way I continue to feel about him.'

'So this is why you broke off your engagement with Purva?'

'How could I marry one man and feel this way about another?'

'I understand that … but … I don't … don't trust Rajeev, Kas … I…' fumbled Pitajee. 'Are you going to...?'

'Yes,' I said. 'Dad would not ask me to meet Rajeev unless he thought it was a good idea.'

Pitajee did not reply for a long time. 'You seem to have made your decision,' he said quietly, a hint of desperation in his voice.

Midnight.

How do I begin?

1.00 a.m.

I cannot write a simple email.

2.00 a.m.

Bleh!

3.00 a.m.

Why am I so wide awake? And why, dear lord, can I not put together a simple email?

4.30 a.m.

So after staring at the screen for four hours and creating 117 drafts, I finally read through the short email once more before hitting the 'send' button.

Hi Rajeev,

I would like to meet you. Are you planning to come to India any time soon?

Kasturi

4.34 a.m.

I was about to log out of the account, when an email popped back in.

I am booking tickets right away for Saturday.

Rajeev

My mouth felt dry; it was Thursday already.

I reminded myself to breathe as my pulse quickened. This could not really be happening.

19

Car Park, Delhi Domestic Airport, 13 May 2013, 7.00 p.m.

I thought hard as I waited for Anu at the airport. Anu was flying in from Pune and my flight from home had landed half an hour ago. Anu should be out any minute, I told myself, getting a little restless. The plan was for us to go home together and, more importantly, catch up. 'Kas!' said Anu, tapping my shoulder.

I turned around to face her and stilled. The first thing about her that struck me was how sad her pretty face looked; there were dark circles under her eyes which looked ready to start watering anytime now. I noticed her hands next, covered in an elaborate henna pattern, a gentle reminder of the ceremony she had just attended. Finally, my eyes fell on the ring on her finger.

I took her hands in mine, feeling the gravity of the situation. She looked at me and shrugged helplessly, not trusting herself with words. She then held my hands in hers, her face registering an emotional struggle as she fiddled with my finger that was no longer adorned with a ring.

'When I met you last, you had an engagement ring on this finger,' she said in a low voice

'When I met you last,' I said, feeling my throat catch, 'you did not.'

'Why?' she asked, half pleading, her eyes shining with a coat of water. 'Purva is ... is ... he is the nicest man we all know.'

I sat down in the driver's seat and Anu sat in the front passenger seat, but I did not turn on the ignition. Instead, I let my hands rest on the steering wheel.

'Anu ... I don't feel sure about ... about Purva ... I could not ... I just couldn't go ahead with the wedding. It would have been so wrong ... to marry someone you're not sure about at all.'

'It is so wrong to marry someone you're not sure about,' Anu repeated ghost-like after me and spared a hand over my head.

'Yes, Anu, it is wrong and unfair on both people who are getting into the marriage,' I said, fully aware that we were now talking about Anu and Saumen.

'What did Purva say?' she asked.

I shook my head. 'I told him what I wanted.'

'And?'

'I guess he let me have what I asked for...'

Anu and I sat in silence for a few minutes, both of us lost in thought.

'Did the surprise engagement freak you out?' she asked.

I nodded my head.

'I thought it was a bad idea,' she said.

I sat there staring at the planet-sized diamond on Anu's

finger debating whether to tell her about Rajeev. I wondered if I felt ashamed of speaking the truth.

'Your story?' I said, turning around to face her. 'What the hell happened? Pitajee just won't talk about it. He keeps saying that everything is fine. I don't know what he means!'

'My parents were very rude to him,' she said.

'Nothing new about that! I don't know how he puts up with that, to be honest.'

'When I went home,' she began, 'I could see that there was going to be a lot of trouble with Mum and Dad about Amay. They insisted that I forget him – after all, they said, girls do have these flings. When I refused to listen to them, they realized that I will only forget him if they place a suitable boy in front of me.'

I stared at her.

'Why did you agree to the engagement?' I asked, a familiar surge of anger now rising in my throat.

'I had little choice, Kas,' she said in a small voice.

'What do you mean by that?'

'Dad.' she said.

'What about him?' I asked and then it hit me. 'His heart?'

'Kas, that night, after I had been forced to meet Saumen – that's the name of the guy, by the way – I threw a massive tantrum. That is when Mum took me to another room and in a fit of mad anger began to fling files at me.'

'What?'

'Medical reports,' she said quietly.

'What medical reports?' I asked.

'Dad has a very weak heart,' she said, tearing up as I shook my head disbelievingly. 'Mum told me that Dad really wants me married to Saumen and could I not forget Amay, whom I have known for only two years, for the sake of my father who brought me into this world.'

I let out another deep breath. I could not contest the logic.

'You should have seen Dad when I was throwing my tantrum! He was so red in the face, I thought he was going to have a heart attack! When Mum showed me the medical reports, she said…'

'She said?'

'She said Dad will die if I marry Amay.'

Oh the drama! 'And then you agreed?' Anu nodded, her head hung low. 'Oh,' I said, lost in thought.

'Amay and I had a long conversation,' said Anu, 'and we came to a conclusion. I told him that I love him, I love him more than I love myself, but I don't love him more than I love Dad. I would not be able to live if something happened to Dad ... because of me…'

I stayed silent for a few minutes. 'What did he say?' I asked.

'He said he understood. And no matter how much he hated my father for doing this, if he were in my place, he would do the same…' Anu trailed off, sobbing.

I have spent years squabbling with Pitajee, throwing pillows and coffee mugs at him. There was something so mature about the Pitajee Anu was talking about that I felt my heart break. I held my head in my hands for a few minutes, the silence of the car park disrupted by a girl shrieking with delight as she leapt into the arms of her boyfriend.

No one deserved this. No one. Not the worst people on the planet and certainly not Anu and Pitajee who could not knowingly hurt a fly.

'Kas, Dad is not keeping well ... he looks fine but his heart is not good. I can live with any man if that makes him happy. I will try to forget Amay. I ... I...'

I lunged forward and wrapped my arms around Anu in a fierce hug. I have known Anu since the day I set foot in Delhi. I have seen her morph from a tomboy to a girl madly in love with my best friend. I can read her expressions like the back of my hand and what I could read now broke my heart again and again. Two years ago, when I was piecing together bits of my life after the Rajeev debacle, Anu had told me that seeing me in such a mess had made her want to cry her heart out. It was only now that I understood what she had meant by that; all I wanted to do was to cry and not stop.

Friendship. How it can double your joy and also double your misery.

'You poor, poor thing,' I muttered into her hair, feeling tears sting my eyes too. 'It's horrible, isn't it?'

I could feel her nod her head. And my heart broke again.

'How will you do this?' I said, my voice cracking as I felt the desperation that Anu had been living with these past few weeks

'I don't know, Kasturi. I have no freaking clue,' she said, now openly sobbing into my shoulder.

'Shh ... Anu ... you will...' I never completed the sentence. Angry, desperate tears clouded my vision and I soon found myself clinging to Anu in the deserted car park, crying my heart out for all four of us.

Love. It's like Father Christmas. A myth.

Vijaywada & Sons, Head Office, Green Park, 20 May 2013.

It is quite ridiculous, you know, this whole thing about being a VP. At Vijaywada & Sons, it becomes even funnier. We have three offices in Delhi and each office is headed by a VP. All three offices are fairly close to each other, so we actually have a vice president – Green Park, vice president – Connaught Place, Outer Circle and vice president – Connaught Place, Inner Circle.

I know. Strange, but true. Some smart MBA grad must have come up with this nonsense.

Even though it is Saturday, I am in the office, mainly because if I had nothing to do, I would die of anxiety. So there I was, grumpy to be at work on a Saturday morning and trying helplessly to drill some sense into the brain of the vice-president-Connaught-Place-Inner-Circle, when I saw Padma walk in, her brand new red stilettos clicking on the tiled floor.

That girl had taken to fashion like a duck takes to water, I thought proudly, as with one swift movement, she took off her Gucci shades.

Oh boy!

'Gucci-shuchchi,' I grinned at her, when I had finished talking to vice-president-Connaught-Place-Inner-Circle and had given up all hope in mankind.

'Kas ... you look a little different today,' she said, narrowing her eyes at me and completely ignoring my comment.

'You look different too, Gucci-shuchchi.'

If anyone could glare, it was Padma, and glare at me she did.

'Nothing … usual stuff.'

'No, it's not,' she said, coming closer to me, pulling a chair and scrutinizing my face as if I were bacteria in a Petri dish.

I remained silent as she studied me carefully for a few minutes. 'You are worried,' she declared finally.

'No … nothing,' I said, looking at my hands. I get uncomfortable around people who can read my face and, since we became friends, Padma had become worryingly good at it.

'Tell me,' she insisted, pulling her chair closer to me.

'Padma, I am meeting Rajeev today,' I said quietly, taken aback that this had tumbled out for I had not even mentioned it to Anu. Funny how sometimes it is easier to speak honestly with people who are not as close to you.

There was silence for a few seconds during which Padma, whom I had spoken to about Rajeev earlier, stared at me, her eyes becoming bigger by the second.

'Did you break off your engagement to Purva because of Rajeev?' she asked. Put so bluntly, I cringed.

But it was time to be honest. With someone, at least.

'Partly yes, partly no.'

'No?' she asked me, in a voice that was surprisingly gentle.

'Because I was getting all worked up about the wedding. I did not feel ready at all.'

'Hmmm … and why yes?'

'Because if Rajeev had not materialized on the scene, I would have grumbled a little bit, thrown a few tantrums, probably gotten the wedding date postponed, but not broken off my engagement with Purva.'

'Do you love Purva?'

'Oh, yes … of course,' I said the next instant and then I

stopped short. What had I just said? The whole idea behind cancelling my wedding had been that I did not love Purva.

'Does he love you?'

'When we were together, I had no doubt that he loved me.'

'Do you love Rajeev?'

I paused. 'Umm ... he ... he is very handsome ... and...'

'Do you love Rajeev?' Padma insisted.

'I am attracted to him...'

'Do you love Rajeev, Kasturi?'

I shook my head. 'I am not sure,' I said.

'Then let me answer it for you,' she said as I looked up at a very determined face staring back at me. 'You don't love Rajeev and I will tell you why I know. When we love someone, Kasturi, we know it even before we know. It's like your soul hears your heart before you hear it. Love reaches somewhere deep inside us long before it becomes apparent. I would not have had to ask you thrice.'

I said nothing.

'Does he love you?' she asked.

'Yes, he says so in his emails,' I said.

'When you guys were together earlier, did he ever tell you that he loved you?' she asked, smiling. I felt better and less like I was being questioned by the police.

'Yes, of course, all the time. I wish Purva had told me more often that he loved me.'

'That Purva did not do the same is good, Kasturi,' said Padma calmly.

'What do you mean?'

'Purva did not tell you each day that he loved you because it was such a big part of his existence that he felt no need to reiterate it. Like, you know, we breathe all the time, but do I feel the need to tell everyone that I am breathing? No. But when I go for a holiday to Chennai, I will tell people about it. Purva may not have told you of his love day-in and day-out but he did not cheat on you. Rajeev might have told you that he loved you each day, but…' she paused, getting up, 'he was cheating on you all the while. That, my dear friend, is the difference between the two men.'

I sat still. The whole atmosphere that Padma had created around me had ensconced me in a bubble of logic and sense. As she walked back to her desk, Padma turned around and raised one perfectly arched eyebrow at me.

'People don't change, Kas, they just don't. Remember that,' she said, shaking her head ominously.

20

5.00 p.m.

I called Dad. Mum picked up.

'Where is Dad? I need to speak to him.' I said.

'Kasturi, he is down with a slight headache, darling. Call later?' said Mum.

'Can he just speak to me for a minute?' I insisted. Dad never had headaches, but of late…

I heard Mum mumble something to Dad in the background. 'He seems to be asleep…' she said in a low whisper.

Drat!

'Okay. Tell him I called when he wakes up.'

5.30 p.m.

There is a lot of noise in my head. I want it to clear up.

6.00 p.m.

Rajeev. Another hour and I will be sitting in front of him!

6.15 p.m.

Oh god. Why am I feeling all weird? Nerves?

6.20 p.m.

Why is my face in a perpetual frown? Is it just nerves?

6.45 p.m.

I sat still in the car, parked outside TGIF. My eyes scanned the parking lot and hands turned ice-cold when I spotted the familiar white Honda Civic. He had a) not changed cars and b) was already inside, just a few feet away from me. I almost began to hyperventilate at the mere thought.

People don't change. Purva will remain honest and nice. Rajeev will remain the cheat that he was.

I looked at myself in the rear-view mirror, barely noticing the make-up I had spent hours putting on.

People don't change. Purva will remain honest and nice. Rajeev will remain the cheat that he was.

I absently looked around for my purse, feeling increasingly restless. My lips felt cold too and I took in deep bursts of air. As I marvelled at how my body was reacting to the situation, it hit me – the reason why this was such a big deal.

By meeting Rajeev I knew I was crossing the Rubicon, the point of no return. I could look back but never come back. I would be pushing Purva to a corner from where I would never be able to reach him. For me he would have to cease to exist. The moment had come when I would have to choose between the two men. And for me, that was a big deal.

People don't change. Purva will remain honest and nice. Rajeev will remain the cheat that he was.

'I will go,' I said, breathing out and settling the collar of my shirt. I grabbed my purse and, as I did so, the glove cupboard yanked open and something fell out.

Before I knew it, Mum and Dad singing happy birthday was gently echoing in the car. I was immobile for a minute as I stared down at the turquoise musical box that Purva had so painstakingly set right for my birthday. It now lay open, upside down. Desolate. Sad.

My brain burst into a whirlwind of emotion and noise. Pitajee's and Padma's words rang in my head. I continued to stare unblinking at the box, transfixed, unable to peel myself away from a force that tugged at me again and again and again.

I picked up the box, dusted off an imaginary fleck of dirt and put it on the car seat. I shut it slowly and the notes died out, leaving behind a silence that threatened to suffocate me. My cell phone beeped, jarring me out of my reverie. It was the reminder that I had set for my meeting with Rajeev.

I opened the box again and the familiar tune started playing, the gentle notes filling the silence in the car. I breathed deeply and closed my eyes, concentrating on each note that was ingrained in my memory and my heart. Thoughts ran around in my head, randomly at first, then aggressively and finally in a straight line as things fell into place. Like magic, in a span of a few seconds, with the music playing in the background, the clouds parted and the sun shone.

I opened my eyes and looked around. The world somehow

seemed different. Something had just happened – something beyond my reckoning and beyond logic – that had helped me make a decision. It was, I realized, an epiphany. In that one moment, I felt closer to God than I had ever before. Dad had asked me to meet Rajeev. Now, finally, as the song finished and the ballerina stopped twirling, I understood why.

With my decision made, I patted the box and smiled for the first time in what seemed like ages. I slapped the steering wheel. It felt nice to be sure. Grinning my widest, I turned the ignition of the car back on. I needed to meet Purva immediately. Meet him and tell him how horribly idiotic I had been.

Only, I never got to do that.

21

7.10 p.m.

I imagined myself to be quite the Bond girl as I swerved my little red Maruti Swift through the traffic heading straight towards AIIMS and Purva. Not another moment should be lost, I told myself sternly. Enough of the madness.

I overtook another car and got screamed at by the driver of another. This whole mad dash across the city thing, it so appealed to my sense of drama. Beautiful girl in a red car, zipping across the city to tell a handsome doctor that it was him her heart beat for. Aah. The theatrical zing.

When I had agreed to marry Purva, I had done so as a compromise. Purva was even sensitive enough to realize that. I remember, he had said, gruffly, 'I know, Kasturi, that you do not love me, but I hope that one day you will.'

My wounds, then, were too raw, the hurt ran too deep for me to be capable of real, true love. Purva, obviously, loved me and, having walked away from a man who did not return my love, all I'd wanted was someone who loved me more than I loved him.

Purva had fit that bill perfectly. Too perfectly. He was a man

I could trust without an iota of doubt. He was a man who would risk his life for me. He was the man every girl wanted.

Except, of course, me. I just wanted Rajeev.

Yet, I egged myself on to forget Rajeev and limped towards Purva, who stood waiting patiently for me, his arms wide open, ready to collect me in a warm hug. Rajeev's treachery aided me and each time I faltered, I thought of him with Teena and ran a little bit faster towards Purva. Initially, I just pretended that Purva made the world all right for me, but gradually I began to forget Rajeev.

Mum, Dad, Pitajee, Anu – everyone loved Purva for his gentle manners and kind ways. They thought I had hit the jackpot with Purva. As I began to forget Rajeev, the hurt and misery began to become foggy as well. However, he was with Teena and that thought alone continued to sear through me as if it were a sword on fire that had been shoved through my heart.

And then, just when I had immersed myself completely in making paranthas, came the emails. Out the blue they arrived, bursting through the fabric that I had woven and wrapped myself in. Simply put, they turned my life upside down. They took me back to a time when I'd had a man in my life whom I had loved so much that I felt I would burst. I recalled how a single look from him could have me smiling for hours, how one hug from him would keep me warm for days and how one kiss from him would linger on my lips for weeks. That made me restless, so restless that Purva seemed like a handcuff, something that stopped me from being with the man I was secretly pining for. Upset, confused, bewildered at the tricks my heart played with me and scared of what I felt, I decided that I should not marry Purva; not in such a state of mind.

Or so I thought.

Then Dad asked me to meet Rajeev.

A lot of people told me that I was being stupid but the words that really hit home were those of Padma's. It was when I was sitting in the car, Purva's box playing the little ditty in the background, that I understood why Dad asked me to meet Rajeev; he had known that it would be the moment of reckoning. Faced with the choice, I would know which man I truly loved. He had been right.

I was so busy trying to forget Rajeev, so engrossed in not letting him overpower everything in my life, that I had not realized something important. Along the way, I had, unknown to myself, fallen in love with Purva. I smiled now, glad that my head was clear. I could finally breathe easy. At last I knew what I wanted and who my loyalties lay with.

My cell rang. Mum's number flashed on the screen.

'It must be Dad,' I said to myself, 'returning my call.'

It was not. It was Mum. Breathless.

Ten seconds later, I had stamped my feet so hard on the brakes that a car behind had rammed into me. My car skidded a few feet before coming to a halt.

'Say that again, Mum?' I said into the phone, feeling the blood drain from my face.

'Dad's being wheeled into the OT,' she said, surprisingly calm.

'Why? What's wrong with him?' I screamed, already hysterical.

'They ... umm ... need to operate.'

'Operate on what?' I asked. Maybe it was his foot, he had had some ligament issue last month. I knew even as I asked the question that this would not be the case.

'Umm ... don't get scared, Kas, it's...'

'It's what, Mum?' I said, getting more restless by the minute.

'It's his brain ... there ... there has been some bleeding... '

I was stunned into silence.

'Don't worry, it's not something major ... umm...' struggled Mum, '... umm ... can you come?'

I had already careened my car around and, pausing only briefly to check if my credit cards were with me, I sped towards the airport, brushing away anxious tears that were already clouding my vision.

'I am on my way, Mum.'

'Central Hospital, ask for the Neurosurgery ICU.'

22

Indira Gandhi Airport, 9.00 p.m.

'Ma'am, I *can* give you a choice,' said the lady in the business suit, in a very important and heavily-accented voice.

Shut up.

'You could … let me see … either take the last flight out; I have an economy ticket available for seven thousand rupees or…'

Shut up.

'…I could give you the next flight out, but we only have a business class ticket available…'

'How much?' I asked listlessly, the decision already made.

'Twenty-three thousand rupees.'

'I want it,' I said, pretty much a second before she had finished speaking.

9.20 p.m.

I have called Mum so many times that she has actually threatened to not answer any of my calls. Even in this situation, she is terrorizing me!

As we speak, Dad is in the OT getting prepped for the surgery. Since Dad had been having headaches which would not go, they had gone for a quick MRI scan today without, of course, telling me. They were expecting the scan to be clean; give Dad a few multi-vitamins and pack him off for the day.

When I had called Mum, they were actually in the diagnostic centre. The scan was disastrous and showed the brain shrivelled and pushed to one corner with the rest of the sac filled with blood from an injury. Mum now recalled Dad hitting his head a few weeks ago and blacking out. Being a doctor, he had simply ignored the whole episode, until, of course, now.

The operation, Mum insists, is very simple, but it's my father whose brain the doctors are fiddling with and it is not cool.

So *not* cool.

9.22 p.m.

'Mummy,' lisped the little boy tugging at his mother's kurta and pointing at me, 'is this didi mad?'

I glared at the little boy who hid behind his decidedly embarrassed-looking mother. I realized that it was probably not the boy's fault. I had been, for the last ten minutes, pacing the airport lounge, wringing my hands and muttering, 'My dad is going through brain surgery,' repeatedly to myself.

I hastily scraped my loose, and by now wild, hair into a ponytail and sat down on my hands, in a desperate attempt to look less mad.

10.00 p.m.

Dad's operation has begun. I am about to board the plane. Mum is waiting outside the OT.

I imagined her alone and the tears, a result of sheer helplessness, refused to stop. I will now be airborne and will not even be able to speak to Mum till half an hour after Dad comes out of surgery.

God, please … please be with Dad.

Midnight.

I am out of the airport but Dad is still not out of the OT. The darkest thoughts have been plaguing me for the last hour.

21 May 2013, 1.00 a.m.

I called Mum from the airport and even her 'Hi, Beta,' sounded different; relieved. I took a deep breath the moment I heard her voice.

'Is Dad out?' I asked. 'Why did they take so long?'

'Seems like there was another emergency.'

'What happened to Dad?' I shrieked into the phone. I was in a car that one of my cousins was driving and we were speeding towards the hospital.

'Naah,' said Mum dismissively, as if no emergency could ever possibly happen with my dad, who was being wheeled out of an emergency neurosurgery operation. 'Some other guy. Dad is fine. They needed the doctors there.'

Another deep breath.

'All went okay?' I asked.

'Yes, Kasturi, all was okay.'

I paused for a second. 'All okay?' I asked, again.

'Yes, Kas,' said Mum.

Another pause.

'All o-'

'Shut up, Kasturi Beta.'

4.00 a.m.

'Only one person can go in,' said Dr Kulkarni, looking at the bunch of us huddled outside the Neurosurgery ICU. Dad had been shifted to the post-operative ICU an hour ago. His extended family were all there, standing with solemn faces.

'You go, Kas,' Mum said, nudging me.

I froze.

I stared at my feet, willing them to move, but they would not listen. An inexplicable sort of fear began to creep up inside me. I had always seen Dad healthy and strong. I did not know if I would be able to take the sight of him in a hospital bed; every cell in my body revolted at the idea.

What a coward.

'Mum ... you ... you go,' I stammered.

Mum smiled benignly, as if she was doing me a favour.

'I know you want to go, Koochie,' she insisted.

For the first time since she had taken to calling me Koochie, I let it pass without comment or fight. I was about to walk towards the grey-blue doors of the ICU when Mum put a hand on my shoulder.

'Koochie?' she said.

'Yes, Mum…' I turned around, my heart and head both feeling heavy and tired from stress and exhaustion. Maybe Mum was going to tell me that I had been a rock? She too, I must say, had been remarkably brave.

'Dad has a little bit of a Prem Chopra thing going on,' she said, patting her head.

'What? What do you mean by that?' I asked, confused.

Then it dawned on me; they had shaved Dad's head for the operation. My eyes were wet but a weak giggle escaped me nevertheless.

A Prem Chopra thing going on! I smiled a weak smile at Mum who returned it.

'We will be okay, Koochie,' she said, patting my shoulders.

'Yes, Mum, we will be,' I said, putting on the plastic bag sort-of-thing that the guard outside the Neurosurgery ICU passed on to me to put on my shoes.

'This way, please,' said Dr Kulkarni. 'Dr Advani is with him, don't worry.' Dr Advani is Dad's friend from medical school who happens to be on deputation at this hospital. This fact alone had made all the difference to us.

I nodded, already feeling my hands go numb. The doors of the ICU opened and with them opened a whole new world. I took in my surroundings, not really believing what my eyes were seeing. There were about ten beds in the ICU, each of them occupied. As my eyes travelled from one bed to the next, I sucked in my breath. Nine very ill people lay in beds, in full view of the nurses and doctors. I almost saw a man with an open brain and instinctively withdrew my eyes before I really registered any details. Another man seemed to be repeatedly having fits. One by one, my eyes scanned each bed, a shudder passing through me each time, along with a whiff of relief that the very sick person was not Dad. I was, with all my heart, dreading the moment I would spot Dad.

Which I soon did. I was surprised that I was not surprised. Or upset. He seemed to be sleeping peacefully, albeit with a heavily-bandaged head.

'Dad,' I said, softly, when I walked up to him. Advani Uncle nodded and mouthed, 'He is absolutely fine,' at me.

Dad's eyes fluttered open a few seconds later. I bent low but Advani Uncle gently pushed me away.

'Did you meet him?' were the first words Dad uttered after coming out of the surgery.

Did you meet him?

It took me a moment to understand that he was asking about Rajeev. All of that already seemed like it had happened a million years ago, in a different, faraway world.

'Uh … no ... no, I did not,' I said, bending closer to him.

'Do you want to meet him?' he asked, closing his eyes now.

I paused.

'No,' I said quietly.

Dad said nothing; his eyes remained closed but a slow, gentle smile gradually spread across his face. I smiled too.

Life, you know, is funny. Funny in its own way. We were in the Neurosurgery ICU, Dad had just had surgery and we were both smiling. We were smiling because, as Dad had hoped, I had not crossed the Rubicon.

4.30 a.m.

This has been the longest night in my life.

It's weird, you know, how life comes full circle. You don't know when or how it happens but one day, you find yourself worrying about your parents, taking care of them and trying your best to do whatever you can for their comfort.

You have known all along that no one will ever really love you the way your parents do and then, one day, you realize that no one will ever love your parents as much as you do.

6.00 a.m.

With the relatives gone, there were a hundred things to be sorted: Mum's clothes, food, toothbrush, soap, Dad's medicines, who would stay with Dad for the night and once he was out of the OT … the list was tiringly endless and my brain was already exhausted. Mum and I were sitting outside the ICU when a doctor came to us with some documents. I looked away in disgust. Another set of papers that spoke about worst-case situations that I did not even want to think about.

'Please sign these,' he said, looking first at Mum and then at me.

I groaned silently. I looked at Mum and she shook her head; she was not going to sign anything that discounted the hospital of responsibility should anything happen to Dad. As the doctor looked expectantly at me, all the weight of the last couple of hours fell on me like a brick and tears began to sting my eyes. Angrily, I willed them to dry up.

This was so not the time for a meltdown.

It was then that an odd yearning seared through me. Very few single children will admit it, but almost all of us deeply feel the void of not having a brother or a sister to fight, play or share our lives and parents with. I felt this so strongly in that moment that another wave of tears was ready to burst forth. What would I not give to have a sibling to share this with? Maybe he/she would be the stronger one and would happily sign documents without batting an eyelid since the mere sight of the papers was reducing me to tears.

'I wish I were not the only child!' I said ruefully, a little too loudly in the silent room.

There was a pause before three sombre voices responded. 'You're not.'

I knew who the voices belonged to even before I saw them. A weird, inexplicable wave of relief was already spreading itself through my being as I turned around and saw Pitajee, Anu and Purva crowding at the door. Without another word, and without even looking at me, Purva stepped forward and took the pen from my hands.

'Papers, Doc?' he said, looking at the doctor and not even glancing in my direction.

Pitajee, who has always had such an easy camaraderie with Mum that sometimes even I have been jealous, stood on my right, his arm around her. Anu, with an arm around my waist, was on my left and Purva, with the pen in his hands, was in front of me.

With Dad in the Neurosurgery ICU, it was possibly the darkest hour of my life. But as with each dark hour that life had, of late, thrown at me, my closest friends had rallied around, ready to offer a steadying hand, should I falter.

A couple of weeks ago, I had called off my wedding to Purva without even giving him a proper reason. Six hours ago, I had travelled across Delhi to meet Rajeev.

6.08 a.m.

'I'm sorry,' said the doctor, looking seriously at Mum and then at me. 'Only immediate family members can sign these papers.'

Purva's pen was about to touch paper when, on hearing the words of the doctor and very familiar with hospital protocol, he paused.

For a few seconds, nothing happened. And then Mum spoke. 'Purva will sign the papers, Doctor,' she said in a low voice that trembled just a little bit. 'He *is* family.'

I looked at Mum, her eyes were now red and wet. Anu sniffed away a tear and I hugged her sideways. Purva, his face grave and serious, bent low to sign the document. I have always loved the pretty, neat cursive of Purva's hand and almost mechanically peeped over to see him write.

Purva had signed and typed his full name in capital letters. Just below that, he was asked to fill in his relationship with the patient.

I saw Purva's pen not hesitate for even an instant as he printed three letters.

SON.

Sometimes you want him to scream at you. Sometimes you need him to be red-faced with sheer anger. Sometimes you want him to tell you that he hates you.

Instead. Three simple letters. Written with earnestness.

The next instant, I had shot out of the room, my face wet with tears that had been threatening to spill over since I'd first heard of Dad's surgery. Guilt choked me breathless and shame made me blind. I ran down the corridor that was teeming with patients, doctors and nurses, brushing aside people who came in my way, tears clouding my vision. I ran the fastest my tired legs could carry me and stopped only when I had come out of the hospital.

I sat down on the stairs, my face in my hands, and cried bitterly. The tears that seemed to begin from somewhere deep inside me, where it hurt so much that the pain was unbearable, would not stop.

23

23 May 2013, 10.00 a.m.

Dad was now well settled in the private room. Family, friends and relatives had all been calling up as news of Dad's dramatic surgery spread far and wide. With Dad out of the ICU and danger, Mum was only too happy to relate the whole sequence of events to anyone willing to listen. There were, of course, some modifications. For instance, the time between the MRI scan and the surgery was reduced from four hours (the real number) to forty-five minutes (the more dramatic number), from two doctors wheeling Dad into the OT, the number theatrically shot up to eleven doctors and – lo and behold – fourteen nurses. If the latest version was to be believed, it would seem that the entire hospital had been in an uproar and Mum was just about managing to keep everything in control.

I found myself shaking my head but smiling nevertheless.

6.00 p.m.

'Subdural hematoma?' asked the nurse, looking at Dad's chart and readying him for another antibiotic injection. Purva, who seemed to know every doctor in the world, had made sure that Dad was getting five-star treatment from everyone, ranging from the head of the department to the nurse.

Dad nodded his head, which at least *looked* considerably lighter, now that the helmet-like bandage had been taken off.

'Today is Monday?' she asked, most casually.

'No, I think it's Tuesday,' Dad corrected her.

'So you are a doctor too?'

'Yes,' said Dad, rolling up his sleeves, ready for the injection.

'Your specialty, Doctor Sa'ab?'

'Ortho,' he said.

I rolled my eyes. This covert way of checking if Dad's memory was working fine was ridiculous. Of course, as soon as Dad had come into his private room, I had asked him what two-plus-two was. He had smiled and rattled off the multiplication table of thirty-seven, which had Mum really worried for a second; after all, seventy-four was not the sum of two and two.

'Your name, Doctor Sa'ab,' she asked again.

Dad looked at her and, with a straight face, said, 'Pintu.'

Pitajee laughed for two minutes without stopping. Seeing him in splits, Mum joined in, as did Anu. Even I managed a small smile. The nurse on the other hand, scuttled out as soon as she could.

8.00 p.m.

I was sitting on the floor outside Dad's room, taking a moment to myself. I rested my head against the wall as sounds of laughter from the room reached me. Purva, Mum, Anu and

Pitajee were inside, entertaining Dad. Eleven times since Dad's surgery, various doctors have tousled my hair and told me that subdural hematoma is an uncomplicated surgery. I am, of course, ready to kill anyone who repeats that to me. It is my dad. Even if subdural hematoma needed the simplest surgery known to man, it happened to my dad and, because of that simple fact, it is, for me, a big deal.

I was thinking these angry, dark thoughts when someone touched my hand gently, startling me out of my reverie.

Pitajee. He joined me on the floor and held my tightly-clamped fist. I smiled weakly at him, eyes tearing up for no reason. Slowly, finger by finger, Pitajee unfurled my fist. It was then that I realized that I had had my hands balled up in a fist pretty much ever since I had got that call from Mum. It is something I do whenever I am stressed.

'Relax now, Kas. We are all here and will see this through,' he said, putting a hand on my head. Snuggling close to him for comfort, I rested my head on his shoulder and we sat like that, watching people walk by.

'Pitajee,' I said, staring at the wall in front of me.

'Hmm?'

'I messed up.'

He said nothing.

'I made a terrible mistake.'

Still nothing.

'I love Purva.'

'What about that scum-eating, cheating bastard?' Pitajee asked finally.

I grinned. 'I would not know.'

A satisfied sigh from Pitajee.

'I won't bug you with questions, Kas, but I do have a comment,' he paused and then continued when I looked at him quizzically. 'You are the biggest idiot on this planet, Kas.'

'Yes,' I said, nodding my head in agreement. There was no denying that now.

'You need to be worried, Kas,' he drawled.

'Why?' I asked, sitting straighter.

'Purva's Mum is keen for her son to be married as soon as possible. She mentioned something about planting a pretty girl in front of him so that he can get over the crazy girl who returned the engagement ring. And,' he continued, mimicking my sing-song voice, 'in case you did not realize it, you, my dear, are the crazy one.'

I slumped back against the wall. I had certainly not seen this coming. 'And Purva?' I asked.

'He is trying his best to get over you, I think,' said Pitajee, the sadness in his voice unmistakable. 'You are so stupid, Kas,' he added, as an afterthought.

I could not agree more, Pitajee.

9.00 p.m.

'Anu?' I said, looking at the tired face of my friend, the daughter of two IAS officers, who had spent the last three nights sleeping on the hospital floor.

'Yes, Kasturi?' she said, smiling. Pitajee, who had maintained a respectable distance from Anu throughout, looked up too. The three of us were in the hospital cafeteria eating paranthas and aloo-tamatar-ki-sabzi. It was odd how this horrible hospital food had become a source of joy and distraction for us.

'I'm sorry,' I said quietly.

'Why?' she asked, looking surprised.

'It's not easy to see a parent unwell,' I said in a low voice.

Anu said nothing. Pitajee looked on, his eyes taking in the scene with much interest.

'I could not understand why you would agree to marrying Saumen just for the sake of your dad, but,' I continued looking down, 'I do now...'

'Come here, Kas,' said Anu, smiling and pulling me into a hug. 'This will be over soon. Uncle will be discharged in two or three days and things will go back to normal.'

'I am sorry Anu, I would do the same ... anything for Dad,' I said, shaking my head.

From the corner of my eye, I saw Pitajee place a hand on Anu's other shoulder. Anu turned around to stare at Pitajee. From where I was, I could only see Pitajee's face and, after a long time, I saw him smile. It was a smile that reached his eyes, a smile that spelt truce. And just like that, I knew, that as tragic as Anu's impending nuptials were, she and Pitajee would remain friends.

For the time being, that was enough for me.

11.00 p.m.

'Kasturi.'

I stopped short, the voice enough to make the hair on my hand stand up. I had just stepped out of Dad's room to get some medicines and before I could say anything, Purva continued.

'Kasturi, that I turned up unannounced like this must be deeply uncomfortable for you, I know. I want to make it clear that I am, in no way, trying to fix things between us. They remain the way you wanted them to be.'

No, you idiot! No!

'Your dad is a lot like my dad,' he said, slowly and with difficulty, his eyes avoiding my gaze. Even when we were together, Purva hardly ever spoke about his father and I had learnt not to ask questions. I knew, even after all these years, that the wound was still raw – a place in his heart had died along with his father. The pain, I knew, was still too fresh and immense. I had not understood it then, and cannot claim to even now, but I know a little better how it feels to see a parent in pain.

Purva continued. 'When I met you and your family, I was immediately drawn to how … how complete you guys were together. You fought with each other, rudely cancelled calls and slammed doors in each other's faces but … you were complete … complete in a way my family will never be. In Uncle, I saw Dad … they are a lot like each other, you know…' he said, with a faraway look on his face. 'It was tough losing mine. If it's okay with you, I would like to be around till yours is absolutely okay. I will leave immediately afterwards,' he concluded, and then looked expectantly at me, half afraid that I would disagree.

In Uncle, I saw Dad.

What else had I taken from him when I returned my engagement ring? The lump in my throat made it difficult for me to speak immediately. I had to tell him, tell him that I was sorry, that I had made a mistake, that…

'Purva … yes, please stay … umm … I … about the engagement … I…'

'Don't worry about that. I have moved on. What's not meant to happen won't and should not,' he said, shrugging his shoulders carelessly.

With that, he left.

24

26 May 2013, 2.00 p.m.

I am petrified. Tomorrow, the doctors will conduct another MRI scan on Dad to make sure that there has not been any further bleeding. The scan is critical because if there is bleeding, that means the surgery was unsuccessful and the entire process will be repeated. Although this is the worst case scenario, my blood runs cold at the mere thought.

6.00 p.m.

I am sitting on the couch next to him, staring at him sleeping. He is refusing to eat anything that I do not feed him with my hands. And here I go again! Why don't these stupid tears stop?

8.00 p.m.

I picked up Dad's previous MRI scan and gulped. The little shrivelled up thing in the top left corner of the cranial cavity was his brain. The darkness all around it was blood from the injury that he had sustained a month back while working in the shed. I will never forget this sight. Please God, please, please, let there be no more bleeding.

9.00 p.m.

An extract from 'Pearls of Wisdom':

> *Your brain is more powerful than you can possibly imagine. It is capable of taking you places. The highest of highs and the lowest of lows. It can make you see things – the most joyful scenes and the most miserable ones. It can, more importantly, also help you see the positive in a miserable situation. It can help you fight off the negativity. It can help you stay sane.*
>
> *It can be your biggest support in a bleak situation.*

Brain, please help me!

10.00 p.m.

I had drifted off to sleep, head in Anu's lap, while Dad and Pitajee watched a cricket match on TV. Mum had returned to spend the night at home – a break for her before we take Dad home and she has to take care of everything.

I woke up to Pitajee and Purva talking to each other in low voices, careful not to disturb me. I squinted and looked at Dad; the TV was switched off and he was fast asleep. Purva was sitting on a chair that he had drawn close to the sofa on which I lay, half asleep.

'Poor thing,' Pitajee was saying.

'This is actually the first time I have seen her sleeping

since the operation,' Anu said. I smiled to myself, feeling wide awake. Few pleasures are greater than overhearing your friends talk about you while you pretend to be asleep.

'I am worried about her now. Have you seen the dark circles below her eyes? And she is hardly eating…' Pitajee said.

'The first night, she just sat on this couch and stared at her dad. Did not sleep a wink…' added Anu.

'Someone needs to talk to her,' said Pitajee.

'You know … I have never seen this side of Kasturi…' continued Anu.

'What do you mean?' asked Pitajee. I felt smug, good to hear them talk like friends again. Like old times. And yes, even I was interested, what *did* she mean?

'Have you seen how her eyes never leave Uncle? She is almost like a mother to her own father right now.'

'She will make one paranoid mother one day,' said Pitajee. I could hear him grin. This is another favourite pastime of his; imagining me as a mother, grandmother and more often than not, great-grandmother with a broken hip and missing dentures.

'And of course, she fainted the other day...' Anu said.

'What? When?' said a concerned voice, that had been quiet all this while. The low baritone of the voice made my heart skip a beat. Purva.

'Yesterday. Late evening. She had not eaten anything the whole day. She was all right after one of the doctors gave her sugar … don't worry,' Pitajee supplied the information.

'Why had she not eaten?' Purva asked.

'Have not you seen, Purva, that the girl is so beside herself with worry that eating is the last thing on her mind?' said Anu, getting a little agitated herself as I felt a warm hand caress my forehead. 'Now ... don't look so worried...'

My eyes were beginning to feel painfully heavy and before I knew it, I was dreaming about Dad's second scan. It still had the brain looking like a shrivelled walnut and the cranial sac was filled with dark shadows.

I woke up, drenched in sweat.

Day 5 in the Private Room, 27 May 2013, 12.30 p.m.

They are wheeling Dad in for the scan. As luck would have it, I am alone with him. Mum and Anu are yet to return from home. Readying the house for Dad's return, which includes cleaning up the house to ensure that it is free of dust and infection, has taken longer than expected. Pitajee, who is officially staying with his bua, is going to return after lunch when, if all goes well with the scan, Dad will be discharged.

Only Purva is in the hospital, but Dr Verma, who heads the hospital and had once taught Purva, has called him away for a quick catch-up before Purva leaves for Delhi tonight.

12.50 p.m.

Dad came out of the room, grinning from ear to ear. Apparently some doctor had told him another joke that began with – 'Four doctors went to a pub' – which, apparently, had had Dad in splits for a whole two minutes. I was too stressed about the report to bother to ask him to repeat the joke to me.

1.00 p.m.

I have asked one of the ward boys to wheel Dad back to his room. I will wait for the report.

2.00 p.m.

When the doctor handed me the large envelope, I wasted not a second in pulling out the report from it. My untrained eyes scanned the report anxiously. It took me a few seconds to figure out what I was looking at.

The cranial cavity still had dark shadows in it.

My heart sank as I realized that my worst fears had come true. The bleeding had not stopped ... Dad would be operated on again, he would spend another couple of days in that horrendous ICU with sick patients all around him...

Thoughts like these created havoc in my head, panic building up steadily inside me. Then, clutching the report to my chest I ran, as fast as my legs could carry me, without really knowing where I was going. It was only a few seconds later that I realized that that odd, unpleasant noise irritating me was the sound of my flip-flops flapping against the concrete floors as I raced across the hallways leading to Dr Verma's room in the other wing of the hospital.

It took me a good few minutes to reach the hallway of Dr Verma's cabin, even though I was running so fast that my stomach was hurting. My legs were automatically taking me to the man I needed to see.

'Purva!' I screamed, as soon as I saw him.

He was walking out of Dr Verma's cabin and stopped

short when he spotted me. I continued to run towards him, gesticulating with the damn report. Purva broke into a run himself and met me midway, a few anxious seconds later.

'Kasturi!' he said, grabbing my elbow, his face white with worry. 'What happened? Is Dad okay?'

'No,' I said, clutching the sleeve of his shirt, all formality forgotten in that moment of sheer desperation. I vaguely recalled gifting him this shirt for his birthday. 'The ... report ... it's happened again ... there is blood everywhere!' I stammered, clutching my throat that suddenly seemed parched, breathing in bursts, tears streaming down my face.

'Give it to me,' he said brusquely and held the report against the sunlight that streamed in from one of the windows. For what seemed like an eternity, he stared at the report, his brows knit in concentration.

'Who said there has been more bleeding?' he asked, turning to face me.

'The cranial sac is all dark...' I said, pointing a shaking finger at the scan. 'It was dark like this in the previous scan too and Dr Advani told me it was so because of the blood that had collected in the cavity,' I rattled off breathlessly, staring at my hand that was shaking like a leaf in the wind.

Purva gently put a hand on mine to stop it from trembling and when he spoke, which he did a few seconds later, his voice was very gentle.

'Kasturi,' he said, bending a little bit so that his face was at level with mine. 'The cavity is dark because it contains water – the same water that was used to wash away the blood. There is no bleeding.'

'Wh … what?' I said, my mouth open, suddenly feeling weak with relief.

Purva hastened to grab me by both my arms, lest I fell in a heap on the floor.

'Kasturi,' he said, almost holding me. 'Dad is fine. With a scan as clean as this, he will be discharged in a few hours. The surgery was successful!'

I stared blankly at him.

'But the brain … it's still in one corner…'

'It will ease into its original size in a few days. It's absolutely normal.'

'Oh,' I said, closing my eyes and, feeling Purva's warm body next to mine, found myself caving into his chest almost involuntarily.

'It's over, Kasturi … he is absolutely fine,' he said as he pulled me closer. His gentle hands stroked my hair for a few minutes and I clung to him, eyes closed, willing my breathing to normalize.

'It's over,' he muttered again, more to himself than to me. That reminded both of us of something else that was now over.

The next instant, we looked at each other and, embarrassed at how close we were, withdrew. Purva looked everywhere but at me.

'I will get going,' he said, under his breath and hurriedly walked away.

2.01 p.m.

Still trying to digest what just happened, I pulled out my

phone and found myself staring at it. Text from Anu. Succinct and shocking.

'My wedding date has been fixed for 9 December.'

I stood still for a few minutes.

25

28 May 2013.

Amidst much fanfare, a cavalcade of six cars brought Dad home. Ours is a quiet neighbourhood where little happens, so Dad's return was much like a highly-anticipated state event. Neighbours stood on their balconies and craned their necks to have a look at 'Doctor Sahib' who had just come from the ICU. I found myself looking around to make sure that there were no cameras. Mum actually waved at the 'crowds' – her word, not mine – as she helped Dad into our house.

Dad has been told to rest as much as he can for two weeks and then resume his normal lifestyle. That had me very worried; for a man as active as Dad, I know the 'resting' bit was going to be the biggest challenge in this entire ordeal.

I did not get to see Purva again after the incident outside Dr Verma's cabin. He bade farewell to Dad and Mum when I was not around. From what I heard, Mum had become all teary-eyed when he was leaving and had blessed him furiously. Dad had had a word with him alone. No amount of coaxing or threatening would get him to reveal what they'd discussed. Pitajee and Anu had left soon after, given that the worst was behind us. They walked down the hall together and then parted ways. For some reason, maybe because it was so symbolic of how things stood at the moment, I felt a lump in my throat as I stared at their retreating backs. Pitajee took the right with his Buaji and Anu the left, where a car with a red light, that Saumen had arranged for, waited to take her to the airport.

What happened to the four of us? Just the other day we were all happy and heading towards marriages that would have lasted us forever. And now this.

It does not help that a lot of this muck is my fault.

3 June 2013.

Another extract from a post on 'Pearls of Wisdom':

> *Close your eyes and think of all the problems that exist in your life. If the list does not include illness, you are fine. And if the list includes an illness, then know that if God gave you the problem, he has also given you the strength to deal with it. Either way, keep the faith.*

7 June 2013.

'You have a job and a life to go back to,' Mum said, physically pushing me away with her hands. Really?

'Mum, another day here ... for Dad...' I pleaded.

'Dad is fine,' she said breezily, as I peeped inside Dad's bedroom, which he was not supposed to leave for another three days. Of course he was not there. The missing parent, who had just spent a couple of days in the Neurosurgery ICU, was found, a few minutes later, in the garden, jumping up to grab a low-lying papaya.

'Thought we could have this fresh for breakfast,' said my father a little sheepishly, scratching the gauze that adorned his head, a small reminder of the ordeal we had gone through.

'Dad,' I said threateningly, pointing towards the door.

'I will go in now and rest,' he said meekly, as if the idea had just struck him.

I sighed.

'Okay, one more day,' said Mum wearily and scuttled in after Dad. Dad was worse than a toddler right now!

9 June 2013, 6.00 p.m.

My little bag, mostly stuffed with laddoos that I have told Mum a hundred times that I do not eat, was in the car. I had had a good cry in the bathroom and was now ready to leave.

'God bless you, Beta,' said Dad, placing a hand on my head.

I said nothing and looked away, lest I teared up, determined to keep the mood positive. Leaving him was turning out to be more difficult than I had imagined.

Dad's hand lingered on my head and I was forced to face him. 'You *are* my son,' he said smiling.

'And you are my father,' I said, giggling. Dad rolled his eyes and then laughed.

6.10 p.m.

Ten minutes in the car and Mum called.

'Kasturi!' she said, sounding very worried. My heart skipped a beat. 'Dad is missing.'

'Again?' I wailed, slapping a hand on my forehead.

'Yes...'

'Check the garden?' I suggested.

'He's not there.'

'The terrace?'

'No, not there either!'

'Umm ... oh god ... the shed?'

'No, not there!'

A nagging suspicion reared its ugly head. 'Is his car in the garage?' I asked.

'No,' said Mum after a pause, sounding in awe of what Dad was capable of. Doctors had strictly told Dad to not drive for another two weeks at least.

'Did you call him?'

'About fifteen times!'

'And?'

'He's not taking the call obviously! What if ... what if something has happened? I don't know why I ever married your father! You know, when your Dadi-Dada came to our house with the proposal, that very day one man had proposed marriage to me. If only I had... '

'Bye Mum, will call you in a bit,' I said, cutting in. I knew the whole story already.

I dialled Dad's number and he picked up in an instant.

'Dad,' I said, exasperated. 'What are you doing?'

'Driving!' he said jubilantly.

'Why?' I asked, shaking my head incredulously.

'Just wanted to check if everything was working all right,'

he said. I knew he was not talking about the car and I could not help but smile.

'Is it?'

'Of course,' he said happily.

I slumped into the seat of the car, a wide grin plastered across my face as I dialled Mum's number to tell her that Dad was all right.

I waited for Mum to pick up the phone and thought about the one thing I had to do.

Get Purva back.

26

11 June 2013, Delhi.

I might be rather thick most of the time but twenty-one unanswered calls are enough to make it abundantly clear to me that Purva does not wish to talk.

Why am I surprised? Did I expect him to welcome me with a jaimala after all the drama I have done? Pitajee told me today that he thinks I have the mental agility of a soap dish. I think I will kill him. Yes, that will be the noble thing to do.

13 June 2013.

I have sent him twenty emails.

And called him thirty-four times.

And visited his hospital three times.

Nothing.

15 June 2013.

Purva walked away the moment he saw me approaching. It hurt more than I had ever imagined anything could.

18 June 2013.

'I am now losing patience with that obstinate man,' I said exasperatedly into the phone.

'Of course,' said Pitajee mildly. 'He is the one who is at fault…'

'Yes!' I said indignantly, conveniently ignoring the sarcasm. 'It's not like I went away and married the first man I found walking his dog on the street outside my house.'

'So, Kasturi, tell me, what *did* you do?'

'I just acted a little … you know … pricey,' I said, delicately shrugging my shoulders.

'And?'

'And threw a small tantrum, which, might I add, we're all allowed, every once in a while.'

'And?'

'Errr…'

'And?' Pitajee insisted.

'Umm … returned the engagement ring,' I replied, my voice tiny now.

'And?'

'And cancelled the wedding…' I said, deflating like a punctured balloon.

Okay, I get it.

23 June 2013.

The latest from our revered doctor is that he has changed his phone number with the primary purpose of avoiding me. Of course, I got his new number from Anu about two milliseconds after he changed it. Ha!

27 June 2013.

I called on his new number eleven times and he did not pick up. I called him from Vijaywada's phone and he answered instantly.

However, Purva stuck to his obstinate guns and cancelled the call the moment I said hello.

29 June 2013.

'Dogs,' said Mr Vijaywada, pulling a chair next to me.

'What about them, Mr Vijaywada?' I asked, trying hard to sound interested. The things I do to keep my job.

'Many years ago I used to live in Calcutta.'

'Very good,' I said.

'And I picked up this stray dog and made him mine.'

The thought of anything becoming his was deeply disturbing but, putting my feelings aside, I continued to look on encouragingly.

'But then, I needed to shift to Delhi … to start a new life.'

'I see.'

'But I could not leave my dog!'

'Oh, of course,' I agreed.

'Do you know what he did?'

'He?'

'The dog was a he.'

'Oh, so what did he do?'

'He went to the kitchen, used his little paws to open the kitchen window and jumped out.'

I spluttered out the coffee I was drinking. 'What do you mean?'

'He knew he was coming in the way of my life, and he sensed my hesitation … and … and he committed suicide, just so that I could carry on with my life. I found his body on the street when I came back from office that day.'

'Your dog committed suicide?' I asked, just to clarify.

Vijaywada nodded his head slowly and sadly. 'Today is his death anniversary,' he added in a despairing voice.

'Anniversary of the suicide of your dog,' I repeated, biting the insides of my cheeks to stop the guffaws.

Vijaywada nodded his head.

'I think you should go home and rest,' I said, trying desperately to control my laughter. 'It could not have been easy for you.'

'It still isn't,' he said, looking forlornly at his hands.

Vijaywada got up and was but a few feet away from us when Padma (who had been listening to the conversation) burst out laughing. 'I know what actually happened,' she said.

'What?' I asked, wiping coffee from the table where I had spilt it in a fit of laughter.

'He pushed his dog out of the kitchen and then pretended it was suicide!'

Another fit of giggles followed this.

30 June 2013.

'Paddy,' I said, looking intently at P.P. Padma's bangs. There was something I had been meaning to ask her for the longest time.

'Hmm?'

'Why did you hate me so much in the beginning? Am I really horrible?'

Paddy put down the cup of coffee she had been sipping from. 'I could lie or I couldn't lie.'

'Don't lie,' I said, meaning it.

'Well … I felt you had everything very easy … too easy.'

'What do you mean by that?'

'You know … how little you worked and how smitten Vijaywada was with you. How you seemed to have this bunch of really cool friends … you know.'

I grunted, not really getting it.

'Okay,' she said firmly, 'I will say it as it is … or was. I was jealous. Plain jealous. I felt you had it all. Good looks, charming personality, fabulous boyfriend, doting parents, great friends...'

I did not know where to look.

'I told myself that obviously something has to be wrong with Kasturi and decided that you are horrible. Which you are not and you went out of your way to help me and really changed my life, in a way, and I … I...' Paddy fumbled, helpless now.

It was my cue to get up and give her a big hug. 'Let's forget all about it,' I said.

'Let's do that, Kassie!' said Paddy, returning my wide smile with an even wider one.

3 July 2013.

I feel absolutely miserable.

It does not help that, of late, Mum has taken to sprouting Hindi idioms at me. Idiom of the day is, 'Jaisi karni, waisi bharni.'

The idiom yesterday was, 'Ab pachhtaye kya hoye, jab chidiya chug gayi khet.'

I get it Mum, I do!

10 July 2013.

Dear World,

I get it. I messed up. Now will you please stop making me feel this small?

World peace and warm regards,

Kasturi

15 July 2013, 10.00 p.m.

I had been dreading this call. Since the day I left him waiting for me at TGIF, Rajeev has sent me many emails. Overtaken by events, I had not had a chance to reply.

Till last night.

I needed closure and I knew, even though I had not spoken to Rajeev in years, that he did too. There was a time, however brief, when he and I had connected at a very deep level. We did not realize it then but I understand it better now. Though we parted ways in the ugliest manner possible, I know I loved him then just as I know now that he needs closure to move on. Just as I know I do too.

I emailed him saying that I would like to speak to him. He gave me his number and that is what I dialled now.

'Hi,' I said, surprised at how nervous I felt.

'Kasturi!' he gushed.

It was odd to hear his voice. Some part of me immediately recognized it as a voice that, at one point in time, had been my most favourite sound in the world.

'I'm sorry, Rajeev, for not turning up that day.'

'It's okay. I've done worse by you. I don't think I have any right to complain,' he said. His voice was heavier than I remembered; more mature, with a warmer ring to it.

'I … I want to keep this short. I don't think I'll be meeting you or calling you. I'm sorry, Rajeev. This is it.' I said, biting my lip.

'Okay,' he said softly.

'Bye,' I said.

'Wait.'

'Yes?'

'Kasturi, if you can, please try to forgive me,' he said, his voice breaking. 'I will always love you.'

I remained silent for a few moments.

'I forgive you, Rajeev. Live well,' I said and hung up.

Somewhere deep inside my heart, a little bit of me broke and I touched my wet face, surprised at the tears. Or maybe not really surprised. This was never going to be easy. You know, I still dream of Rajeev sometimes, vague dreams,

dreams where nothing happens, but he's in them. I wake up feeling as if I'd just met an old friend. With time, I find myself forgetting all the bad things that happened between us. The good times live on, not in a hormone-crazed, I-want-Rajeev way, but in a more quiet, dignified manner.

Rajeev probably thinks I am severing all ties with him.

I am not. I cannot. No matter how hard I try.

He is part of my past, a past that was, in most bits, very beautiful. He is a part of my subconscious because, when I loved him, I loved him with a fire I had not known existed inside me. He will remain there, probably for decades, as a beautiful memory that might begin to fade with time and one day vanish completely. Other stories from my life will overwrite Rajeev's memory.

Maybe. Or maybe not. Maybe he will always be there, a gentle reminder of a love that once was.

Either way, I accept memories of us and the place in my life that they choose to occupy. And for all those wonderful memories, I forgive him the deceit.

I loved Rajeev, but I love Purva.

Live well, Rajeev, live well and prosper.

20 July 2013.

An extract from Mum's blog-post titled, 'True peace and Aradhya Bachchan':

By the time I die, which I hope is a long way off – I need to first see Pimple get married and then ensure that she gets her children married on time. I am also, and understandably so, very curious to see if Aradhya Bachchan will become an actress like her parents and grandparents – I want to have found my peace. True peace.

That is also my biggest hope for you. For you to find peace.

What is true peace, I hope you are asking yourself now.

True peace is knowing that you have followed at least some of the dreams that you have held closest to your heart. True peace is knowing that you have nurtured at least some of the people who have been closest to your heart. True peace is knowing that you have expressed at least some of the feelings that you have felt closest to your heart.

True peace comes from the quiet in your heart, so take care of it.

As of today, 435 people follow her blog – twenty more than last month. Mum is already on her way to cyber stardom.

25 July 2013.

'Errr,' said Pitajee.

'Stop err-ing and start speaking,' I snapped back at him. With Purva acting the way he was, patience, let us just say, was a rare thing to come by.

'Umm…'

'I will murder you now,' I said in a voice thick with emotion.

'It's been three months now, Kas,' he said hesitantly.

I sighed. I had never imagined that Purva would prove to be such a difficult man to win back. 'Pitajee,' I sulked into my phone.

'Kas.'

'He won't even talk to me.'

'I know.'

'He won't even look at me.'

'I know.'

'What do I do? I've tried everything in the world,' I moaned.

The proverbial pause, pregnant with meaning.

'Have you, Kas?' he asked, in a sage voice. 'Have you?'

11.00 a.m.

With renewed vigour, I have set on the most difficult task life has thrown at me. And as with most difficult tasks, my first stop was Google.

'How to get your boyfriend back' threw up a couple of depressing articles which preached patience and extolled the healing abilities of time. What utter rubbish!

'How to win back upset bf' produced another couple of articles that made me want to kill myself.

'How to make up with bf' ... What? Did I just fall asleep? Arrgghhh.

I muck up stuff in original ways so I must un-muck stuff the same way.

1.00 p.m.

Though I have a fertile, imaginative mind, nothing strikes me at the moment.

3.00 p.m.

No, nothing yet.

5.00 p.m.

I was watching reruns of the *Great British Bake Off* when it hit me.

An idea! Voila!

A few hurried texts were exchanged with Pitajee and Anu and it was agreed that the idea was undeniably cute. If this did not melt Purva's heart, we could conclusively agree that he did not possess one.

6.00 p.m.

On a Great-British-Bake-Off-induced high, I bought all the things one would need to bake a simple vanilla sponge cake. The idea is to keep it basic and create the best, yummiest sponge cake that ever existed on this planet. For the plan to really work, I have to simply outdo all the bakers in this world. Given that I have never baked before, this will be a cakewalk for me. Pun intended.

With this noble thought in mind, I set to work, vowing to follow to the last word the recipe that Pitajee had emailed me. I religiously sifted the flour, added sugar and eggs and beat them to the right consistency.

That man, my friend Pitajee, is a national treasure. His support and enthusiasm for this baking project has been infectious. What else are friends for, he said philosophically, when I called him to tell him that all the mixing was almost done, and I agreed.

Proud of myself, I read the last line in the recipe and groaned.

'Place the baking tray in the oven for 45-50 minutes till the cake rises.'

My phone rang. Pitajee.

Instead of the expected hello, what I heard was maniacal laughter that could only come from a man possessed.

'Did you put the batter in the *oven*?' howled Pitajee.

'Shut up and don't you dare ever call me again,' I said. Just before I cancelled the call, I heard him burst into a fresh bout of the aforementioned maniacal laughter.

I had forgotten that I did not have an oven. Pitajee, that scoundrel, obviously had not.

26 July 2013, 9.00 a.m.

I got a store-bought sponge cake, cut it in the shape of the letter 'I', put it in a pink cardboard box, decorated the box with a huge pink ribbon, drove to AIIMS and left it with ward boy Ravi Singh for a certain Dr Purva Dixit.

27 July 2013, 9.00 a.m.

Sponge cake cut in the shape of the letter 'A' has been left at AIIMS with ward boy Ravi Singh for Dr Dixit.

'Did he take the box I left for him yesterday?' I asked Ravi Singh, as he patted the pink box I had just handed him.

'No, Kasturi Didi,' Ravi Singh said dolefully.

'Did he at least open it?'

'No.'

That grumpy man! Hmph!

28 July 2013, 9.00 a.m.

Letter of the day – M.

'Did he take it?' I asked Ravi Singh.

'No.'

'Did he open it?'

'No,' he said, shaking his head.

'Life is very unfair, Ravi Singh,' I said balefully.

'It sure is, Kasturi Didi,' said Ravi Singh, looking wistfully at a young, pretty nurse who was walking past us.

29 July 2013, 9.00 a.m.

Letter of the day – S.

'Did he…' I began, as I dropped off the pink cake-box for the day.

'No.' Ravi Singh said.

'Oh,' I said, shaking my head with sheer, unadulterated misery. The plan was already falling apart and I had barely reached 'S'.

'But…'

'What?' I exclaimed.

'Nurse Julian had kept the pink box in the cupboard, so obviously it was not in full view of anyone walking past the counter. Dr Dixit came to me late in the afternoon, after his rounds, and asked if there was anything for him.'

I was already mentally doing a tribal victory-dance. 'Oh my god! Then? Then? Ravi Singh, what did you say?' I asked, grabbing his arm in excitement.

Ravi Singh smiled a benign, Mother-Teresa-ish smile.

'I said yes there is and handed him the box.'

'OH MY GOD!' I shrieked. 'Then? Then? THEN?'

'Nothing,' Ravi Singh said, his face falling.

'Oh!'

'He looked at the box, shook his head and left.'

'Looked *in* the box, you mean?' I asked hopefully.

Ravi Singh shook his head. 'At,' he clarified.

'Oh.'

'I know.'

'A word?'

'No, Kasturi Didi.'

'A smile?'

'No, Kasturi Didi.'

I sighed.

'Life is very unfair, Kasturi Didi,' Ravi Singh said philosophically.

'It sure is, Ravi Singh,' I said, nodding my head in melancholic agreement.

30 July 2013, 9.00 a.m.

Letter of the day – O.

'HE OPENED IT!' Ravi Singh was already shouting at the top of his lungs by the time I reached him. His eyes were shining with wild excitement and, to my surprise, along with him stood the same pretty nurse I had seen his eyes follow the other day.

'Did he? He opened it?' I shrieked in delight.

'Yes, he did,' Ravi Singh smiled happily. The nurse also nodded her head vigorously.

'Did he say anything?'

'No.'

'Did he smile?' I asked again.

'No.'

'Did he take it with him?'

'No.'

'Who cares, Ravi Singh? He opened the box!' I grabbed Ravi Singh and twirled him around. The pretty nurse stared at us with wide eyes and Ravi Singh tried to look very familiar, as if girlfriends of senior surgeons regularly twirled him around.

31 July 2013, 9.00 a.m.

Letter of the day – R.

Ravi Singh and the pretty nurse were waiting for me when I reached with my box. An elderly nurse, whom I had sometimes seen in the hospital, was with them. I had not even handed the cake-box to Ravi, when he said, 'He opened yesterday's box as well!'

'And?' I said, shouting with happiness.

'He said… ' continued the pretty nurse.

'He said…' repeated Ravi Singh in a teasing voice, exchanging a look with the pretty nurse.

'Ravi Singh! And you!' I cried, jabbing a finger at the pretty nurse. 'Speak up!'

'Did anyone get a chance to open the first few boxes?'

My heart leapt with sheer delight. At least I had his attention.

'What did you say?'

'What would I say Kasturi Didi? I said I had.'

'And?'

'He asked me if they were alphabets too and I said, yes, they were I, A, M, S, O.'

I beamed back at the three faces that smiled excitedly at me.

Could this work? Would it be cakes that would break the wall the angry Purva had constructed around himself? Cakes?

1 August 2013, 9.00 a.m.

Letter of the day – R.

Today when I reached the hospital desk, Ravi Singh, pretty nurse, elderly nurse and another orderly were waiting for me, smiles plastered on their faces.

'He opened it, saw what was inside and left the box at the counter,' Ravi Singh said. I no longer had to even ask.

2 August 2013, 9.00 a.m.

Letter of the day – Y.

A little group, consisting of no less than seven members of staff, was waiting for me when I reached the hospital today.

'He said…' began Ravi Singh.

'That, that…' said pretty nurse.

'Please see…' interrupted the elderly nurse.

'...that the cake...' said the orderly.

'...is not wasted!' concluded a nurse with long hair, who pumped her fist in the air.

I looked around at the faces that crowded around and an odd, warm, fuzzy feeling enveloped my heart. Many faces were unfamiliar and most were lined with worry, and yet in all of them I saw something that made me want to burst into tears.

27

3 August 2013, 9.00 a.m.

Letter of the day – A.

Ravi Singh wants to become an actor. The nurse with long hair, mother to two rowdy boys, is desperate to have a baby girl who might deign to listen to her once in a while and the old orderly is still grieving for his wife who died four years ago. These were all nameless faces I had barely registered in the two years I have been regularly visiting the hospital. Now they know a little bit of my story, just as I know a little bit of theirs.

Odd, the friends you make. Very odd.

4 August 2013, 9.00 a.m.

Letter of the day – N.

5 August 2013, 9.00 a.m.

Letter of the day – D.

Today, instead of Ravi Singh – who had taken a day off to

audition for a role in a television serial – the head nurse of the nephrology ward met me at the gate to collect the box.

'Kasturi Beta?' she began hesitatingly.

'Yes, Sister?' I asked, jiggling the car keys.

'Umm … do you … do you think you can get chocolate cake?'

'What?'

'I mean … vanilla gets boring after a while,' she replied, shrugging her shoulders.

Ji, Madam, ji.

6 August 2013, 9.00 a.m.

Letter of the day – S.

Flavour of the day – Chocolate.

Number of people who came to receive the cake – eleven.

7 August 2013, 9.00 a.m.

Letter of the day – T.

Flavour of the day – Chocolate.

Number of people gathered to take the cake – fourteen.

4.00 p.m.

I was strolling aimlessly in Khan market, thinking about ways to tell Purva how much I loved him and how sorry I was, when my eyes fell on three people walking towards me. I choked on the coffee I had just taken a mouthful of and the American in front of me turned around curiously. I couldn't care less, for, walking towards me, in deep conversation with each other were Purva, Vikram and Anju Aunty.

Someone – read: yours truly – has correctly said that the wrath of a woman scorned is nothing compared to the wrath of a mother whose child has been scorned.

These days Anju Aunty is a regular fixture in my nightmares. In one of the more violent ones, she dangles me by my throat over a steep cliff that rises above a sea of demons, hauls me up just before I die and chops me, alive and kicking, me into pieces which she later feeds to snakes.

Within seconds, I had ducked and hidden behind the only object of reasonable size I could spot – a remarkably smelly dustbin that was overflowing with choicest rubbish that Khan Market could come up with. Needless to add, the next thirty seconds, during which I tried my best to become one with the dustbin reeking of kebabs and urine, as the trio walked past me, were the longest of my life.

Once they were safely out of sight, I emerged from behind the dustbin and was taking in long, deep and much-needed breaths of fresh air when I felt a pair of eyes on me.

Vikram.

I had no doubt that that I looked mentally deranged, sheepishly walking out from behind the dustbin. She cancels her engagement without proper reason and then goes around the city crouching behind dustbins; decidedly mad as a hatter. I prepared myself for whatever abuses Vikram was going to hurl at me for breaking his brother's heart. Maybe I could explain to him. The chances were slim but I could try…

'Bhabhi,' he said simply and I looked up, stunned, my mouth open in sheer surprise.

Bhabhi. The word that I had once run away from was now music to my ears.

'Vikram,' I said stupidly.

'I saw you hide,' he said, grinning.

Why do I do such things? I craned my neck to make sure that Purva and, more importantly, Anju Aunty were out of sight.

'I have to go but we need to talk,' he gushed. 'If, of course, you don't mind?'

I nodded my head, vigorously. A piece of stale bread fell off my shoulders. Vikram stifled a laugh and pulled out a piece of green pepper from my hair.

'Just tell me when and where,' I said, grinning too.

'I will text,' he said hurriedly. 'I've got to go now.' He walked away, giving me a quick smile.

He had walked but a few feet when he abruptly turned around, came to me and enveloped me in a tight hug.

'I missed you, Bhabhi,' he said, avoiding eye-contact and leaving immediately without waiting for me to say anything. Which was a good thing, because his quick hug and earnest words had left me with a lump in my throat. Scream and shout at me and I will throw water bottles at you in retaliation; that is the kind of fight that I understand. Forgive me with a smile and I am as lost as a bright orange fish in the desert.

I don't deserve to be forgiven so easily. Not this time, Vikram.

10.00 p.m.

I have not been able to push the little incident in Khan Market out of my mind. It is so true that sometimes a bigger lesson is taught by forgiving than by punishing.

I went to bed with a wide smile on my face, but only after having typed a lengthy email to the municipality of Khan Market, complaining about the unhygienic waste in dustbins that line their prominent streets.

8 August 2013, 9.00 a.m.

Letter of the day – U.

Flavour of the day – Chocolate.

Number of people gathered to receive my cake – sixteen.

I have been dropping off cakes at the hospital long enough for us all to have a schedule. The first thing I am told is Purva's reaction to the box, which remains the same. Each day, after his rounds, he comes and has a look at the box. He never eats the cake and leaves the box at the same counter where I leave it each morning.

One of the ladies, whom I suspect is a convalescing patient, has recommended that I get pineapple cake instead of chocolate. Three others vehemently disagreed.

9 August 2013, 9.00 a.m.

Letter of the day – P.

Flavour of the day – Pineapple.

Number of people gathered to receive my cake – seventeen.

8.00 p.m.

Pitajee, Anu, Vikram and I sat in the living room looking at each other.

Love. A simple, four-letter word, yet it is so complicated and complex in its origins and ramifications. The things it makes the most rational of us do! And how docile it can make even the most boisterous of us. The power of love. The madness of love.

Case in point being Anu and Pitajee. Since Dad's operation, they have been trying to behave as normally as they can, given that Anu is about to marry Saumen. An unhappy truce seems to exist between them, where they both pretend to be immune to the other's presence.

Only they are not. The way they grab opportunities to just be near each other breaks my heart every time.

Every time.

'He is just very quiet,' said Vikram, telling me about Purva. 'Not that he wasn't before … but … just a lot more … you know … sad…'

I knew.

'Vikram,' I said, looking intently at him. 'I'm sorry.'

'Bhabhi,' he said, looking decidedly uncomfortable 'Don't say that … it's okay. I understand … girls have doubts when they're about to get married…'

'I'm sorry, Vikram,' I repeated, putting my hand on his and meaning each word.

Vikram was quiet for a minute. 'It's all right, Bhabhi. You were my bhabhi then and we need to make sure that you continue to remain that,' he said, winking.

'In that case,' said Pitajee, taking over. 'We really need your help.' Needless to say, Anu, Pitajee and I had plans. Devious plans.

'Sure,' said Vikram, more than eager to help. 'Anything to get them back together. What do I have to do?'

'Nothing much ... you just have to lie, spy and steal,' I said, shrugging my shoulders nonchalantly.

28

10 August 2013, 9.00 a.m.

Letter of the day – I.

Flavour of the day – Coffee and walnut.

Number of people who came to receive the cake – Twenty-two.

'Kasturi Didi,' whispered Ravi Singh conspiratorially to me as he and the pretty nurse came running after me.

'Yes?'

'Umm...'

I looked curiously at ward boy Ravi Singh. The pretty nurse nodded encouragingly at him and placed a tender hand on his shoulder. I could see that Ravi Singh almost died then and there with sheer joy.

'Has ... has Dr Dixit responded in any way?' he finally blurted his question.

'What?' I asked, shocked at the audacity of the question.

'I mean...' fumbled Ravi Singh, 'do you guys stand a chance of getting back together?'

'What?' I asked, shocked further. 'Why do you ask?'

'Er… you see, Kasturi Didi,' he said, shuffling his feet, 'people are betting.'

To say that my jaw dropped to the floor would not be an exaggeration. 'Betting on what?'

'On whether you will be able to win Dr Dixit back.'

I continued to stare open-mouthed.

'So … if you … you know … give us insider information … we could … you know … make some money. There is a lot riding on this. We expect almost everyone on the staffing register to place bets, and then there are the patients too…'

'What? The patients?'

'Yes, yes,' said Ravi Singh, 'in fact, Sharda Aunty, the diabetes patient,' he said, as if I would know her, 'even pretended to have a fainting fit last night just to make sure they wouldn't discharge her.'

'Why?'

'Just so that she can stay!' chipped in the pretty nurse.

'And do what?' I asked, weakly.

'See if you get the doctor and,' she added ruefully, 'then she can make some money.'

I was feeling very, very faint.

1.00 p.m.

'Vik,' I hissed into the phone.

'Bhabhi,' he hissed back. Right after my heart, this man, I thought warmly to myself.

'Any news?'

'No, Bhai has been in the OT the entire day.'

Today is the day we put our plan into action. To facilitate ease of communication, a WhatsApp group – rather optimistically titled 'Mission (Let's make it) Possible' – has been created. We have been buzzing each other on the group the whole day and it is clear that all of us are on tenterhooks. The necessary things have been given to Vikram and now it is up to him and … well … Purva.

6.00 p.m.

WhatsApp messages on Mission Possible –

Pitajee – 'Vik, has the spider entered the web?'

Anu – 'What?'

Me – 'What?'

Vikram – 'What?'

Pitajee – 'Just asking if Purva is home yet.'

10.00 p.m.

Vikram – 'The spider is in the web.'

Me – 'LOL.'

Anu – 'LOL.'

Pitajee. '…'

11.00 p.m.

I am breathing easier now. After what seemed like an eternity, Purva reached home, tired and exhausted from the surgeries of the day. Once dinner was done and Anju Aunty had retired to her room for the night, Vikram went to Purva's room and, without another word, handed him two bowls. Each of the bowls contained water and in the water happily swam a goldfish each.

'What the hell is this, Vikki?' Purva exclaimed, watching his brother place the two bowls next to his bed.

'Gifts for you,' he said.

'Gifts? Fish? Have you lost it?' Purva asked, laughing.

'They are not from me,' Vikram said.

'Then?'

Without another word, Vikram handed him the little note I had written.

Purva,

The fish are a gift from Pitajee and Anu (not from me, so please keep them). The note is just to tell you the names of the fish. They do not respond to names other than the ones we have kept and the names have to be taken in a particular order. First the name of fish number one followed by the name of fish number two. Always together and always in that order.

Without further ado, here are the names –

Fish number two: Kasturi.

Fish number one: Silly.

Say the names together and in the correct order.

Love,

Kasturi

Vikram tells me that Purva stared first at the fish swimming gleefully in the clear waters and then at the letter.

He tried very hard not to, but, a few seconds later, he burst out laughing.

Strike one.

Smug look

Now for strike two.

29

11 August 2013, 9.00 a.m.

Letter of the day – D.

Flavour of the day – Banana.

Number of people receiving the cake – twenty-five. (Dear lord!)

Today is the day when we set part two of 'Mission (Let's make it) Possible' into motion and, needless to say, the stress levels are sky-rocketing. I had spent countless nights awake and in deep thought, trying to come up with something suitable for today, without much success. Without any solution in sight, I was very close to giving up when, one day, it took me one glance at a newspaper Anu was going through to slap the table and shout 'I've got it!' in sheer jubilation.

It remains to be seen whether my plan is half as good as I hope it is.

3.00 p.m.

Restless.

4.00 p.m.

Very restless.

6.00 p.m.

Purva should be home anytime soon. I hope Vikram can somehow put that paper in front of him.

10.00 p.m.

Anu, Pitajee and I were sitting at the dining table. The food lay in front of us, cold and untouched. I was exchanging another miserable blank stare with Anu, when our cells beeped simultaneously.

Vikram.

Vikram – 'Bhai is home and I have placed that sheet in the newspaper.'

Pitajee – 'Why the newspaper?'

Vikram – 'Bhai always reads the newspaper before going to bed.'

Pitajee made a face and said, 'Kas, are you sure you want *this* guy? He reads the newspaper before going to bed. I mean, really, he needs to get a life, you know.'

I managed a weak grin.

10.05 p.m.

Vikram – 'I have told Bhai that I want to spend some time in his room while he reads the newspaper.'

Anu – 'What did he say?'
Vikram – 'He never says no to me ☺.'

10.06 p.m.

Vikram – 'The sheet fell out of the newspaper.'

A collective gasp at the dining table as Anu dramatically brings her hands to her mouth.

10.07 p.m.

Vikram – 'He has picked up the paper.'
Me – 'What is he doing now?'
Vikram – 'He is staring at it.'

10.08 p.m.

Vikram – 'Bhai is looking very restless and has just grabbed a pencil. He is scribbling something on the paper, thinking and then scribbling some more.'

I crossed my fingers and smiled in spite of myself, when I saw Anu do the same and Pitajee follow suit.

10.09 p.m.

Vikram – 'OMG! Is he solving a crossword puzzle?'

Yes, he is. The sheet of paper that I asked Vikram to put in front of Purva looked like this.

PURVA'S CROSSWORD

1. Kasturi learnt to make these for Purva's Mum (8)
2. Purva loves Kasturi's ____ (5)
3. Doodh is actually known as ____ (4)
4. Your smile fills my heart with ____ (3)
5. Kasturi loves Purva's ____ (5)
6. Govind Goswami eats like an ____ (2)
7. To cut a long story short Kasturi ____ Purva more than anything else in the world (5)
8. And wants to just say this ____ (8)

10.10 p.m.

Me – 'When he puts his pencil down, please tell me.'

10.14 p.m.

Vikram – 'He has.'

Me – 'What is he doing now?'

Vikram – 'Staring at the piece of paper, his face is expressionless and he won't even blink.'

Pitajee looked at me. 'Call him, Kasturi. Just call him,' he said, earnestly.

'Is this like you telling me to put the cake batter in the oven?' I asked.

'Shut up! No!' he said, putting a brotherly hand on my head. I looked at Anu and she smiled too.

'Call him, Kas. Fight for him. Don't let him go,' she said in a quiet voice.

Pitajee looked up at Anu with a startled look on his face – a look that I saw but did not pay much attention to.

'Show me the completed crossword, Kas,' Anu said.

I silently handed another sheet of paper to her. If Purva had filled his in correctly, the sheet of paper in his hand would look a lot like the one that Anu was now staring at.

She read through the clues and the correct answers and then silently handed me my phone.

'Call him, Kas. You guys need to talk,' she said.

I picked up my phone and slowly started punched in the numbers. My heart was beating furiously as the call went through. What would Purva say? Will he … won't he?

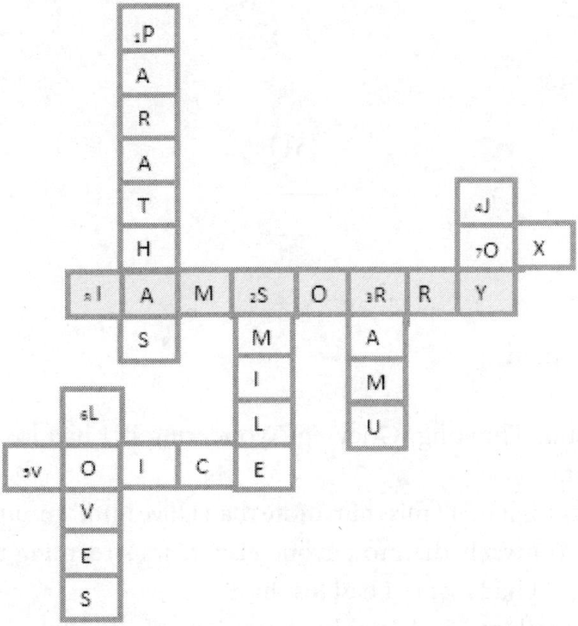

10.15 p.m.

Vikram – 'Someone just called on his phone. He stared at the phone for a minute, looked at the sheet of paper, paused for a few seconds and then cancelled the call.'

Pitajee, looking at me – 'And now, what is he doing?'

Vikram – 'He says he needs to head back to the hospital. I have never seen him so agitated.'

Pitajee, continuing to look in my direction as Anu wiped the silent tears that were streaming down my face – 'And I have never seen Kasturi look so agitated either.'

30

10.30 p.m.

I sat still. Thinking. Grieving. Wondering if I had lost him forever.

'How is it that I miss him more than I love him,' I muttered, more to myself than to anyone else, tears streaming down my face. I had lost it. I had lost him.

'Go to him,' said Anu, her voice low.

Pitajee and I turned around to face her at the same time.

'Kasturi,' she said, her face grave, 'if Purva is truly lost, you will lose him but not the memories. The memories will haunt you, day and night, and whoever you finally end up with will never be as good as the memories in your heart. Do yourself a favour – spare yourself the torture, and go fight for him.'

I knew that Anu was speaking from first-hand experience. Pitajee shuffled his feet and stared uncomfortably at the floor.

'He will reject me again,' I said, feeling it in my bones.

'Then you go to him again. You don't stop till the world ends,' she said, dramatically slapping the dining table.

The three of us stared at the table which rattled its indignant dissent.

'Come on,' said Pitajee, gently pulling me by the arm

'Come where?'

'To AIIMS. You have to fight him to get him, kid.'

11.00 p.m.

As I ambled along the corridor leading to Purva's office, I was too scared of how the night was going to end to notice Ravi Singh. Ravi Singh, however, almost doubled up in shock when he saw me approach.

'Kasturi Didi? Cake? Right now?'

'No cake,' I moaned to Ravi Singh. He was almost as good a buddy now as, say, Vikram. 'I wish I had come to leave cake.'

'Then?'

'Purva?'

'Oh.' His eyebrows shot up.

'I don't know where this will go, Ravi Singh. I wish I could help you win more money but I can't,' I said ruefully.

'I don't care about the money, Didi,' he said in a low voice. Startled, I looked up at the concerned face of the Bollywood-crazy Ravi Singh and felt my throat tighten. Ravi Singh nodded towards Purva's office. 'Dr Dixit just went into his cabin.'

'Does he have rounds?'

'No.'

'Surgery?'

'No.'

I took a deep breath.

'Is he inside?'

'Yes.'

'Okay,' I said and stood at my spot.

'I think you should go inside, Kasturi Didi.'

'I think so too,' I said and stood still.

'Now?' prodded Ravi Singh.

'Now?' I asked.

'Yes.'

'Okay.'

'Okay.'

'Okay.'

I exchanged a look.

'I will go in now.'

Ravi Singh looked exasperatedly at me and, before I could stop him, he had opened the door and announced my arrival to Purva.

Scared and anxious I stood at the door with no idea of how the night would end.

11.10 p.m.

Purva's usually cheerful office was eerily quiet and dark, except for a lone lamp that lit his table. He sat there, my crossword in his hand, his face expressionless. On seeing me, he put on his glasses and got up.

I swallowed hard.

Being goofy, fooling around, silly antics – all of that came naturally to me. This did not. Not at all. I cleared my throat. As I mustered up courage, the image of an angry Purva dragging me out of this room flashed out of nowhere and I shut my mouth.

My throat felt dry. The room was too warm. My cheeks felt very hot. My heart beat too fast.

Purva, meanwhile, had come up to me.

'How can I help you?' he asked formally, his face giving away nothing. Had he told me to get lost, I would have, without giving this matter another thought, about-turned and left. That is how much I wanted to avoid what I knew was on its way: a confrontation.

I said nothing. I stood still. Not because I wanted to but because I was singularly incapable of either movement or words.

'Umm…' I ventured after a little bit.

Purva looked questioningly at me, his x-ray-like eyes scanning my face so intently that I felt like I did not belong in my own skin.

I looked down at my hands, at the carpet, at my shoes, at his shoes … and then my mind wandered … wandered to Purva … I began to imagine how it would have felt to be in his place – to have loved someone with such honesty and have her do what I did to him. How would he have told his family that I did not want him? The friends, relatives, colleagues … the embarrassment, the sorrow, the heartbreak. And yet, he had come when Dad had needed him. How difficult would that have been?

'Purva…' I said, looking up to see him still gazing at me. 'I'm sorry, Purva,' I said, looking down and trying to gulp away the tears that now threatened to spill over.

Purva looked away. I gently pulled his face towards mine, faltered for a minute when I saw his eyes all red, gathered myself and said, 'I am sorry, Purva. I am very sorry.'

'Go away, Kasturi,' he said, turning away again.

'I will, I promise I will, but just let me tell you a few things … one last time? Please?' I begged.

Reluctantly Purva turned to face me.

'I am sorry, Purva, for all the hurt and the pain. I was scared … very scared … and confused. I could have talked it out with you, Mum, Dad anyone … but I chose to do the one thing I should not have. I hurt you. But I love you. I love so much more than I thought I did … and it took all this for me to figure that out. You don't hurt people you love… but I did and I am sorry.'

Purva shook his head, his face giving away nothing.

'I wish I could go back to the past and change what I did. But I can't. So I have no choice but to live with the consequences … I have no one to blame but myself.'

Purva stood still, looking down now.

'Can you forgive me, Purva?' I asked, my voice cracking now, afraid that I knew the answer.

'Kasturi ... I … I can't…' he fumbled.

My heart sank. This was really happening.

'I don't think…' Purva stammered, his face red now.

'It's okay,' I said hurriedly, every cell in my body revolting at the idea of even hearing the full sentence. 'It's okay, it's okay,' I said more to myself than to him and tried in vain to wipe away the tears that had my face all wet now.

'It's okay if you can't get back with me. I don't deserve someone like you,' I said, in a trance. It had happened but I still could not believe it. Purva had said no. He did not want me back. Well done, Kasturi Shukla, very well done.

Purva said nothing. I brushed tears away with the back of my hand.

'I will always love you,' I said, one last time, and ran towards the door desperate to get out of the room.

31

I had barely touched the cool metal of the doorknob when a firm hand grabbed my wrist with such force that I winced in pain. Before I knew it, two strong arms had wrapped themselves around me. Tears had already blurred my vision and now grief clouded any semblance of logic and reason. All I wanted to do was curl up and cry. Cry my heart out for all that had happened.

And that is exactly what I did.

With strong arms wrapped around me and a broad chest against my face, I curled up in the warmth that surrounded me and cried bitterly and without stopping. A gentle hand caressed the back of my head which only made me cry harder.

'Shhh, Kasturi,' said Purva in a gentle voice into my ear.

I cried harder.

'You will dehydrate yourself!' said the alarmed doctor a few minutes later.

And I cried harder.

'Okay, okay. Cry as much as you want,' he said resignedly and clasped his hands tighter around my waist.

Time stood still. I don't know how long we stayed like that. Not saying a word. Not moving. Not talking. My sobs broke the silence of the room like small waves crashing on the beach. I cried into his right shoulder and, when his shirt there was too wet for my comfort, I shifted to the other shoulder and cried harder than before. He simply held me without saying another word, without telling me to hush, without trying to stop me from it ... just holding me, one with me and my grief.

When I was done, I withdrew a few inches so that I could see his face in the gentle glow of the lamp.

'I am sorry, Purva,' I said, between sobs.

Purva's large black eyes stared at me for a few seconds before he spoke. 'Do you have any idea how adorable you look when you cry like this?' he said, gently brushing away some tears.

'I am so sorry,' I said, breaking into another fresh wave of tears.

'How did you even think for a minute that I would ask you to leave?'

Another fresh wave of tears. 'I'm sorry,' I said again. How many times would I have to say this for me to feel okay?

'I know you are,' he said and took my face in his hands. With his fingers he brushed away strands of hair that were now wet with tears.

'Purva!' I exclaimed, gulping in some air and readying myself for another monologue to explain what had happened.

He placed a finger on my lips and, boring his dark eyes into mine, he whispered, 'I love you, Kasturi, and that is all that matters.'

That shut me up and for some time I simply stared at him, taking in the simple beauty of his dark, intelligent eyes and the poetic curl of the longest eyelashes I had ever seen. Why had I not noticed them before? And why did each word from him sound so earnest, so sincere and so true? How did each word find its way to my heart, searing it with a pain that I found difficult to swallow?

'I love you too, Purva,' I said and felt such a powerful rush of love for him that my eyes pooled with tears again. I knew, in that moment, that there was something that needed to be done and now was the time to do it.

I disengaged myself from Purva, went down on one knee and, staring at the most astonished man I had ever set eyes on, asked the following simple and direct question:

'Dr Purva Dixit, will you marry me?' It was definitely my turn now.

'What?' he said, his eyes the size of saucepans.

'Will you marry me?' I repeated, crying and laughing at the same time now.

'Wait a second!' he said, bending low and inspecting the ring. 'This is my ring!'

'Yes.'

'How did you get it?'

'Vikram got it for me.'

'That slime! He stole it from me?'

'For me,' I said, smiling sweetly.

'You scoundrel!' he growled and then laughed my favourite laugh, the one that started somewhere at the back of his throat and filled me with the purest kind of joy. A laugh that I had not heard in weeks.

However, practical matters took precedence.

'Purva, you really need to say something! My knee is killing me!' I groaned, laughing, tears still fresh in my eyes. 'Purva!' I wailed impatiently.

He laughed for what seemed like a good hour before giving me his hand.

'Yes, I will, darling. Of course I will,' he said softly, holding on to my hand to help me get up.

'You will?' I asked just to be sure as I put the ring on his finger

'Kasturi,' he said, looking earnestly into my eyes, 'if there is one thing I have realized in the last few days, it is this – I cannot live a few days without you. How do you think I will live a lifetime without my daily dose of madness, you crazy, goofy and absolutely adorable woman?'

Delighted and beyond happy, I threw my arms around his neck. Yahooooo!' I yelped, as I smacked one big, wet kiss on his lips.

Laughing, Purva wrestled out of the kiss and held me in a long, warm embrace. Almost making up for the distance of the last few weeks.

Words fail me here, they do. For it is so difficult to describe the simple joy of being able to love the man you love. Of being able to look into his eyes and find them filled with love for you. Of being able to kiss his lips and know that he loves you more than any other. Of looking for his eyes to see that they have already found you. Of extending him a hand to see that he is already offered you his...

To be in love with a man who loves you with all his heart, that is, without any doubt, the most wonderful thing in this world.

32

12 August 2013, 1.00 a.m.

Purva and I spent more than an hour together, simply talking … trying to catch up on the weeks we had spent apart. I curled up in his lap, sitting cheek-to-cheek, taking in the familiar smell of the disinfectant, refusing to let go of his hand even for a second.

Purva's strong arms clasped my waist and pulled me closer to him, his eyes boring into mine. I let him pull me to himself, feeling snug and comfortable in his arms. Wrapped in them, I felt fully aware of how much he loved me. Purva traced my face with his finger, staring intently at every patch of skin that his fingers touched and then leant in for a kiss. He kissed me with an urgency that I was not familiar with, probably making up for the time apart. There was something about being kissed now that was in stark contrast with the kisses before our break-up. These seemed more urgent, more passionate, less doubtful. He kissed my eyes, brows and forehead and I let him, revelling in the love of a man I knew for sure I loved in return.

'Your alphabet cakes were very cute,' he said, looking

indulgently at me. I was already revelling in the attention that Purva was lavishing on me. How I had missed this!

'I know,' I said coyly, shrugging my shoulders, 'and the fish?'

Purva laughed out loud. 'Silly Kasturi!' he said, tousling my hair.

'Did you solve the crossword?' I asked.

'Of course I did. It took me less than a minute.'

'Was it then that you decided to forgive me?' I asked, more out of curiosity than anything else. What had finally worked?

'You had me much before that,' he said, smiling a slow smile.

'When? The fish?'

He shook his head.

'The cakes?'

He shook his head.

'The very, very first cake?'

'When I left Dad,' he said and I noticed how he left out 'your', 'in the hospital, he told me that you were already sorry about what had happened.'

'Really?' I asked, surprised.

'Yes. He asked me if I still loved you.'

'Oh!' I said, taken aback. 'And what did you say?'

Purva smiled and his eyes shone. 'That I could never not love Kasturi,' he said, shrugging his shoulders. It took a moment for realization to dawn upon me. So Dad knew all this while! I had been on the phone with him pretty much every day, fretting about Purva, and he would tell me to be patient and to understand how much Purva meant to me.

'Even when I do stupid things?' I asked, wide-eyed.

'*Especially*,' he said, smiling, 'when you do stupid things.'

'Why?'

'Because that's the way it is.'

I smiled a wide, happy smile and promised myself that I would never again take for granted the love that I am lucky to get from Purva. It is pure and genuine and people die many deaths to have this in their lives.

'So you were never really angry with me?'

'For a bit I was. You know, when things seem to fall apart, I often try to let go of the idea of how I think things should be. Maybe there is a bigger picture I cannot see? I know you well enough, Kasturi, and the more I thought about you, the more convinced I felt of your love for me, though you seemed very unsure. So I decided to simply wait for you to figure things out in your head. If you did not love me, I could not force you to be with me, and if you realized that you did, I was right here, waiting for you.'

My mind inadvertently went back to the misery I had to go through during the time Purva had refused to talk to me and a chill ran through me. That was a part of my life I did not wish to relive.

'Of course, I am sure, Purva … very sure of how I feel about you,' I said, my heart melting like warm wax with love that really knew no bounds. 'I love you so, so much.' I added, spreading my hands wide to show him how much.

'Silly girl!' he laughed and kissed me on the forehead. We chatted more – about Dad's surgery, about Pitajee and Anu.

When I glanced at my watch, it was already one. 'Will you drop me home?' I asked.

'Yeah, of course,' he said, getting up.

Hand in hand, we walked out of Purva's office but stopped short when I opened the door. The sight that met my eyes stunned me into immobility.

Ravi Singh and Pretty Nurse were pacing the corridor, their body language giving away their anxiety. Behind them stood about twenty people, staring expectantly at the door that had just opened to reveal us.

'They're holding hands!' someone shouted.

'Oh yes! I win!' someone else shouted

'I win too! Five thousand rupees!' another woman screamed.

'What's going on?' Purva asked me, looking bewildered.

Ravi Singh and Pretty Nurse ran up to me and, after hesitating for less than a second, gave me a quick hug.

'Kasturi Didi! I am so happy for you. Dr Dixit is the nicest man. You are very lucky!' he gushed.

'I know,' I said, grinning as Purva continued to gape.

'What is happening? Will you please explain?' he mumbled. Someone came and shook his hand.

'Thank you, Doctor Sa'ab,' another man said. 'I made three thousand rupees thanks to you.'

'Err… okay… you are welcome,' mumbled Purva.

I nodded my head absently, distracted, for I had just spotted two of my most favourite people in the world standing at the end of the corridor. Anu, laughing and crying at the same time, looked first at me and then at Purva. The sheer delight on her face made me well up.

And that is when, in a moment of rare clarity, the thought hit me. That a friend feels sad for you when bad things are happening is *not* a mark of true friendship. When unfortunate things happen to people we dislike, we find enough humanity in us to be sympathetic. Great things happening to one friend is the litmus test of the friendship of the other. Mostly, that is when the green-eyed monster raises its head and gobbles up the friendship. There is only one mark of a true friend. She feels genuine happiness for you when good things happen to you. Period.

'Bhaiyya! Bhabhi!' yelled Vikram, as he came bounding in, interrupting the little moment I was having, delight written all over his face.

'You guys!' Anu squealed, clapping her hands with glee. I stared, amazed at the transformation. The glum, sad Anu was nowhere to be seen. Purva grinned at her, a glorious grin that made my heart melt all over again, and bent low to give her a hug. Instead, Anu clasped his face in her hands and kissed him on his forehead. Pitajee's eyes grew to the size of saucepans when he realized what had just happened.

'I love you guys!' Anu said, pulling both Purva and me into a big hug. Vikram snuggled in.

'I love you guys too,' mumbled Pitajee, staring at the four of us. 'And I'm feeling very left out at the moment.'

'You idiot!' said Anu, yanking him into the group hug and soon it was like old times.

Anu, Pitajee, Purva, Vikram and I. In a group hug, happy, laughing and crying at the same time, celebrating another beginning.

33

12 August 2013, 2.00 a.m.

'What?' shrieked Mum.

'Yes!' I shrieked back. I could easily imagine her sitting upright in the bed, rubbing her eyes.

'Are you serious?' she shrieked again.

'Yes! I am!' I shrieked in return.

'Oh my god! I am so happy!' she shrieked in response.

'So am I!' I shrieked.

Pause.

'This means,' she said, her voice low as realization dawned upon her, 'I have a wedding to shop for ... errr ... I mean ... plan again?'

'Yes, Mum, I think you do,' I said, grinning.

'Oh ho,' she mumbled to Dad, who was obviously trying to sleep. 'Let me talk to my daughter. Go outside and sleep on the couch.' And then to me. 'Yes, Koochie, tell me how it all happened?'

Poor Dad, I thought, trying hard to stop the grin that seemed stuck on my face now.

14 August 2013.

It was not our first. Yet it felt like it. Purva always kissed very slowly as if, and I have said this before, the world around him ceased to matter. For the first time, the world around me blended into oblivion as well. Tender, gentle and always asking if I was okay. Endearing even when making out, I thought to myself with a wry smile.

'Is Anu coming home tonight?' he asked, his eyes dark with an intensity I had not known.

I tried to speak but nothing came out. I shook my head.

A small smile from Purva. With nimble hands, he unbotted the top button of my shirt and planted a tender kiss on my collarbone.

15 August 2013.

On the occasion of Independence Day, the readers of 'Pearls of Wisdom' are in for a treat. Purva has made a glorious debut on the blog under the rather inglorious pseudonym of 'Dimple'. It makes more sense – if you can dare to call it that – when you read the title of the post announcing our wedding: 'My Pimple to wed Her Dimple.'

I am not even sure I know how I feel about this and am trying to make sure that Purva does not go online.

Ever.

16 August 2013, 10.00 a.m.

'You look happy, Kassie,' said Padma, flicking aside her hot new bangs and grinning her widest. Of course she knew already. Pitajee and Padma have become too thick recently for her to not have found out within minutes of us getting back together.

'Yes! Yes! Yes!' I said, throwing my arms around her.

'You silly girl,' said Padma, wrapping her arms around me. 'That doctor guy is perfect for you, you know that, don't you?'

'Yes, I do! Yes, I do!' I yelped, grinning from ear to ear.

20 August 2013, 11.30 p.m.

After her last post on our pending nuptials, Mum has been inundated with questions from despairing mums from across the world, all worried about getting their daughters married to suitable surgeons with high networth.

Mum called today to comment philosophically on how borders are but lines on the maps and how mothers from all over the globe seem to have the same problem – difficult, obstinate daughters.

Her readers seem to treat her with an inexplicable air of reverence. Mum treats them with an equally inexplicable I-am-shri-shri-shri-Prabha-Shukla-esque superiority.

25 August 2013.

'We might have a problem,' said Purva, looking seriously at the faces before him.

'What?' Anu and I said, in unison.

'My mum.'

'Oh dear!' I said, slumping back into my chair. I had completely forgotten about her.

Pitajee giggled.

'And what is that for?' I asked.

'From what I know, her conclusion, when you called off the engagement, was that you are off your rocker.'

'What?' I wailed. The problems just don't seem to end.

'If I remember correctly, she lamented that Agra was too far, else the mental asylum there would be the perfect place for you spend the rest of your life,' said Pitajee, now howling with laughter like a madman.

'Pitajee,' I said, the tone of my voice heavy with threat. 'Stop it or I will throw this coffee at you.'

By now, Purva was trying hard not to laugh and that infuriated me further.

'I mean, only a few days ago, after due deliberation, the consensus was that you are as mad as a hatter. And now, to tell her that you are back in her son's life ... can I be there when she is told of the return of the madwoman?'

Even though he had a point, a promise was a promise, and I picked up my latte and threw it at him with a sweet smile on my face.

Once the commotion that obviously arises when someone throws coffee at someone else had subsided and Pitajee had glared at me to his heart's content, we settled back to discuss the matter.

'Really, Kas,' Purva said, straightening up. 'We will need to work on Mum.'

'But how?' I said, looking around.

'I have no clue,' said Purva, shaking his head.

'Neither do I,' said Anu, biting her nails.

'Me neither,' said Pitajee.

'I,' said Vikram looking quite superior, 'may have an idea.' Attentively, we all leaned in to listen to his masterplan.

30 August 2013.

'Don't you have any shame?' I asked Pitajee.

'No,' he said, his mouth full of chips.

'There is a girl in this room trying to sort out her sari,' I tried again, as Anu fiddled with the two hundred safety pins that were holding up the proverbial six yards of grace.

'Who? Where?' he asked, looking around, unable to spot the 'girl'.

I picked up the bottle of talcum powder and threw it at him. He ducked artfully to dodge the flying weapon.

'Arre, Bahu,' said Pitajee, coming closer and amicably placing the talcum powder back on the dressing table where it belonged. 'What about the ghoonghat?'

Grinning idiotically, he placed the aanchal of the sari over my head. I stared at the reflection in the mirror and had to admit that I looked tense. It was, after all, only the most important day in my life and nothing was in my control.

'Pitajee,' I groaned. 'I look so silly.'

'No,' he said firmly. 'It's fine. Anju Aunty will like this.' Anu, who was helping me with the bangles, now nodded her head in vehement agreement.

I sighed and stuck a safety pin to make sure that the pallu did not slide off. Today was a big day. Anju Aunty had only this morning been informed that Purva and I were back together. Before she could have a shock induced heart attack, Purva had invited her to my place for dinner.

She would be here anytime now.

7.00 p.m.

You could cut the tension in the room with a blunt knife. The air was heavy with suspense. The only thing missing was a suitably goose-bump-inducing background score from a B-grade horror flick.

Anu, Pitajee and I sat in the living room looking nervously at each other. Pitajee was chewing his lower lip, Anu was biting her nails and I was trying to manage my sari. Anytime now…

The bell rang shrilly, cutting through the blanket of anxiety we were all wrapped in, making us jump.

Purva, Vikram and Anju Aunty had arrived. And with that, it began.

'I don't think this is a good idea,' I heard her saying when I walked into the drawing room. She was clearly still recovering from the shock of having me back in the life of her precious son. Oh, well.

Anju Aunty stopped mid-sentence the moment her eyes fell on me standing shyly at the door, clad in the yellow sari, head covered in a pallu, bangles adorning my hands. I was, let's face it people, any potential mother-in-law's sweetest dream.

'Umm … Kasturi,' she said, staring at me from top to toe. 'You are wearing a sari and bangles.'

'Ji Auntyji,' I said, primly settling the pallu over my head and walking towards her, Anu by my side. 'Charan sparsh, Auntyji,' I said and bent low to touch her feet. Pitajee had spent two hours with me the day before, helping me perfect the charan sparsh.

'Charan sparsh to you too, Beta,' said Anju Aunty, obviously bewildered at what was happening. For a moment, I wondered if I should bless her with a 'doodho nahao, puto phalo' just for kicks, but one glare from Anu, who knew exactly what was going on in my head, and I shut my mouth. The whole idea behind this was for me to *not* be me.

'You … err … look different…' Anju Aunty mused.

'Ji Auntyji,' I said, nodding my head and looking down at my hands. With the TV awash with perfect daughters-in-law, Anu and I had to but watch a few hours of saas-bahu serials to perfect my imitation of the ideal bahu. I looked up at the ceiling and sent a silent thanks to Ekta Kapoor.

For a few minutes, no one spoke. Vikram then nudged me. I had almost forgotten. 'Oh!' I said out loud, and everyone looked at me. 'I almost forgot.'

'What? What did you forget?' asked Vikram, looking innocently at me.

'Time for puja,' I said.

'Who is Puja? Are we expecting someone else?' asked Anju Aunty.

'Oh no, Auntyji,' I tittered. 'It's time for my puja. Prayers. Worship,' I clarified. Purva shook his head, disbelieving.

Anju Aunty stared at me. 'You do puja?' she asked.

'Every day at err…' I paused and glanced at my wrist watch, 'at 7.17 p.m.'

'Oh.'

'If you don't mind, Auntyji, please can I be excused for a few minutes?' I asked politely.

'If you don't mind, can I join you?' Anju Aunty asked, not to be outdone.

'Sure,' I said and got up. Soon we had all trooped into the box room which had been hastily, over the last few days, converted into a puja room.

Having practised this all week, I knew exactly what to do and quickly set to work. I lit the diya and incense stick. Anu had arranged a huge metal tray with fresh flowers and fruit, which I placed in front of the idols.

'Auntyji,' I began hesitantly.

'Yes?'

'Umm…' I pointedly looked at her head.

'Oh! Of course, of course,' she said, and quickly covered her head with the pallu of her dupatta. Pitajee had a coughing fit that subsided as abruptly as it had started.

When everyone was ready, I folded my hands and began to sing *Om Jai Jagdish*, the only bhajan I had been able to learn by heart in the short time that I had been given.

'Purva!' hissed Anju Aunty, who stood next to me limply watching me sing. 'Sing with her!'

'Are you kidding me, Mom?' asked Purva, staring at me and shaking his head.

'Bhaiyya, you should!' said Vikram and joined in, as did Anju Aunty. By the time the bhajan concluded, I was standing with folded hands, profusely apologizing to the gods for using them like this and hoping that they understood. In that moment of remorse, I promised weekly attendance at the local mandir for a month.

Anju Aunty's eyes had turned glassy with wonder by now. We left the box room and trooped into the dining room where the table had been set. Flowers and candles added elegance to the whole setting and Anju Aunty stared at the table for a few seconds before taking her seat.

'I am sorry, Aunty, the puja took longer than expected,' I said, turning to face Anju Aunty. 'I just get so lost in my prayers sometimes…'

I saw Anju Aunty gulp visibly. 'That's fine, not a problem,' she said with obvious difficulty.

'Let us sit down for dinner. It's ready,' I said to everyone and pointed towards the dining table.

'Who cooked?' Anju Aunty asked Anu as I busied myself in making sure that everyone was comfortable.

'Kasturi did, Aunty. She's a fantastic cook!' Anu said loudly. 'Though of course, I am sure you know that already.'

'Oh, come on,' I said piously, dismissing her carefully practised compliments with the wave of a hand.

'Have you made the daal and paneer?' said Anju Aunty, staring at the delicious-looking food that was already on the table.

I nodded my head. 'And the kofte, the kebabs, chicken biryani, butter chicken and Konkani fish that I am about to get from the kitchen,' I added.

'Oh, wow!' said Anju Aunty. 'Maybe someday you can share the Konkani fish recipe?'

'Of course, Aunty, of course,' I said, gushing.

There was another coughing fit from Pitajee, whose mother had spent the better part of the morning cooking the food. Anu and Vikram both glared him into feeling healthier again.

'You cooked all this?' asked Anju Aunty again, not quite believing what she was seeing.

I nodded my head shyly, settling the pallu over my head. I noted that Anju Aunty still had her head covered as well.

'You ... you seem very different now,' she said as she sat down. I flitted around her, fussing over the food and her plate.

This was it. My cue.

'Aunty, I *am* different now. Let us just say...' (pause, count till three, look far away, resume) '...being away from Purva taught me a big lesson. I am sorry for all the trouble I caused. Each day ... each day ... each day...' I paused, panicking as my brain froze. The next few words that Pitajee and Vikram had written together for me refused to come to me. I stood still, not moving, and stared helplessly at Pitajee. I could not forget my words now! No!

'When you pray,' he said and then had another coughing fit.

Yes! Bless you, Pitajee!

'Each day,' I continued jubilantly, 'when I pray, I ask God to forgive me. I don't know if He will, or when He will, but till then ... I am guilty...'

Then, most dramatically, I gave a little sniff and, covering my mouth with one end of the pallu, rushed out of the room.

'I think she became a little emotional,' said Anu in a sad voice.

'Oh...' said Anju Aunty, quite bewildered.

'I will go get her,' Anu said.

'Yes, do that please,' said Purva, covering his face as Vikram grinned.

'Don't grin like that, Vikram,' said Anju Aunty angrily. 'The girl is emotional. You have to be more considerate.'

Pitajee had yet another coughing fit. A little later, I came out, looking more composed and we all finally sat down to dinner.

'Paranthas, Auntyji,' I said, smiling at her.

'Mughlai?' she asked, laughing.

I nodded my head. The only thing at the table that I had made.

Pitajee and Anu exchanged a look as Anju Aunty laughed delightedly and picked two fluffy, round and soft paranthas for herself.

'So Auntyji,' I said chattily. 'How is Lata Taiji?'

Anju Aunty looked at me, surprised. 'You remember her?'

'Of course!' I said, indignantly. 'You were telling me once how well her boutique was doing.'

'Yes, yes, of course.'

'The one that Betu Didi is helping out with these days,' I said.

'Is she?' she asked me, her eyes growing bigger by the second. 'I *knew* someone was helping her! Lata Didi is incapable of doing this on her own! How do you know?'

'Betu Didi told me.'

'When? How?'

'We are Facebook friends…' I lied.

'Oh, yes ... of course,' she said, her eyes growing bigger.

'And Beti Didi?' I asked, nonchalantly breaking a piece of parantha and dipping it in the daal. 'How is her course coming along?'

Anju Aunty did not speak for a few minutes and stared first at the sari-clad girl sitting in front of her with her head covered, then at the various dishes on the table. She even peered in the direction of the box room from which the aroma of burning incense was wafting in. To put it mildly, I think she was overwhelmed.

'Kasturi Beta,' she said, putting a hand on my head. 'Do you think I should speak to your Mum about the wedding date?'

Purva stared open-mouthed at his mother and Vikram nudged his brother, arching his eyebrows, a superior look plastered all over his face.

'Oh Auntyji,' I said, following it with a half giggle and looking down at my plate.

'GOAL!' shouted Vikram, and when we all stared aghast at him, he grinned and pointed towards the TV.

Once Anju Aunty had left, and before we all collapsed on the large sofa in the drawing room with sheer relief, the first thing I did was send Betu Didi a Facebook friend request.

11.35 p.m.

'Beta,' said Mum when I picked up the phone.

'Mum?'

'What did you do to Anjuji?'

'Worked my magic. Why?'

'She has already spoken to her panditji.'

'For?'

'The wedding date.'

'Whose wedding date?'

'Kasturi!'

'Oh sorry, my wedding date!'

'We have one date available in December and nothing for

six months after that. For obvious reasons, we all think it's best the wedding date is set for as soon as possible.'

'Oh my god!'

'Should I say yes?' she asked, her voice a little bit on edge. We all knew what had happened the last time the parents had agreed on a date.

I grinned. 'Mum, say yes! December is fine!'

'Are you sure?' she asked, laughing.

'Yes!'

'Okay, bye then!'

11.36 p.m.

Arrggghhh.

'Mum,' I said into the phone as soon as she picked up.

'Beta?'

'When am I getting married?'

'Why?'

'Mum! The date! At least I should know the date?'

'Oh sorry, yes. The ninth of December. Just finalized it with Anjuji.'

Why was the date so familiar, I wondered to myself as I cancelled the call. Then it hit me a few seconds later. Anu was getting married to Saumen on the ninth of December!

34

15 September 2013, 8.00 p.m.

Purva, Pitajee and I were sitting in our living room playing Scrabble. Let me rephrase that. Purva and I were playing Scrabble while Pitajee was playing another form of the same game, the rules of which changed every now and then as per his convenience. To show his displeasure at me pointing this out to him, Pitajee had just picked up a cushion and was aiming it at me when Anu burst through the door, her face awash with tears.

She sank to the floor, her face in her hands, her body racking with sobs. Pitajee reached her first, sank to the floor with her and held her in his arms. For a few seconds, no one spoke.

'What's wrong, Anu?' said Pitajee as he gently rocked her. Purva and I looked on, worried and helpless.

'My wedding lehenga is ready,' she said simply and sank further into the ground, crying harder than before.

It was only when Purva wiped the tears off my face that I realized that I was also crying.

20 October 2013, 2.00 p.m.

'Kasturi Beta,' said Vijaywada, coming to my desk and placing a paternal hand on my head.

Now what was wrong?

'Yes Sir?'

He heaved a deep sigh, sat down and then proceeded to stare at me with undisguised pity in his eyes.

'You are getting married, Beta, are you not?'

I had distributed invitations and a box of sweets to everyone in office. Of course I was getting married.

'Yes Sir. I hope you will be attending the wedding. It will mean a lot to both Purva and me,' I said primly.

'I have been thinking...'

Never a good sign. 'And?' I probed, worried.

'I think I have figured out the perfect gift for you.'

'Okay? What is it?' I said cautiously. Anything could happen now. I did not trust the man sitting across the desk from me.

He smiled. 'My brother who lives in the US is visiting India.'

'Okay? So?' Oh my god! Gifts from America?

'He is a famous ENT surgeon.'

I gulped with slight difficulty.

'I told him about your ailment, my child, and he is very curious about your sporadic deafness. He has offered to examine you next week! Who knows, if all goes well, you will be perfectly fine before the wedding!'

What? WHAT?

'Kasturi Beta...' prodded Mr Vijaywada, no doubt a little concerned by my lack of enthusiasm.

'Sir ... umm ... thank you. I cannot thank you enough, but I won't be here next week. I was just about to book my holiday dates.'

'Beta,' said Mr Vijaywada, 'don't worry. Look at the worry lines on your face! Don't worry, beta, don't worry!'

Don't worry? Was he kidding me?

'Just let me call Bhaiyya and I will see what I can do.' And with that, Mr Vijaywada pulled out his phone, dialled a number and spoke briefly.

'Now!' he said triumphantly.

WHAT?

'Let's go,' he said with a wide, victorious smile.

'Oh my god!'

'God, my child, *is* with you. In the form of my world-famous ENT-surgeon brother.'

I am so losing my job today.

4.00 p.m.

I sat on the cold steel stool, allowing one of the best ENT surgeons in the world to peer into my fully-functioning ear. On the outside, I was sure I looked confident, but on the inside, I was trembling with unadulterated fear.

Whatever would Mr Vijaywada do when my lie was exposed? Fire me? Shout and scream at me? Hand me over to the police? Oh, the number of sickies I have applied for because of my 'ear problem'.

'So you can't hear sometimes?' Dr Vijaywada asked.

'Yes Sir,' I mumbled, looking at my hands. I will stick to my story for the longest time possible, I promised myself.

'Can you hear now?'

'Yes Sir.'

'Is there a pattern to this illness?' he asked.

My Vijaywada butted in with, 'Yes, yes, I think it is more on Mondays and Fridays ... what do you think, Kasturi?'

I gulped. I hate working on Mondays and Fridays.

'Emmm ... possibly,' I said, feeling remarkably weak. I toyed with the idea of pretending to faint.

'Let me look again,' said Dr Vijaywada, a kind, distinguished-looking man, a little older than Mr Vijaywada. 'Which medicines have you tried?' he asked me after a minute.

'Erm ... Calcical ... err... 500 and ... and ... Avomine 200,' I said helplessly.

'I see,' said Dr Vijaywada, his face expressionless.

'Poor girl, she has been to so many doctors,' said Mr Vijaywada. 'Bhaiyya, you have to do something for her. Please do something!'

For a few minutes, no one spoke as Dr Vijaywada investigated the matter.

'I am done,' he declared.

So am I, I thought to myself, crossing my fingers. Where is the last copy of my CV stored? I will, of course, have to lie about this to Pitajee, or else I will never hear the end of how I was fired from my job for lying about an imaginary ear infection.

'Yes, so what can we do?' asked Mr Vijaywada.

I did not feel up to hearing it. Should I just run for the door and make a dash for it?

Dr Vijaywada looked at me for a moment. 'Nothing can be done,' he said.

'What?' exclaimed Mr Vijaywada.

Of course nothing could be done. There was nothing to be done. Come on, say it, Dr Vijaywada. I prepped myself for a hearty round of tears. Maybe they would help?

'The eardrum has been irreparably damaged, I am afraid. Such episodes of deafness are generally cyclical in nature. In Kasturi's case, they happen on Mondays and Fridays. All you can do, Bhai, is be as supportive as is possible.'

What? WHAT?

'Are you sure, Bhaiyya?' asked Mr Vijaywada, crestfallen.

'Are you sure, Uncle?' I asked in a small voice, just to confirm before I started the mental somersaults.

'Bhaiyya, this poor girl is getting married in a few days. Which mother-in-law will put up with a half-deaf daughter-in-law? India may have progressed but still, girls are girls.'

I am sure the image of his four girls swam before Vijaywada's eyes as he sniffed away a tear.

Dr Vijaywada sighed. 'Doctors are not gods. This is incurable. I have seen a few cases before this and…' he shook his head sadly, slowly, '… no, nothing can be done.'

'Oh.'

I tried hard, very hard to look half as crestfallen as poor Mr Vijaywada.

'You will have to be supportive. Please make sure you do not give her too much work on Mondays and Fridays,' Dr Vijaywada said.

Mr Vijaywada nodded his head. 'Of course I won't, Bhaiyya.'

'And the stress of making that weekly report on Thursdays does not help much either,' I added helpfully.

Dr Vijaywada gave me a look.

'But it's fine! I deal with stress just fine,' I said hurriedly.

Dr Vijaywada looked like he was about to smile.

'Are you sure, Bhaiyya, that nothing can be done?' Mr Vijaywada asked again.

'Yes, I am quite sure.' Dr Vijaywada turned towards me. 'Kasturi?'

'Yes Sir?'

'Just add cod liver oil to your diet ... it may help, but may not also. You know how tricky this illness can be.'

'Yes, of course,' I said, shrugging my shoulders barely able to keep my face straight.

'I am sorry I could not be of more help,' he said, shaking his head seriously.

'It's okay, Doctor Uncle. I have heard the same prognosis from too many doctors now for it to affect me much. I just want to thank you! Thank you *so* much, Dr Vijaywada,' I said, meaning it.

Dr Vijaywada shook my hand solemnly. Just as I was about to turn and leave the room, he winked at me. 'My brother talks rubbish all the time,' he whispered in my ear. 'Maybe I have just caught this disease from you.'

'What?' I exclaimed, my voice barely audible with the shock.

'Go away now, I need to laugh,' the elder Vijaywada said to me and I scuttered away before he changed his mind.

35

26 October 2013. Forty-five Days to Go for the Wedding.

I returned home to do the shopping. Given that we have such little time to shop for the wedding, time has been allocated to specific items. The wedding lehenga gets three whole days. No more, no less.

We went to eleven shops today and I tried on thirty-four red lehengas (I am not exaggerating) and liked none. It has to, has to, has to be a red lehenga and I am refusing to even look at other stuff.

27 October 2013. Forty-four Days to Go for the Wedding.

The usual is as follows.

I spot a lehenga that I think I might consider if the world were ending. The moment the shopkeeper senses this, he goes into overdrive. After all he has just fed us samosas and chai.

'Chotu,' he barks at the thin man standing in the corner with a sullen look on his face. 'Wear this!'

I double over in shock. 'What?'

'Ma'am, he will wear the lehenga,' says the shopkeeper with a nod of his head. 'So that you get an idea of how this will look.'

Really? No, I mean, really?

And soon, in front of my horrified eyes, stands a thin man, clad in a lehenga with the ghoonghat draped over his head.

I mean, like, really?

We went to ten shops today and I tried on seventeen lehengas. I liked two. Mostly because the shop waale bhaiyya looked so downcast, as time progressed, that I refused to like any.

28 October 2013. Forty-three Days to Go for the Wedding.

We went to eight shops today, tried a million lehengas and bought one. It is cream-and-golden in colour. They draped it around me and covered my head like a dulhan, which made Mum get all teary-eyed. To be honest, I barely recognized the flushed girl who stared back at me in the floor length mirror. The two hundred people in the shop all nodded their heads and said that I looked very beautiful.

Mum put up a post on her blog titled 'How to buy a lehenga'.

31 October 2013. Forty Days to Go for the Wedding.

Do I like being the bride-to-be or do I like being the bride-to-be? Anju Aunty, Purva and Vikram spent the whole day shopping for me!

Anju Aunty chatted the whole time about Pinku Mama (the first I had heard of him) who is down with flu but redeemed herself by buying me a gorgeous pink-and-yellow lehenga for the wedding reception.

Vikram, in spite of my protests, bought me a Rolex. I asked him if he was rollexing in money and, believe me, he laughed.

Purva, after I pestered him, bought me lots of candy. I was, of course, most excited about the candy and ate so much of it that I felt quite sick afterwards.

2 November 2013. Thirty-eight Days to Go for the Wedding.

Does the shopping ever end? It is now becoming quite tedious.

3 November 2013. Thirty-seven Days to Go for the Wedding.

I stood in the corridor of the hospital, staring at Purva talk to the family of a patient. The mother was in tears and repeatedly tried to touch Purva's feet. Purva tried his best to not let her do that, patting her back and even giving her a hug.

As I inched closer to them, I heard the last few words she spoke before leaving. 'My son has two gods, Doctor Sa'ab,' she said with earnest tears in her eyes. 'One that created him,' she said, pointing heavenwards, 'and another that gave him life,' she said, looking at Purva.

Purva smiled and shook his head, looking decidedly uncomfortable. 'It's my job,' he tried to say but the lady would not hear any of it.

I stood there, watching the little scene, my heart full of love for him.

5 November 2013. Thirty-five Days to Go for the Wedding.

After due deliberation between the parties involved, it has been decided that it will be most convenient if the wedding takes place in Delhi. Both sides have a lot of relatives in Delhi and it all seems to add up well. However, the tragic irony of it all is not lost on me; Anu and I will be getting married on the same day in the same city. I look forward to the day with joy and anticipation for I will be starting a new life with a man I love whereas Anu is readying herself to brave married life with a man she will never be able to love.

In other news, thanks to some very highly-placed contacts of the Dixit family, the venue for the wedding has been confirmed. The gentleman who will be decorating the venue sent me a PDF file with options of various flowers to choose from.

'Brides are so particular. They seem to know exactly what they want!' said the man, winking at me as I looked at him blankly.

After getting about eleven reminders from him, yesterday, I finally opened the file. Frankly speaking, they *all* looked the same to me.

'Paddy?' I said to Padma, looking over my laptop.

'Huh?' she said, flicking away her bangs.

'Choose a number between one and sixty-seven?'

'Twenty-three,' she said.

That is how, on the day of the wedding, the venue looked hideous – 'decorated' with an abundance of disgusting-looking orange and purple flowers. Not my fault, I would say then and you now know why.

7 November 2013. Thirty-three Days to Go for the Wedding.

Mum is writing a series on her blog titled 'Getting Pimple married!' where she speaks openly about the challenges of being the mother of an obstinate bride-to-be. The readership has swollen to about fifteen hundred followers and someone has created a fan page on Facebook.

I just shake my head in disbelief.

10 November 2013. Thirty Days to Go for the Wedding, 10.00 p.m.

Anu and I sat cross-legged, face to face, on my bed. A disgusting green face mask covered most of my face. Mum has insisted that I put this on each day before my wedding to get the glow that has so far eluded me (because obviously I have not been listening to her).

One month to go and life as we know it will change forever. For both of us.

'So tell me more about the suitcases that Aunty bought for you,' she asked, her eyes shining with excitement. It's silly, the amount of interest she has in my wedding preparations when she hardly ever bothers with her own.

I said nothing and she put a hand on my arm.

'You feel uncomfortable talking to me about your wedding, don't you?' she asked, looking at me with a gentle smile. I stared at the dark circles under her eyes; she had not been sleeping at all. I hear her toss and turn every night.

I did not say anything.

'Please don't do that,' she pleaded. 'You know your wedding is like a kaleidoscope through which I see the simple joys of a marriage. I try to imagine what it would feel like to marry someone you love … I live my wedding with Amay, the one that will never happen, through your wedding with Purva … let me live it. Please, Kasturi?'

I stared at the girl sitting in front of me in wonder. It would be very easy for her to be jealous, sarcastic and acidic; most girls in her shoes would be just that. I am, after all, getting something that she wants but cannot get. And yet, there she is, eyes shining, eager to hear all about my silly red suitcases, in the process opening her fragile broken heart in front of me. I paused to wonder, yet again, what I had done in my previous birth to have found friends like Anu and Pitajee, and why God had to do something so horrible to them.

'Yes, of course, Anu,' I said, and hugged her tight and long. 'Something good will come out of this, Anu,' I whispered into her ear. I felt her nod her head. Neither of us were, however, convinced.

'Now, about the suitcases,' she said, withdrawing, a little too hurriedly.

I continued to stare at her, spellbound. It is true, you get to know the character of a person not when the sun shines but when dark clouds gather.

'I love you, Anu,' I mumbled, more to myself than to her.

15 November 2013. Twenty-five Days to Go for the Wedding, 6.00 p.m.

I nearly died of shock today when I got a friend request from Lata Chaturvedi. *The* Lata Taiji wants to be my friend on Facebook.

She turned seventy-two last month.

Are you kidding me?

18 November 2013. Twenty-two Days to Go for the Wedding, 8.00 a.m.

I am back home – the last time I will be here as an unmarried girl. While most of my three-day trip will be used in giving measurements to the tailor (seriously, going to the tailor is as bad as going to the dentist these days), shopping and trying to make my face glow, there is another thing I want do to.

I want to go around the house and hug each room and thank each chair and kiss each bed. Okay cross that, I sound deranged, but you get the drift, don't you?

8.01 a.m.

My bedroom. It still has a poster of the Spice Girls from the second century BC and a desktop computer from a thousand years before that. Mum had tried to sell it but finally decided against it when they refused to offer her anything more than two thousand rupees. I am half afraid that she will hand it over to me after my wedding, as a treasured family heirloom.

The number of hours I have spent in this room, eyes glued to the Physics textbook, trying desperately to mug up theorems that made no sense, knowing that mugging won't get me through the hallowed portals of IIT. The fights with Mum, the gossip sessions with aunts and cousins, the gyaan session with Ramu … it has all happened here.

8.04 a.m.

The kitchen.

The countless hours Mum has spent pleading with me and threatening, in vain, to teach me how to cook. For further and more embarrassing details, please refer to a post on Mum's blog titled, 'Getting Dimple to Cook (it must be easier to climb Mt Everest)'.

The countless hours I have spent here, chatting with Mum, filling her with the details of my day.

8.06 a.m.

The living room.

Sitting cross-legged on the now slightly frayed sofa as one of the parents hand-fed me dal-chawal.

Sitting at the dining table, bawling my head off, because I had scored an eight-on-ten and not a ten-on-ten, as Mum and Dad looked on bewildered, desperately trying to pacify an inconsolable teenager.

The television, my good, old, faithful TV. *Dilwale Dulhaniya Le Jayenge*, reruns of *Friends*, MTV…

The recliner. Hours curled up on it with a book in my hand. From Enid Blytons to Nancy Drews to the Brontë sisters to Sidney Sheldon and John Grisham.

Oh gosh, the overwhelming memories of my childhood home.

8.10 a.m.

The garden.

The banana tree that Dad had planted with me. I had then proceeded to religiously water it three times a day and had almost killed it. It survives only because Dad had the wisdom to order me to stay at least ten feet away from it.

The strawberries that excite the entire family more than man reaching Neptune will.

The soft green of the grass that I have sat on, soaking in the weak winter sun.

The little brown bird that builds a nest every year in that tree, by the gate. The memories…

8.15 a.m.

Mum and Dad's bedroom.

The countless nights I have trooped into this room in the middle of the night, groggily dragging a pillow with me and snuggling in between Mum and Dad.

The dreams and the comfort…

I know I am not leaving any of it … I know, I know, I know. I know!

I am going to be someone's wife, someone's daughter-in-law, there is a boy who calls me Bhabhi, there are snotty-nosed little kids who call me Chachi. I will be a part of their family, another set to love and be loved by. Yet it all feels so heavy and sad … a chapter of life is about to begin but another is about to end. I cannot help but feel this huge burden of emotions that weigh heavy on my shoulders. Why does life have to change? Why can't it all remain the same? Why do we have to grow up?

How we fight to let go and how we fight to keep.

21 November 2013. Nineteen Days to Go for the Wedding.

Anu and I shopped for bangles today. For me.

She refused to buy anything for herself. Pitajee came to pick us up and did not, even for a second, take his eyes off Anu.

It broke my heart.

3.00 p.m.

'Mum,' I said, into the phone.

'Is it important?' she barked. 'I am out shopping for the wedding. I have no time.'

'Well, no one is dying,' I said, sarcastically.

'Good. Talk later then.'

What?

23 November 2013. Seventeen Days to Go for the Wedding.

The wedding shopping is like this treacherous monster that attacks every positive feeling in your soul. I rebelled today by refusing, point-blank, to shop for pumice stone that Mum insists I need to buy. Before the day ended Mum had posted a long-ish blog titled, 'Managing difficult children: Twenty things I have learnt as a parent'.

She goes on to list about sixty things.

In other news, it's my bachelorette tomorrow. Yahoo!

25 November 2013. Fifteen Days to Go for the Wedding, 9.00 a.m.

Worryingly, I have no recollection of what happened at my bachelorette.

11.59 a.m.

Oh.

Now I do. And so do 879 others.

Noon.

'Paddy,' I try to yell into the phone, only the voice that comes out is nothing but a hoarse whisper.

'Shut up, da,' Padma says, her voice groggy. 'Stop screaming. My head hurts.'

'Take those bloody pictures off Facebook!'

'Which pictures?'

'Pictures of my bachelorette ... the ones where I am dancing on top of a table,' I say.

There is stunned silence.

'You danced on table-tops?' a shocked voice asks.

'With you by my side,' I reply despondently.

'Are you kidding me?' Her voice is a stunned whisper.

'And you have shared them on Facebook!'

'Dear lord,' says Paddy.

'Dear lord it is,' I say, nodding my head and hoping fervently that neither Anju Aunty nor her hundred sisters/ brothers have been on Facebook in the last two hours.

12.02 p.m.

Self-explanatory text from Pitajee: 'Bawahahahahaha.'

How I hate him!

2.00 p.m.

The pictures were taken off Facebook, but not before a couple of incidents took place.

Since I was tagged in the pictures, I have received about ten friend requests, including one from a certain Raju Ban Gaya Gentleman.

Hotty Singh also wants to be my friend.

Just before we took the pictures off Facebook, a couple of notifications popped up. Lata Taiji had 'liked' a picture – one that had me sitting cross-legged on a table, looking dazed and drinking from a jug that was larger than me.

The head hurts; I think I should sleep.

36

28 November 2013. Twelve Days to Go for the Wedding, 9.00 p.m.

The café was an odd choice for our last huddle before the two weddings but, we all agreed, we did not want to meet anywhere else. The café had witnessed me falling in love with Purva, heard the many sweet nothings that Pitajee had murmured to Anu, seen me walk away from Purva, looked on, amused, as I'd tried to win him back, been aghast as Anu and Pitajee parted ways and smiled indulgently as Purva and I got back together.

Now it looked at us, the bittersweet memories hanging heavy in the air.

'I won't be present at your wedding ... that is tragic!' said Anu, smiling weakly at Purva and me. Without another word, Purva got up from the chair that he had pulled close to me and went to sit next to Anu. The two of them stared at each other, speaking to one another without saying anything. They do that sometimes.

Purva ruffled Anu's hair. 'Silly girl,' he said, smiling and pulling her into a hug.

Anu smiled as well. She was determined to be happy this evening but there was something wrong.

'Is everything okay, Anu?' I asked.

Anu laughed bitterly and I looked down at my hands, mentally thwacking myself on the head with a rolled up newspaper. What a silly question to ask! I should not be allowed to speak.

'Honeymoon tickets booked?' she asked, changing the subject.

'Yes,' I said. 'Brazil it is!'

'I hope you guys have a great time,' she said, putting a hand on mine 'I will probably see Dr and Mrs Dixit when they come back, all tanned, from Brazil!'

I inched closer to her. 'Anu…' I said, my eyes pleading and unwilling to even look at the stone-faced man who sat next to me. 'Think this through … please … the wedding is still a few days away … anything can happen … if … if the two of you want to…'

Anu stilled, her face paled.

'Wha…' I began, but Pitajee cut in.

'Let's not go there again, Kas. It's all been decided.'

Helplessness filled me with despair. 'So … what now? The two of you never meet?' I asked angrily.

'Relax, Kas,' said Pitajee. 'We'll be friends … if, of course, Saumen does not have a problem…' he said, looking at Anu.

'Friends?' I repeated, tears welling up in my eyes. Anu and Pitajee were parents who were divorcing each other and I was their child whom neither knew what to do with. I smiled as my fertile brain sketched images in my head.

'And now you are smiling,' said Pitajee, inching closer to

me. 'You *are* deranged, you know.'

'Shut up!' I said and hit him on the back of his head.

Before I knew it, Pitajee had pinned my hands behind my back. 'Say you're sorry!'

'Never!'

'Now.'

'I will die before I say I'm sorry,' I said hotly, enjoying every minute of this. As we fought, from the corner of my eye, I saw Purva stare at Anu, an odd expression on his face. He had seen something. Something that had made him still, something that, for a second, gave me chills and made the hair on the back of my neck stand up. Before I turned away, I saw Purva murmur something to Anu.

Later, as Purva and I walked to his car, I looked back to see Anu and Pitajee who had fallen behind. The two seemed to be deep in conversation.

'What did you say to Anu when I was beating up Pitajee?' I asked Purva.

'To speak up and not bottle things up inside her,' he said, shrugging his shoulders.

'Should we wait for them?' I asked, not really sure of what he meant.

He looked at the two silhouettes in the dimly-lit parking lot of AIIMS.

'No, let them talk,' he said quietly and opened the door of his car, beckoning for me to hop in.

11.30 p.m.

The car came to a neat halt in front of the house that, for the first time, I no longer shared with Anu. She had left to move into a five-star hotel that her mum was already settled into, in preparation for the wedding. Speaking of parents, mine arrive tomorrow, armed, I have been told, with six huge suitcases and seventeen boxes of mithai.

Purva rested his hands on the steering wheel and looked at me, a slow, beautiful smile lighting up his face. He stared for a few seconds, not blinking.

'Hi,' I said brightly, uncomfortable with the silence.

Purva threw his head back and laughed. 'In time, Kasturi,' he said, letting a hand rest lightly on my cheek, 'the Delhi government will slap an entertainment tax on you.'

I tried to look indignantly at him, but could not, with that idiotic grin plastered across my face. Instead, I took his big, wide hands into my tiny ones and stared right back at him. Increasingly, these moments, where it was just us, were becoming rare and I fiercely treasured the little time we managed to get together. Honest and simple, kind and gentle – Purva, the man who was to be my husband in ten short days. I searched myself for doubts and breathed easy when I could not find any. It is funny, sometimes, the confidence you can find in the peace of a decision well made.

I slowly fingered the scars on his hands, as always, fascinated by them.

'I love your scars,' I said, grinning at him.

'I love the whole of you,' he said, grinning back. I made a face at him – my usual response when he said something filmy. There was a moment's pause before he spoke again. 'Are you stressed about the wedding?' he asked gently.

'No, not at all,' I said, already feeling sick at the thought of being surrounded by a hundred relatives who would, no doubt, scrutinize everything from the flowers in my hair to the little ant that dared wander into the living room. Bleh!

He smiled, seeing right through the lie.

'There is something I want you to keep,' he said, still not switching on the light in the car. Bathed in the yellow glow of the rickety street lamp, Purva untied the watch on his wrist.

I gasped theatrically, bringing my hands to my face, much like a newly crowned Ms Universe. Under the Bollywood-esque drama that I was shamelessly indulging in, I hoped I was disguising genuine surprise. Purva, for reasons best known to him, has never been seen without this watch. We have teased and bullied him about it and received no response other than a quick, hurried smile that never quite reached the eyes.

'This,' he said, handing the watch to me.

'Your watch?' I asked, perplexed. 'Why? I mean…'

He shook his head.

'Eh?'

'Dad,' he said, in a voice so low that I had to strain my ears, 'died in a car crash.'

My heart skipped a beat for this was only the second time Purva was speaking voluntarily about his father. Anju Aunty had mentioned his untimely death to me once but, not wishing to upset her, I had refrained from asking her anything more.

'I was thirteen,' Purva continued, his large expressive eyes boring into mine. I felt his fingers clutch my hand tighter and a lump appeared in my throat.

From the dark clouds that now gathered in his eyes, I knew he was briefly reliving the horror and the pain. I gulped as I recalled what a wreck I had been, at twenty-seven, when my dad had had to spend a few days in the hospital. Thirteen is so young, it is so cruel.

'And Vikram was nine.'

I tried to not imagine the two boys, aged thirteen and nine, dealing with such an immense loss.

'I … I'm sorry … it could not have been easy,' I mumbled uncomfortably. Where was my brain when I needed it to come up with something comforting? Where were the bloody words? I looked on helplessly.

'When you look back, Kasturi, can you think of a moment that completely changed your life and defined you into becoming the person you are now?'

IIT Jee results? In spite of my best efforts I had not gotten through, but my idiotic study partner had somehow managed. I vaguely recalled crying non-stop for fourteen hours. The entire household had come to a standstill. The drama!

'No,' I said, shaking my head.

'I can,' he said softly. 'We were to head to Disneyland in a week's time when it happened. I grew up in an instant – went from being a child to head of the family with a mother and brother to take care of in a matter of minutes.'

Silence.

'Dad was the only earning member and he was gone…' he said, more to himself than to me. 'I don't even know how we survived till Mum started working again. I tutored kids for the money…' he said and then smiled a slow smile. 'I was such a horrible teacher!'

In my head flashed the image of a scared thirteen-year-old

taking charge of his mother and brother, the boy-man. The head of a shattered family.

People are not born beautiful. They become beautiful. Through despair and struggle, pain and suffering, they come out armed with a kind of sensitivity that enables them to empathize with the pain that others are going through a lot better than the rest of us. As I sat there listening to Purva, his ways began to make sense to me.

'I worked very hard for so long and from such a young age that I don't know any other way now,' he said, almost by way of an apology.

I nodded my head. I understood. Finally.

'Vikram is only four years younger but you know…' he struggled, looking for the right words. 'I think, no, I know … I am sure … he is like a son to me. I knew that he would follow my footsteps, so I wanted to do everything correctly, for my sake and for Vikki's.'

And he had. His younger brother was also a doctor, a promising surgeon, saving lives, just like his Purva Bhaiyya.

I took Purva's troubled face in my hands and kissed him on his forehead, my heart welling up for the thirteen-year-old boy that still lingered somewhere in those dark, deep eyes. From tutoring kids for money to becoming an incredibly successful surgeon, Purva's journey suddenly weighed more. It had to be a story of grit and gumption; a story that, if I'm lucky, someday the shy, quiet man in front of me will share with me. Till then, I shall wait.

I could now understand why he liked me best when I was goofing around, laughing carelessly and why he would smack Pitajee for upsetting me. For in my madness, he glimpsed a freedom he had never had the luxury of. It was a madness that could only be a part of you if you never had to teach to support your family, if you grew up with both parents at your beck and call, if did not live your entire life feeling completely responsible for your sibling.

'You make me happy, Kasturi ... happier than I ever thought I could be,' Purva said, bringing me back to the present. His face looked a little relaxed now.

I traced his eyebrows, lost in thought. I wished I could go back in time and give the thirteen-year-old Purva a hug, hold his hand, tell him that it would all be okay … or wait, would it?

'Don't let anything take your spirit away from you, Kasturi. Not your work, not family, not me,' he said, holding my hands tighter.

'Yes, boss,' I said and forced myself to grin.

'This watch,' he said nodding at the watch that he clutched tightly in his hands, 'survived the crash without a scratch. I have never voluntarily taken it off … till now.'

And then he put the watch in my palm.

'You want me to have this?' I asked, shocked and touched and teary and perplexed. This was the man I walked away from? Really, Kasturi Shukla? Really?

He smiled and pulled out my hand. Tying the watch on my wrist he looked critically at it.

'It's a man's watch, so you may not want to wear it … but I want you to keep it.'

'Why? It is your most prized possession, Purva!'

'You never met Dad,' he said quietly. 'He would have loved you like the daughter he never had. I want a bit of him to be with you.'

No, I am not going to cry.

'And you?'

'I have the memories,' he said, bending low to plant a kiss on my cheeks and lingering there. 'You take the watch.'

Mum, in a fit of wisdom, once said that simple words, because they are simple, find it easiest to reach the soul. I think that explained why I pulled a surprised Purva into a fierce hug and cried bitterly into his shoulders. I cried for the helpless thirteen-year-old boy, I cried for the selfless twenty-nine-year-old man and I cried because my heart ached.

Maybe this is love?

Maybe I am finally, truly in love?

37

6 December 2013.

Three masis and two chachis stood around me in a circle and continued to exchange quizzical glances. Clad in a yellow salwar-kurta, as instructed by Panditji, I was sitting in front of a kalash that had been stuffed with neem leaves.

'Do you know what to do?' I asked a bewildered-looking masi.

'Not really … I think the plan is to simply make up the rasams as we go along,' she said, shrugging her shoulders.

'What? What? What?' said the balding panditji, who had overheard our conversation.

'The rasam, Panditji,' Mum said with folded hands.

'Kanya koh prastut kiya jaye,' he said in a monotone, staring at me. Insolently, I stared right back.

'No, not Kanya! It's Kasturi!' said Padma, quite scandalized at the faux pas. The masis and chachis burst out laughing. Panditji, disapproving of all laughing that was happening, cleared his throat.

'Haldi, haldi,' he shouted and proceeded to bark out instructions to all and sundry. Today was the day of the haldi rasam and, before the hour had passed, five aunts with their heads covered and with many fond words of endearment, had delicately put haldi on my forehead, shoulders and knees.

Mum cooed in the background and Dad, clad in a posh kurta-pyjama, behaved like a man possessed by his SLR camera.

Pitajee, for whom Mum has a very soft corner, was the only man invited to put haldi on me. Both Mum and I were very aware that similar ceremonies were taking place in Anu's house as well. The burden that the smiling Pitajee carried was not lost on us and we had pledged to do whatever it took to keep him distracted. Pitajee proceeded to daintily touch my forehead, shoulders and knees with haldi, then, grinning his most evil grin, he smeared the yellow paste on my face with one grand sweep of his hands.

The aunties howled with delight and I screamed my lungs out. Panditji shook his head.

'Children these days,' he said ruefully as, leaving aside all the coyness of a bride-to-be, I charged towards Pitajee.

Anything to keep him distracted, I thought to myself. Even if it means wrecking my haldi ceremony.

Anything to keep him distracted.

4.00 p.m.

I was looking at the pictures that Dad had taken during the ceremony. The ones that really made me smile were the ones where Pitajee and I were at it again. Beating each other up, I realized with a start, has pretty much been the backbone of our friendship. Purva told me once that he did not know who was a worse influence on whom between the two of us. And I guess it's true.

7 December 2013, 8.00 a.m.

Some puja.

Noon.

Another puja.

2.00 p.m.

I am just getting out of a family meeting that lasted an hour. Before we left the meeting room, Mum huddled us together for a picture that would go on her blog as part of a post titled 'Dimple's wedding: Organizational skills needed'. Most of us – well, everyone except yours truly – came out of the session with at least one list and one duty. Here's a sample:

- Ila Mausi responsible for Purva's naniji. Fuss around her and make her feel important.
- Mukund and Bikram to man the food stalls. Please make sure caterers do not distribute, and then later count, more plates than are needed. If possible, try and stop people from using more plates than necessary.
- Prabha and Vineeta responsible for Anjuji. Fuss around her and make her feel VERY important.
- Abhi to make sure Panditji is awake and not drunk. Also make sure he has all the samagri.

The last one on the list caught my attention:

Pitajee to make sure Kasturi does not run away from her own wedding (Just kidding).

I laughed out loud when I read it. The 'Just kidding' in brackets. It's *so* Mum.

3.30 p.m.

Dear lord, another puja!

6.00 p.m.

'What pattern do you want?' asked the boy who had come to apply mehendi on my hands. More girls than I bothered to count – and Pitajee of course – gathered around me, chattering excitedly like little monkeys.

'Can you make a hospital?' I asked brightly. Pitajee led the guffaws. 'No, really. I really want a hospital on my hands,' I tried to say, but my voice was drowned out in the racket.

'What?' said the young boy, shocked out of his wits when I insisted vehemently. 'Auntyji,' he bleated for Mum, scared to be left alone with me.

Mum's rather short post on the blog today was titled, 'What to do when the bride is trying her best to be difficult'.

8.00 p.m.

Why doesn't anyone tell you how much hard work getting married actually is? I have been sitting down for two hours with my hands stretched out, the wet, cold mehendi making it all the more uncomfortable. They are now beginning to feel very numb.

As are my feet.

The others are feasting on a delicious dinner of aloo-puri. Every once in a while, someone comes and pops a little bit of food in my mouth. Pitajee, on the other hand, walks around munching slowly on the gastronomical delight that is aloo-puri, smirking meaningfully and purposefully avoiding eye contact.

Bugger!

8.30 p.m.

Extract from a post that Mum put up on her blog today titled, 'Pearls of wisdom for brides-to-be':

Pimple, darling, I hope you are reading too.

1. *Love between husband and wife is not unconditional. It has to be earned, continuously.*
2. *While people cannot be perfect, relationships can be.*
3. *In being all of the things that you become after marriage, mother, wife, daughter-in-law, sister-in-law, do not forget that you are also you.*
4. *Have arguments with the aim of solving the problem, not just for the sake of having an argument.*
5. *If possible, get a house with two bathrooms. Men really do have a sprinkler attached somewhere.*

9.00 p.m.

Anu has had her mehendi done as well. Instead of Saumen, she got Amay written in one little corner on her right hand.

I almost teared up as I read her text.

Sangeet, 8 December 2013. 8.00 a.m.

I get to see Purva today! Yahoo!

Buckets full of cousins from across the country and the world are pouring in. Most of the guests are staying in my apartment and the one adjacent to it that has been kindly lent to us by the landlord for the wedding.

There is bedding on the floor everywhere. In various corners of the two houses, extended family members sit in cozy clusters and gossip over a million cups of chai. Ramu has taken the position of Head Chef and has a team of three people under him.

It's not easy to get a girl married!

Noon.

'Sleep!' barked Mum, looking darkly at me.

'But I don't feel like sleeping,' I said.

'I don't care, just sleep,' she said dismissively. 'You need to look rested for your sangeet in the evening.'

At that moment, Dad barged into the room. He looked a little bewildered. 'Is Badi Buaji flying in or taking the train?' Dad asked, looking at Mum, who had about ten lists in her hand.

'Buaji is already here,' said Mum.

'Oh dear!' said Dad, wiping his forehead. 'Then someone is waiting somewhere. Get me Pitajee! We need to find out who is where!'

And with that, he rushed out of the room.

6.00 p.m.

A dazzlingly beautiful, even if I say so myself, yellow anarkali, hair set in gentle curls, hands resplendent with bangles, mehendi and the huge diamond engagement ring.

Flanked on either side by Paddy, Pitajee and my cousins, I walked into the brilliantly decked hall for my sangeet in a trance, not believing that it was all finally happening!

Incidentally, Purva was the first person my eyes fell on as I looked around. Clad in a cream, understated kurta, he looked so utterly elegant and handsome that I almost gasped in shock. When did he start looking so gorgeous, I wondered to myself.

'Jiju!' squealed one of my younger cousins. 'He is so handsome!'

'He *is* looking dapper, isn't he?' said Paddy, unable to keep the surprise out of her voice.

'The ladki,' said Purva, coming closer and winking at me. 'And the ladki waaley,' said Purva, slapping Pitajee on his back. I grinned. After very little debate, Pitajee had decided that he would attend the wedding as *my* guest. Hence the ladki waaley jibe.

Anju Aunty came to me and smothered me with kisses in front of a very amused Purva.

'Leave her alone,' he said, laughing and pulling us apart.

'Why? Why? Is no one else allowed to kiss her?' said one of Anju Aunty's cousins, winking at Purva and me.

'No, no, Auntyji. Why don't you kiss her as well?' said Pitajee, poker-faced.

6.30 p.m.

Purva's family was given the front row, a stage was set and the music blared from every corner.

I felt excited as I munched on bread pakoras, all the while texting images of my sangeet to Anu.

7.20 p.m.

As men with trays of delicious fried food made sure everyone was fed, the masis and chachis (known to not get along), in an exemplary show of solidarity, danced to 'sasural genda phool'. They missed steps, looked around sheepishly, but finished the song to thunderous applause.

The momentum had kicked up!

8.00 p.m.

Friends from B-school, who had travelled from across the country to be in Delhi for my wedding, performed an absolutely crazy dance to a medley of songs that had everyone wanting more.

A chachi, who wanted to sing a ballad about a daughter leaving the proverbial Babul ka Ghar but had been told not to because we had all collectively decided to not make my wedding a teary affair, showed her rebellious side and sang 'Disco Deewane'. Dadi almost spasmed in shock and I doubled up in laughter.

The wedding photographer went mad and took about four thousand pictures.

8.30 p.m.

'Ladies and gentlemen,' bellowed my mamaji, who was hosting the event. 'For a girl in her parents' house, her sister is said to be her confidante. When she weds and goes to live with her husband's family, it is the devar, who takes the sister's place!'

Shouts of 'Yes! Yes!' from the now very animated crowd.

'What happens when the sister of the bride and brother of the groom get together for…'

The thunderous cheering that followed drowned his last words, as strains of 'Waah Waah Raam Ji' from the epic *Hum Aapke Hain Kaun* began trickling in, much to the delight of everyone in the hall. Nothing like a good old Bollywood song!

And in front of our delighted eyes, onstage appeared Vikram, clad in a white kurta-pyjama and brown sleeveless jacket. Next to him stood Mili in a brown lehenga. The bride's sister and the groom's brother. Our very own Madhuri and Salman.

I yelped in delight as the two swayed to 'Bhaiyya Aur Bhabhi Koh'. The two were good dancers and swayed effortlessly to the music, imitating steps from the movie. The cheering that started when the song was announced did not stop even during their performance.

10.15 p.m.

Friends from AIIMS, Purva's batchmates from the various courses he had done, friends from my B-school and engineering college, neighbours and family members, all set aside pride and dignity and danced with abandon to Bollywood numbers for hours.

The night, already a big hit, reached its crescendo when Purva and I were dragged onto the stage and surrounded by enthusiastic aunts and uncles who insisted we jiggle to the beats of 'Daaru Desi'.

'And so,' said Mamaji as Purva and I settled back into our chairs and awaited the announcement for dinner, 'the night comes to an end…'

I cheered along with others, mildly surprised at how much I had enjoyed my own sangeet. I was getting up when I realized that Mamaji was not finished. A few more words to wish me luck maybe?

'But before that happens,' he said, smiling broadly, as three microphones were brought and placed about five feet from me, 'maybe we all have time for one last performance?'

Everyone, except me, cheered.

Who was going to perform now? Hadn't everyone already been onstage? I looked at Purva, who shrugged, looking puzzled himself. A lot of cousins were missing, I realized with a start. Were they eating already?

'Amay on the tambourine,' boomed Mamaji as Pitajee got up from right behind me, tambourine in hand, a smug you-have-no-clue-what-is-coming-your-way grin on his face.

'Vikram on the guitar,' said Mamaji, as I gasped.

'Purva, what's going on?' I hissed at him, but he looked as lost as I did.

'And the lead singer, Dr Purva Dixit,' Mamaji hollered, to thunderous applause. I was stunned, as Purva, who had been pretending to be as bemused as I was, winked and slowly got up to stand behind the microphone.

I realized that I had both my hands to my mouth in shock. I know that Purva sings, of course, but I also know how much he hates singing in public.

'For you, Kasturi,' said Purva into the microphone, his eyes boring into mine, 'from all of us.'

By this time, I realized, almost everyone was standing in their places. Sitting there, in the midst of silence, shocked out of my wits, I waited.

Vikram began strumming the familiar tunes of one of my all-time favourite songs. 'I'm Gonna Be...' I looked on stunned and Pitajee beat the tambourine to the tune with a grin plastered on his face.

I gasped as realization hit home. This was the song Dad had once, many, many years ago, sung for Mum. Purva knew this and was recreating the same moment for me. In front of the whole world! Purva had not opened his mouth yet, but tears were already pooling in my eyes. It could not get any more perfect!

Only it would.

'When I wake up, well I know I'm gonna be, I'm gonna be the man who wakes up next to you,' Purva sang in his golden voice, mimicking The Proclaimers so well that I wondered for one mad minute if he was just lip-syncing.

In that one instant a little charpai had materialized next

to the trio, and Veena, my littlest cousin, and Rahul, Purva's little nephew, were just waking up. Little Purva looks at little Kasturi who is trying her best to make her yawn look believable and gives her a big hug.

'Aww!' I heard someone say.

'When I go out, yeah I know, I know, I'm gonna be the man who goes along with you,' crooned Purva to the beat that Vikram and Pitajee provided.

The charpai had vanished and in place of the little kids, Mum and Dad stepped out of a door cut out of cardboard. Mum had a little pink purse slung around her shoulders, ready to go out. Grinning at me and singing the song, hand in hand, Mum and Dad walked past me, looking giddy like teenagers.

'Mum!' I screamed in delight, along with others.

'If I get drunk, well I know I'm gonna be, I'm gonna be the man who gets drunk next to you,' sang Purva as his mausaji appeared, pretending to be intoxicated next to a stern-looking Mausiji. The look on Mausiji's face was so disapproving that we all collectively burst out laughing.

'If I haver, yeah I know I'm gonna be I'm gonna be the man who is havering to you,' sang Purva, grinning at me again. His cousin Utkarsh appeared, talking rubbish to a seemingly irritated Padma. Padma, mock anger written all over face, thwacked Utkarsh with her hands, making all of us laugh again.

By now everyone was on their feet, clapping to the music in unison. Every eye was on the three men who were performing a few feet away from me. Purva, Vikram and Pitajee sang the beautiful, gorgeous chorus, hitting the right notes, the right voices all put together so beautifully, that I had goosebumps on my hands as I listened to them, enraptured.

'For I would walk five hundred miles and I would walk five hundred more…'

And then just Purva. 'It's the beat of a man who walks a thousand miles,' sang Purva, his solo voice ringing out loud and clear to the rhythm that had everyone mesmerized, 'and fall down at your door.' And with that, twenty of our friends and cousins, who had been gathering around the boys all this while, came forward and fell down at my feet, much to the amusement of the other guests. Mad cheering followed this, but Purva continued.

'When I'm working, yes I know I'm gonna be, I'm gonna be the man who is working hard for you.' Dad again appeared, this time wearing his doctor's coat, stethoscope around his neck, and as Purva sang this line, he winked at me and pretended to quickly perform one surgery after the other, eliciting much laughter from everyone around.

'And when the money comes in for the work I do, I'll pass almost every penny on to you,' Purva crooned into the microphone, his body swaying to the beat. His confidence and charisma had me completely shocked. This man was born for the stage! Where was the shy, quiet doctor I knew?

To my utter astonishment, Mr Vijaywada emerged from the crowd as Purva sang this, showering fake currency notes at his delighted wife.

'Mr Vijaywada!' I yelped, laughing and crying at the same time, stunned at all the people who had got together for this little act.

'When I come home, yeah I know I'm gonna be,' sang Purva, his melodious voice ringing across the hall, and his

Tauji appeared and started running Bollywood-style towards a cardboard cut-out of a house, beside which stood Taiji smiling with a cup of tea in her hand. 'I'm gonna be the man who comes back home to you.'

'And if I grow old, well I know I'm gonna be,' sang Purva as, to my absolute delight, my nanaji came forward, limping a little. This was the first time that I had seen him walk without his walking stick but that was not what had my eyes popping out. Nanaji was clad in a beige kurta exactly like Purva's.

'Oh my god,' I cried, laughing like a madwoman, making no attempt to hide my tears now.

'I'm gonna be the man who is growing old with you,' he sang as Naniji, clad in a yellow anarkali, identical to mine, walked in and shyly stood next to Nanaji, in the midst of deafening hooting.

'Naniji!' I screamed in delight, as the two of them grinned back at the screaming, shouting, clapping, hollering audience. Nanaji and Naniji, dressed like Purva and me, looking so darn cute with their white hair and gentle smiles that I could just hug them for hours. How much planning had this taken? And how the hell did they convince Naniji to wear an anarkali?

And before I knew it, it was time for the lovely, fun-filled chorus that I had heard at least a gazillion times before. The three men synchronized perfectly. 'I would walk five hundred miles and I would walk five hundred more. It's the beat of a man who walks a thousand miles to fall down at your door.' Purva used both his hands to point at me and again twenty cousins and friends, giggling uncontrollably, tumbled at my feet.

'Tadalala.' Forty people took the cue to join in the chorus and surround me in a circle.

'Tadalalalala. Tadalalallala. Tadalalalla.'

By now, pretty much everyone in the hall was surrounding me, singing the chorus. That was a spectacular moment. About a hundred people, singing together the chorus of a song most had probably never heard of before.

Purva silenced everyone with a gesture and sang the last two lines alone. My hands had not left my mouth since the song had begun. This was beyond anything I could have imagined.

'I would walk five hundred miles and I would walk five hundred more,' sang Purva, pulling out the microphone from the stand and walking towards me, his eyes not leaving mine even for a second. 'It's the beat of a man who walks a thousand miles to fall down at your door,' he finished with a flourish.

And then it was, for a few seconds, mad.

I was laughing and crying, and suddenly everyone had pulled the nearest person into an embrace. There was not a single dry eye and not a single face that did not bear a wide smile. I may not say this enough, but Dr Purva Dixit, you are, indeed, one special man!

The man I was about to marry was not the romantic sort, really. He was simply a hard-working doctor who would much rather be in the OT opening hearts than in front of a hundred people singing. Yet he sang for me! Not only that, he chose a song that he knew held special meaning for me and my family. He got both families to participate and managed to get more than thirty people to fall at my feet, not once but twice.

I felt like the luckiest girl on the planet.

10.17 p.m.

I was brushing away happy tears when I saw Pitajee sneak out of the group hug, phone stuck to his ears, his face white.

'Is everything okay?' I tried to ask over the din that surrounded us.

When Pitajee turned around to look at me, his eyes were large with amazement.

'Kas...' he was about to say something but seemed to change his mind. 'Er ... Mum wants me home, I think,' he mumbled hurriedly. He looked around and, seeing Purva busy with everyone, pulled Vikram out.

'Come with me please, Vik?' he asked Vikram, who readily agreed.

'Pitajee!' I shouted, as someone pulled me back into the hug.

'Kas, it's fine, it's fine,' Pitajee shouted, hurrying away, a bewildered Vikram at his heels.

38

9 December 2013, 11.00 p.m.

I sat there wondering.

The day had been eventless, well as eventless as it could have been, given that it was my wedding day. I had had a meltdown early in the morning – the whole thing was getting a bit much for me – followed by some more puja and then hours in the parlour getting ready.

A lot of guests had left after dinner and many had commented on the ... err ... *original* orange-and-purple flowers used for the decorations

Purva and I were half married. The jaimala had happened with us airborne. Vikram had picked up Purva and some cousin hoisted me even higher. Eight feet up in the air, I almost fell on top of Purva, much to the sadistic delight of everyone else.

We spent two hours after that grinning like idiots for the photographers and then wrapped up by feeding each other. No accidents there, thank god.

Now, I had an hour to change into the yellow sari for the

pheras. Panditji would use this time to get himself organized for the long night ahead of us.

However, my mind was elsewhere. Something was wrong. Very wrong.

Pitajee had been acting very suspicious the whole day. Don't get me wrong. Obviously today is a difficult day for Pitajee, yet something did not make sense. I was sitting in front of a mirror taking off my earrings, mulling things over, when Pitajee burst through the door, his eyes wide. 'Where is Vikki?' he blurted out.

'Certainly not here!' I retorted.

Pitajee was about to rush out when, displaying agility James Bond would have been proud of, I rushed ahead of him and spread my hands wide to block the door. 'Don't you dare move an inch,' I said, jabbing a threatening finger at him.

Pitajee groaned loudly. 'I am not in the mood for any drama, Kas,' he said, half-cross, and that confirmed my doubts. Something was definitely wrong … and no, it was not Anu's wedding. Pitajee would never be cross with me on my wedding day.

'I will not move an inch. Not before you tell me exactly what's going on,' I hollered.

Pitajee paled and I knew I had hit the nail on the head. Something *was* going on. Before I could say anything, the door behind me burst open and Vikram and Purva tumbled in.

'Here he is!' said Vikram, spotting Pitajee.

'What's going on?' I said, now looking at my half-husband and his brother.

'What did you find out?' shrieked Pitajee.

What the hell is happening?

'It is not his,' said Vikram, slapping the bed. The words seemed to have a marked effect on Pitajee who, in a matter of seconds, began to tremble with rage.

'What is not whose?' I repeated, but the three men were too busy staring stupidly at each other to bother with me.

'What is not whose?' I asked again, my voice dangerously calm.

No one paid any notice.

'WHAT IS NOT WHOSE?' I yelled at the top of my voice. *That* brought them back to the present.

'The medical reports that Anu's mom showed her…' said Pitajee, looking strangely at me as if it were my fault, 'are not Govind's.'

Excuse my French, but what the…

11.10 p.m.

Within minutes, the startling story tumbled out. Anu had been clearing up her room after her mehendi ceremony late last night, when she chanced upon some papers – her father's medical reports that Ahya had flung across the room a few months ago in a fit of rage. Surprised that such important documents had not been missed, Anu began to look at them, when her eyes fell on what looked like a blood sample report.

The patient's name was Govind Goswami. Blood type A+. Interesting, because Anu knew for a fact that her father's blood type was not A+.

Intrigued, she called up Pitajee, who left my sangeet immediately and got her to fax all the documents to him. He then had Vikram take a look at them. Vikram had concluded that the reports did not belong to Anu's father.

'Do … maybe … I … I think there is some mix-up … just the wrong reports…' I stammered.

'Nope,' said Vikram, shaking his head. 'I spoke with lab technicians at the hospital; professional etiquette can go to hell. Those reports are fudged. They never got any tests done; some Raam Lal was paid a thousand for these.'

'Does this mean…' said Padma, who had been urgently called inside the room as well.

'Yes,' said Pitajee. 'Anu's parents lied so that she would not marry me.'

'Has Anu felt any change in her father's health … does he look weak?' Vikram asked Pitajee.

'That man is an ox! Nothing about him is weak!' he thundered and I stepped back. I had never seen Pitajee's eyes look as dark and dangerous as they did now.

'So,' I asked, looking around, the yellow sari that I should have worn by now lying forgotten on the bed. 'What do we do next?'

There was silence.

'Call Anu. Right away,' said Purva. 'Put her on speaker.'

I did as told. One ring. Two rings. Three rings.

'Oh god, what if Anu does not pick up the phone?' said Padma, wringing her hands with worry. We all looked at each other, tense, unsure of what the night now held in store.

'Hello,' came Anu's voice a few seconds later. Nothing had ever sounded sweeter. You could feel the relief in the room.

'Anu!' I said.

'Anu!' screamed Purva.

'Anu Di!' shouted Vikram.

'Anu!' said Padma.

'Pumpkin!' exclaimed Pitajee.

'Why did you guys take years to call?' she hissed angrily. Lovely Anu, she was back and how I had missed the sharp tongue! 'The reports?' she asked, in a low voice. It was obvious that there were people around her and she did not wish to attract attention.

'It *is* fake,' said Pitajee in a grim voice.

There was silence on the other end.

'Are you married, Anu?' Purva asked. That was something I never thought I would hear Purva ask Anu. As I waited for Anu to reply, I crossed my fingers. Purva, Pitajee, Vikram, Padma all followed suit. And that is how we stood, in a circle, our eyes boring into the phone, heads bent low in concentration and fingers crossed for luck.

This could go either way now.

39

'The baraat has not even come yet,' said Anu disdainfully.

I held my head in my hands and exhaled a big sigh of relief. Vikram pumped his fist in the air and Padma clutched my half-husband's hand in delight.

Purva looked at me and smiled a slow smile. His gaze then met Pitajee's.

'What?' asked Pitajee, looking at all the faces that stared expectantly at him for a few seconds before realization dawned upon him and he gasped.

'You guys were doing this for the parents, who … well … lied,' said Vikram.

I heard Anu take a deep breath. What could be done now? What *should* be done now? Pitajee's face clouded for a few moments and he chewed on his little finger. Then he looked up at Purva, who was already smiling. Purva somehow knew what was going on in Pitajee's head and he nodded, encouragingly. I stared blankly, first at Purva and then at Pitajee.

Taking a moment to steady himself, Pitajee sat down, cleared his throat and spoke. 'Anu, we did this for Govind,' he said.

'Yes,' she said in a small voice.

'And now it is clear that Govind and Ahya lied to us.'

'Yes,' she said again.

'It changes everything ... doesn't it?' he asked, his words laden with meaning.

'Yes,' said Anu.

A moment's pause. I caught Padma's face, steeped in concentration, focused on the conversation between the star-crossed lovers.

'Everything, they say, is fair in love and war. I love you and hereby declare war on Ahya and Govind,' said the gallant knight.

'Oh ... okay,' said Anu, slowly.

'Anu darling, I can just think of one thing that can be done now. Would you,' continued Pitajee, 'consider running away from your wedding?'

'Wha...' I said, feeling my eyes grow in size.

'And marrying me tonight?' he finished.

Padma gasped. These north Indians, her eyes seemed to say.

Vikram and Purva exchanged a look. I crossed my fingers yet again, waiting for Anu to reply. You could have cut the tension in the room with a knife. Vikram spared a hand over his forehead, Purva put a comforting hand on Pitajee's shoulder and I just prayed.

For a few seconds, no one spoke.

'Yes,' said Anu, her voice resolute.

'Dear lord,' Padma and I said in unison, as the meaning of the words sank in. Anu was going to run away from her wedding.

Ananya Goswami was going to run away from her own wedding.

Ananya Goswami was going to run away from her own wedding.

Like, now!

40

11.15 p.m.

Pitajee was about to rush out of the room when Purva yanked him back.

'What do you think you are doing?' he asked Pitajee.

'Eloping with Anu,' he said, obstinately jutting out his chin. No one could stop him.

'And how will you do that?'

'Err … I will … I…'

'Stop stuttering. We need to discuss this.' said Purva, ably taking control of the situation at hand. We all huddled on the single bed.

'First,' I said importantly, 'has anyone done this before? Or knows anyone who has?'

The looks that were most unceremoniously hurled at me shut me up.

'Pitajee, take my car. It's smaller and will make for a quicker getaway,' said Purva.

Pitajee nodded his head as Vikram flung the car keys in his direction.

'Are you doing this alone? I think someone should go with

you,' said Purva again. I vehemently nodded my head.

'Yes,' said Pitajee, the next instant. 'I want Kasturi to come with me.'

'Awww,' I said, clutching my hand to my heart. You know you are someone's best friend when they ask you to accompany them on a life-changing adventure such as this.

'Are you kidding me?' exclaimed Padma. 'Kasturi has to get married!'

Oh. I had quite forgotten all about my wedding.

'I need someone mad enough to do this with me. And you don't get madder than Kas,' said Pitajee, shrugging his shoulders. Everyone in the room, much to my indignation, nodded their heads in silent agreement. I settled the hundred-kilo pallu of my red lehenga over my head, crossed my hands, offended, against my chest and pushed myself against the wall.

No one noticed.

Really, these people need to have more respect for me! At least on my wedding day!

'Purva will plan too much, Padma will think too much, Vikram knows too little about Ahya and Govind…' Pitajee explained.

'I agree,' Purva said, after due deliberation. 'Kasturi should go.' And then into the phone, he said, 'Anu. Kas and Pitajee are coming.'

'Yay!' she said feebly, her voice shaking with both fear and excitement. 'I can't believe we are doing this!'

'Padma, you wear the yellow sari and stay in this room with Vikram,' said my competent half-husband.

Padma looked questioningly at Purva and he explained his contingency plans.

'The bride cannot possibly go missing. If Kas takes longer, then we will say Kas is in the room with Vikram. Worst case scenario, we will have to just tell our parents, but the longer we can avoid doing that, the more time we buy.'

'Right!' said Paddy.

'And after picking up Anu?' asked Vikram.

'Good question,' said Pitajee, looking at Vikram. He had definitely not thought this far. I mentally LOL-ed.

'Get Anu here. The panditji will be waiting, I will make sure that he is,' said Purva.

I felt goosebumps on my hands. This could not really be happening.

'Now go, we don't have much time. If we can get to Anu before her baraat does, it will save us a lot of trouble.'

Pitajee nodded his head, looking a little nervous now that the moment was upon us. So bizarre was the whole idea that I think we were collectively trying not to think too much lest we thought the better of it. Hurry it all up, lest someone begins to think sensibly. How mature!

I put my arm around Pitajee's shoulders. 'We will do it!' I said, pumping my fist in the air.

'Let's go, then!' said Pitajee and I kicked off the heels and quickly put on tennis shoes.

As the two of us rushed out of the room, Purva put a hand on Pitajee's shoulders. Pitajee looked back at him.

'That's my bride there with you,' he said, grinning. 'Get her back on time.'

'Aye, aye, captain,' said Pitajee, as nervous laughter filled the room.

Taj Delhi, Wedding Grounds, 10 December 2013, 12.14 a.m.

'Walk in like you belong,' I whispered to Pitajee as the two of us walked inside the wedding hall. The guards at the gate had looked weirdly at us, unsure about letting another woman in a red lehenga inside.

'Now you take the right and I will take the left. Whoever sees Anu whistles and the other joins. The idea is to run away with Anu flanked on either side by you and me. Remember, you and I, on either side of Anu,' I reminded him.

Pitajee nodded his head absently and cast one look at the sumptuous-looking array of food not too far from us. The gardens were huge and decorated opulently for the wedding of the daughter of Ahya and Govind Goswami. Red-and-gold drapes hung on the walls, pretty flowers decorated the intricately-set tables. One of the many fat and well-dressed aunties walked by me.

'My designer,' said one such aunty – who probably weighed a hundred kilos – to another who seemed to weigh at least a hundred and fifty, 'says I look slim in pink.'

One-fifty-kilo Aunty, looked enviously at the svelte figure of hundred-kilo Aunty. I gulped. It seemed like I had entered a whole new world.

I stealthily walked past another group of aunties.

'Ritu Kumar?' said one aunty, fingering the sari of another one.

'Oh no!' said the lady, quite horrified 'Sabyasachi! Vidya is also a client, you know,' she said with a dainty shrug of her shoulders.

'Vidya? From our building?' said the first aunty, not quite understanding.

'Oh ho, Vidya Balan!' said aunty-in-Sabyasachi, rolling her eyes.

I felt a little faint and quite homesick for my own banal, middle-class wedding which was ... well ... taking place without me for the time being.

The things I do for friends!

I was thinking these thoughts with a fairly philosophical air when I saw her. In the middle of a group of elegantly-dressed people, resplendent in red, stood my beautiful, gorgeous Anu. I looked dismally around her. A well-decorated boy, who could only be Saumen, stood by her, garland in hand. The jaimala was about to happen! The timing could not have been worse!

Anu was walking slowly, talking in hushed tones to her little sister, Anjali, who walked next to her. The two seemed to be in deep conversation. I had no doubt about what was being discussed. Anjali's eyes grew large as she spotted me. As if in slow motion I saw her look left and then right. She then elbowed her sister and pointed in my direction.

'Oh!' I said, hyperventilating as I spotted, from the corner of my eye, at least twenty policemen who had been on duty all along. I am now going to help my friend run away from her own wedding! In front of the police!

Oh dear! Oh dear! Oh dear!

12.18 a.m.

In front of my horrified eyes, I saw Anu press Anjali's hand one last time, hitch her lehenga up and begin to run towards me with all her might.

I heard the crowd gasp collectively.

'Bittu Beta!' said Bunty Mama, who was closest to Anu. I have met Anu's corpulent uncle a couple of times, and felt sorry for the ninety-eight-kilo man as he tried to waddle towards Anu. Anjali politely but firmly pushed him to one side. Bittu Mama looked at Anjali, a mixture of indignation and hurt written all over his round face and three chins.

Anu ran in my direction. A sea of people stared as one bride ran to another. I looked on, a little bewildered, as Anu's strong hands clasped mine and, as if on cue and very much like the climax of a Bollywood movie, the two of us started running towards the gate, hand in hand.

'What?' said one aunty bringing her hands most dramatically to her mouth. 'Goswamiji's daughter is running away with another girl?'

I get it now, I do. Looks really suspicious if you have two women dressed as brides running away hand in hand.

'You never know what kids are up to these days,' said another aunty, shaking her head sadly, 'MTV single-handedly corrupted an entire generation.'

Before anyone could say 'runaway bride', Anu and I were out of the wedding grounds as restless murmurs grew louder in the background. What was really funny and made me giggle was the guard at the gates saluting the moment his eyes fell on Anu. And it was then that it struck me. For all practical matters, Anu had eloped with me and we had not only left Pitajee inside, but had, till now, completely forgotten about him.

The excitement of the night does not end!

'Pitajee!' I said, panting. 'He's still inside!'

'And I am outside!' Anu said, rather meaninglessly.

'Yes, you're outside,' I agreed with her. Both of us were running the hardest we had ever run and talking to each other in hurriedly-caught breaths. The brain is not at its sharpest on such occasions and I forgave Anu immediately for inane remarks.

'I eloped with you, Kasturi,' Anu shrieked, as the realization hit her too. I think neither of us was sure whether we should laugh or cry.

'Annnnuu,' came a loud wail from behind, and Anu and I turned around simultaneously. As if on cue, Pitajee appeared from seemingly nowhere, running his hardest, his arms flailing wildly around him, making him look more comical than heroic, which was not the effect he was trying to achieve. I vaguely noticed the guard saluting him too. For god's sake, had the guard not figured out what was happening?

Pitajee stopped two short steps away from us. For obvious reasons, he had eyes only for Anu who glowed in the bridal attire.

'You are beautiful, Ananya,' said Pitajee, his voice thick with emotion, eyes red and face dripping with love. To my horror, the two of them stood there, most ironically right under a glittering board that announced Anu's wedding to Saumen, and stared at each other, love-struck.

Pitajee was back to looking all woolly and goofy. Anu had just fallen in love all over again.

'Guys ... errr...' I said, trying to gingerly break the spell, 'Err ... really sorry to break this to you, but if you look behind you, about fifty men have just come out of the gates and are attempting what I can only describe as a chase! So really ... I mean ... this is not the time for puppy love...'

'Anu, I love you,' Pitajee said, as Anu's eyes dutifully brimmed with tears. Pitajee clutched her hands with all his might. 'I would have died had you married Saumen. I would have died!'

'I love you too! I love you too!' yelped Anu, and threw her arms around Pitajee.

'Oh, pumpkin!' said Pitajee.

'Cupcake!' murmured Anu and I almost threw up. I had forgotten how disgusting those two could be.

'Guys!' I tried again, mercilessly separating them. 'Look!' I pointed towards a crowd that was now running out of the wedding grounds towards us. Ahya, having kicked off her golden heels, was leading the pack. One look at her set face and I knew I would soon be running the fastest I have ever run. 'We need to run!' I said, with all the wisdom I could muster.

'I agree,' said Pitajee, 'but one moment.' And with that, under Anu's beatific smile, Pitajee went down on one knee.

'Will you marry me, darling?' he murmured dreamily.

Did these guys not know that we were running away from a wedding? From Anu's wedding?

'Yes, she will,' I barged in hurriedly.

'Yes, I will,' said Anu.

'Now give her the ring,' I said to Pitajee, who turned to look blankly at me.

This man!

I yanked my own engagement ring off my finger. 'Here! Use mine!' I said, thrusting it in Pitajee's hands.

'Now you wear it! Quick!' I hissed and literally put the ring around Anu's finger and began to run towards the car.

A sardarji walking past us poked his wife and pointed at the three of us – Pitajee in the centre, flanked on either side by Anu and me, running towards the car with a small mob chasing after us.

'Oye teri,' I heard the sardarji exclaim in awe. 'I have heard of one man running away with *one* girl. But look at this man! He is running away with two brides!'

I stopped running only when we had reached the car. Pitajee took to the wheel and I sat next to him, pushing Anu into the backseat. Adrenaline pumped through the car as Pitajee now took control of the situation and pushed the accelerator hard.

'Kas,' came a small voice from behind me a few minutes later.

'Yes?'

'You put a ring on my finger,' Anu said. 'I hate to break it to you, but I think *we* are engaged.'

I slumped into the seat laughing, weak with relief, and Pitajee joined in. There was just one thought in my mind. Anu and Pitajee would be together now. With my faith in love and destiny restored, I yelled at Pitajee to drive more carefully.

41

Indira Gandhi International Airport, Delhi, 16 December 2013.

'Be good, Kasturi Shukla Dixit!' said Vikram, winking at me.

The million bangles on my hands jingled happily, as Purva and I bid our final farewells to all the people who had piled into the four available cars to drop us off at the airport. I absently fingered the watch on my wrist, Purva's dad's watch, the watch I had not taken off since the day Purva had gifted it to me. With one swoosh of my heavy Kanjivaram sari, I turned around to make my way to the check-in desk. Pushing our humungous suitcase with ease, Purva put an arm lightly around my waist. Just the two of us now.

'Cannot wait to get on that flight to Brazil,' he said lazily. 'It has been so crazy, these last few days.'

Oh, yes. Crazy it had been.

The night of the wedding, worthy of a full-fledged three-hour Bollywood movie, now flashed before my eyes. The mad car-ride across Delhi, rushing to my wedding just as Mum and Anju Aunty … err … I mean Mummy … were about to throw screaming fits, given that they had just realized that the dulhan was absconding, their horrified faces when they saw that there were more brides than expected.

'When He gives, He gives with an open hand,' said Purva's naniji on seeing two brides in place of the one that was missing.

Pitajee's parents had been pulled out from the crowd. Pitajee quickly told them the whole story and asked for their blessing. Too shocked to say anything else to their son who stood next to the girl he loved, pleading with them, they had nodded their approvals. I felt for them. I did. They had, after all, only come to attend a wedding, not take home a daughter-in-law.

Purva, barking at the panditji, had insisted that the sindoor ceremony and pheras be done right away.

The Goswamis had finally barged in, threatening to call the police. Which was ironic, since twenty policemen had accompanied them anyway.

Anu, sitting next to a horrified and clueless panditji, had had a hysterical meltdown, wedding lehenga and all.

Ahya had had the grace – at least momentarily – to look shameful at what she had done, but later had asked the police to arrest Pitajee, which had Pitajee and me very scared for a minute.

Anu had got to her feet in sheer anger and screamed at the top of her lungs, quite like a banshee, 'I am an adult! No law in this country can stop me from marrying the man I love!'

In the end, it was glorious Paddy who came to the rescue. Clad in my yellow sari, she drew herself to her full height and said, 'Here, my boyfriend, Tiger, works for *News of India*. And boy, would the media lap up a story about a lying parent who also happens to be an esteemed IAS officer! Tiger does what he's told, what do you want me to tell Tiger to do? Pretend this never happened? Or go tell the world about it?'

Stunned silence met these profound words. I almost clapped with delight when Padma finished. That girl is worth her weight in gold.

'Thanks, Paddy,' I said to her.

'I owed you one, Kas,' she said, flicking her bangs.

Mum and Dad had performed Anu's kanyadaan when her parents stoutly refused to. Worth *their* weight in gold too, Mum and Dad.

I had spent the last few weeks imagining a very emotional scene of my vidai. My vermillion-smeared forehead covered in a pallu, tears flowing unabated, family and friends queuing up for that hug, a sad song playing in the background.

Well ... none of that happened. The four sets of parents were all too dazed to react. Purva, Pitajee, Anu and I squeezed ourselves into one car and we dropped Anu and Pitajee off at their place first, before heading to Purva's house.

An overwhelmed Pitajee had mumbled, 'Thanks guys, I ... I ... I love you!' as he'd got out of the car, looking away, a tad uncomfortable.

'Just return the ring when you feel like it,' said Purva, and everyone had laughed and huddled for one last hug before the most eventful night of our lives came to an end.

The guests at my wedding went back very content, to say the least. They had come to see one wedding and had seen two, plus some drama and some more drama. One aunt, who had gifted me a pair of gold earrings, came afterwards with a gold pendant. 'After all, itna maza aya,' she said, earnestly.

The next few days are now a blur.

Pitajee's mother, who has always been very fond of Anu, has taken to referring to her new daughter-in-law as the 'return-gift from Kasturi's wedding'.

Anu, obviously, now has a very complicated relationship with her parents. Both parties think they are victims. My mother told Anu that she and Pitajee need to have a baby as soon as possible. 'Babies,' she said, looking pointedly at me, 'are so dear to grandparents, after all.'

I had been married for four days then.

By the end of this month, Pitajee's family will be hosting a proper reception for the wedding. We are all hopeful that Anu's parents will attend the function, though I have my doubts.

Mum, obviously, posted details of the wedding on 'Pearls of Wisdom'. There are three posts dedicated to how Pimple helped her best friend run away from her wedding and, in the process, united true love. To be honest, I come across as quite the hero and have therefore shared links to the post with everyone. In a matter of days, the number of followers of the blog ballooned to 3988, as some small websites picked up on the series and people began to share it on Facebook. Last I heard, a local newspaper was going to cover Mum's stellar rise to cyber stardom through a three-part interview. Mum is already talking about writing her first book, which will be titled *Pearls of Wisdom*.

Dad is doing fine, thank you. The surgery and the trauma of it all are past us and we have collectively decided to move beyond it.

Anu and Pitajee. Purva and I. It's funny how our lives are now entwined in one fabulous, dramatic, Bollywood-esque story that we will probably never tire of discussing. Not only do we share the same wedding date, but also the wedding venue, panditji, puja samagri and, lo and behold, engagement ring as well!

'What are you thinking, Kas?' asked Purva, bringing me out of the past.

'Nothing,' I said smiling. 'Ready?'

'Yes,' he said.

The honeymoon had been paid for by Purva, but planned entirely by me. There have been ... errr ... let's just say, some changes. I felt a little nervous as we made our way to the check-in desk.

'Flight BA 345 to Brazil, please,' said Purva, blindly handing to the lady behind the desk the tickets I had just passed on to him.

The lady looked confused.

'No...' I said. 'These are for the US.'

'The US?' asked Purva, looking in bewilderment first at me, then at the lady.

I nodded my head. 'We stop first at Disneyland and then head to Brazil,' I said, smiling. 'It's high time you got to do that trip.'

Purva stared at the tickets in his hand, then at the lady at the desk and then at me. And before I knew it, my brand new, anti-PDA husband had lifted me off the ground in a fierce hug.

'I love you, Kasturi Shukla!' he said.

'Let me down,' I squealed, kicking my feet with delight.

'These newly-weds!' murmured the lady at the desk, pretending to be exasperated but unable to hide her smile.

Acknowledgements

I have to, just have to, acknowledge it. 'It' is probably destiny or a super-power that we cannot quite understand or God or sheer will or hard work or maybe it is just chance. Whatever 'it' is, a heartfelt thank you.

Thank you, Siddharth Vajpayee, for putting up with a wife who dabbles in far too many things for anyone's good. I love you.

Thank you, Rachana Misra (who is, thankfully, not at all like Kasturi's Mum) and Nisha Kant Misra (who is, thankfully, a lot like Kasturi's Dad), for collectively being my shrinks, my wise saints, my best friends, my comfort blankets.

Thank you, Amita Bajpayee and air vice-marshal (retd.) Shyam Bihari Bajpayee, AVSM, for your love and support.

Thank you, Diva Kant Misra and Neharika Neeraj Kalra. What would Kasturi not give to have a brother and sister-in-law like you?

Thank you, Nikhil Agarwal, for reading everything I write and for being the creative genius behind the names of both my books.

Thank you, Alan Cartwright, for your invaluable inputs on my manuscripts, published and unpublished.

Thank you, Neelini Sarkar, Manasi Subramaniam, Ramona Sen and the rest of the team at HarperCollins, for all the hard work you have put into this book. It has been such a delight to work with you.

And finally, to the readers of *The (In)eligible Bachelors*, thank you for your kind words of encouragement. It has been an incredible journey thus far because of you. I hope I have done justice to Kasturi, Purva, Pitajee and Anu in *~~I Do!~~ Do I?*